OUTLAW
GAMES

OUTLAW
GAMES

VICKI LINDNER

The Dial Press
New York

Published by
The Dial Press
1 Dag Hammarskjold Plaza
New York, New York 10017

Manufactured in the United States of America

First printing

Library of Congress Cataloging in Publication Data

Lindner, Vicki, 1944–
   Outlaw games.

   I. Title.
PS3562.I511409   813'.54   81-17459
ISBN 0-385-27417-3   AACR2

To J.Q.

I would like to thank the Yaddo Foundation for November 1979; the Ward family for The Pond House, September 1980; Berenice Hoffman for orchestration; Joyce Johnson for astute editorial suggestions; my family and friends who read the manuscript, especially Virginia Sharkey, Betty Tompkins, and Esther Wanning, for support.

Some men take pleasure in fantasies whose basic contents are not celestial delights.

Jean Genet, *Miracle of the Rose*

OUTLAW GAMES

CHAPTER

1

*A*T eleven fifteen Dolores wearily retyped the first three pages, fourth draft, of Chapter IV of *High Styling Your Face,* breathed a thread of semipure air, curling chilly and thin beneath the cracked window of the room she called her "office," and believed she detected the last whiff of fall, the final leaf of a nonexistent tree, in this stale draft. That was all it took to launch her from her imprisoning chair and send her squinting into the daylit streets, minus her gloves, umbrella, wearing worn Kung Fu shoes with disintegrating rubber soles, improper for the wet November pavements and the persistent drizzle falling since yesterday. Having escaped her miserable dungeon and its principal instrument of torture, her typewriter, the murdering boredom drained from her bloodstream, and the wads of cotton batting stuffing up her air channels began to fall away.

Sitting on a chair hour after hour, the backs of her thighs spreading numbly into the first phases of puckering cellulite, bored her more than describing the so-called miracles of eye shadow itself. She had been condemning the colors blue and green with raving spite, according to the instructions of the world-famous Hollywood makeup artist, peon to the stars, for whom she ghosted the masterpiece, and though eye shadow per se did not interest her, the shrill voice of spite and condemnation did—her own terrible voice.

No woman who read *High Styling Your Face* would dare use blue eye shadow again, a tacky, unforgivable color that did nothing, *nothing,* Nothing, darling, to enhance the natural shade of the eyes but drowned them out in a glare of false neon. Dolores had even given her own blue eye shadow the heave-ho, the one filched from a designer's special collection of "Haute Couture Tones for Fall," first maliciously scratching the powdered contents from its plastic case with the point of a nail file. Six fifty for that shit, she'd thought, glad she hadn't paid for it, glad it had given her the chance to learn what a potent high it was to steal.

The walls of gray buildings pressed up solidly on either side and the drizzling sky hung low, like a sagging tent's ceiling. There was no escaping this metaphoric prison, she thought, since it began and ended with the parameters of her own body. She was obviously imagining the cellulite, and such narcissistic preoccupations would destroy what was left of her intellect and sanity. Outside, free soul in the rain, she at once felt guilty; the rest of the world labored at nine-to-five jobs five days a week, punched time clocks in real offices, and she couldn't bear her relatively painless free-lance gig, quite well paid, for more than two hours. Undisciplined! It only took a modest exertion to write the dreck she wrote for money; its neat expressions and syncopated phrasing ejected themselves effortlessly in a form and structure that seemed preconceived by another mind, unlike her poetry, her talent, her vocation, which emerged so painfully she felt she tore it out of her cerebrum with bloody fingernails, and could barely tell the difference between the joyful termination of the agony and the quality of the finished poem. In any case, she rationalized, the "Eye Design" chapter was one sixth done and only two more, "Luscious Lips," and "Glamorous Touches for Evening," remained; with minimal discipline she could finish the entire job in three weeks, take the final half of the advance and split for Bolivia, which she would do, yes, unless she fell in love.

She walked toward the subway and was halted by a crowd around a carton waiting for the garbage truck. Women who worked in Soho's fast disappearing factories were picking through a box of castaways evacuated from a posh residential loft. Dolores joined them eagerly, burrowing through the pile of damp discards to the bottom, where the real goodies hid, beating out competitive brown hands. I am a chump for garbage, she thought, using one of Julio Bravo's prison lingo terms, which sounded tough and wise in her mind, put whatever they designated into a forever appropriate frame. The woman next to her held up a soiled, wet tablecloth. "Look at that!" she exclaimed. "That is linen! You know how much my mother pay for a tablecloth like that?"

Dolores displayed her own find, a brown and pink ruffled blouse, dirty with some orange liquefied muck it had contacted in the bin. "That's pure silk," she announced.

3

"Perfect condition!" She stuffed it into her purse along with the Dior Ombre eye shadow she had extracted from the box in the exact color of *braungris* she had just been recommending to the women of America, minus its sponge applicator, but so what, she could use a Q-tip! Another dive, hand surfaces alert for an intriguing texture, and up to the light with a white duck A-line skirt, wriggled over her jeans, tight and grease-stained; no, it would be too small even without stains and besides she didn't need it. She didn't need anything, obviously, except these mad, acquisitive compulsions. The woman next to her found a black leather belt, totally unscarred, the exact width and color Dolores had been contemplating buying, twelve bucks, minimum.

She looked up and hallucinated Vasco, "The Portuguese Artist," in his impeccable four-hundred-dollar fur-lined Italian raincoat and silver sunglasses, his chin and neck extended like a Thoroughbred racehorse, or running chicken's, depending. He was the only person she knew, still important (she had to admit), who would not relish capturing the essence of her unique personality if he happened to spot her grubbing through a carton of soaked garbage, would not think clawing through filth "cute," "eccentric," or significantly antibourgeois, not even amusing; his face would achieve the sour contours of revulsion he reserved for phenomena that offended his clearly defined aesthetic sensibility—an ugly fork, a flowered slipcover, an imperfect female form, her own. No, thank God, it wasn't Vasco, but a short semilookalike in an ordinary raincoat. He was on her mind, unfortunately, so she imagined him everywhere. "Whenever I'm involved with someone and it looks like it could really turn into something I become impotent," he'd explained in his careful, accented diction with perfectly enacted rue, and had set about to prove it. As usual she had selected a warped soul to summon passion for. He had undoubtedly feigned impotence. She would wash the garbage blouse and wear it to his dinner party, a minute secret revenge. What had she created for herself by maintaining him as a friend, listening to the tales of his still troubled love affairs, but more misery, a twinging reminder of rejection (a perverse form of joy?). Yet the thought of Vasco catching her up to the elbows in shit made her question her garbage habit and simultaneously dislike herself for letting the thought of this snob aesthete make her question it. Was dredging for castoffs giving her real satisfaction? Yes and no—the idea of it giving her satisfaction satisfied her, identified her as an anti-establishment stalwart she could almost admire in her mind. She had, in fact, found worthwhile stuff on the street—an antique mirror, a Philippe Venet white blouse with a small stain, easily bleached away.

Enough! She extracted herself from the carton and headed for the Prince Street BMT. She would check out the cosmetic counters at Bloomingdale's; since she planned to advise the female suckers of the world to dust their mugs with translucent powder for a romantic, obscure, phony glamorous evening look she should have some translucent powder of her own, for experimental, if no other purposes. She might be able to charge it to the expense account the publisher had given her, at least deduct it from the taxes she would have to pay this year, and have lunch, deductible as "lunch while doing research," then go to the Guggenheim.

At Bloomingdale's, however, she skipped the cosmetic counters, climbed the escalator two steps at a time to the third floor, mobbed beyond belief. She had been to Bloomingdale's no less than four times in the last month and a half to check the progress of their sales, and now rushed straight to the department that had been steadily reducing the Kenzo Jungle Jap corduroy vests she had craved since they first appeared on the racks in August, part of the fall line. No one in her right mind would fork over eighty-eight bucks for a simple cotton vest, or even thirty-nine, which they had dipped to in October, or for that matter, the ignominious twenty-four ninety-nine of the beginning of the month. To her relief there were still loads of vests on the racks, jammed between the soiled arms of blouses and pilling wool-blend sweaters, raked and creased by thousands of grabbing, materialistic hands throughout the season, still pathetically un-bought—fascist Bloomingdale's should ask itself *why*. She yanked up the ticket on the nearest Kenzo and saw that patience had paid off and the vest was now fourteen ninety-nine, poor Kenzo, overpriced creep; red lines had been vehemently drawn through the diminishing series of higher prices.

She extricated at least six vests from the tangled sweater-blouse arms and empty hangers, dumped them on a chair, threw her heavy mouton coat, too hot for November, on the floor, and keeping a wary eye on her purse, pulled the first vest, an exquisite bright turquoise, over her old black work sweater with the holes under the armpits she had bought two years ago at Gabay's, Bloomingdale's First Avenue outlet for damaged goods. The fine French corduroy was soft, firm, supple, slipped gracefully along the cells of her fingers, suggesting an ideal sensual texture just beyond mortal reach. She raised her eyes to the mirror and confronted her image, vest included, with horror.

She had forgotten to comb her hair before barging out the door or to wash the heavy dosage of Acnomel off her

6

face, applied with hope it could miraculously cure her (imaginary?) blemishes before Vasco's dinner party tonight; her sodden curls, mashed to her head on the left side where she slept, stuck up in matted configurations on the other, and the thick beige patches of medicine shredded on her sallow winter complexion. She should not be caught dead wearing this sweater outside of her apartment or these jeans, her oldest and baggiest, coated in spots with the congealed flour she had used to make bran muffins a week ago, healthy muffins she had eaten four of at one sitting, undoubtedly the reason she looked so fat. Mad bag woman, beggar poet, bloated apparition; she should have cleaned up before heading for Bloomingdale's, but then she hadn't planned to come here; she had unconsciously escaped.

She removed the turquoise vest and rapidly tried the gold and smoky-blue versions over her dirty black sweater, all gorgeous, impeccably cut, revealing her small rib cage, broadening her narrow shoulders and, by comparison, increasing the size of her bust. She began the tedious psychic process of trying to choose one and eliminate the rest. The turquoise would go with her brown pants and her black velvet skirt and her . . . what? The rest of her wardrobe vanished from her mind's eye. Actually the gold would look better with jeans and with black; she had black wool pants, seldom worn, and was thinking of buying a black wool skirt with knife-edge pleats, no matter how much it cost. She'd read in some silly article in one of the silly ladies' magazines she wrote for that a black skirt was the Rock of Gibraltar of any professional woman's wardrobe, which made sense, though despite her so-called professional status she almost never left her apartment and didn't need skirts at all. She eliminated the smoky blue immediately, but then, after a second trial, decided it was the most subtle color; it would go with everything and enhanced the gray-blue of her eyes, barely visible through the grotesque mask of Acnomel. Yet the turquoise was the one she liked the best; naturally, it was the least practical—another "logical" addition to her large, illogical wardrobe, full of random, absurd rags that didn't go together, bargains she was always ironing and mending and forcing into incompatible combinations, bought more because they were reduced in price than for any other reason. No matter how much dough she wasted on clothes, she never looked particularly well dressed or had anything to wear at crucial moments, admittedly few; she constantly purchased sedate business separates for her mythical "lunches with editors" that occurred, at most, twice a year, and when they did she found everything she had bought for such occasions didn't quite mesh or was slightly out of style or fundamentally inappropriate. She should get the gold vest, but she didn't take to it, it didn't *please* her indefinable yearnings as much as the turquoise or even the smoky blue, really blah, boring.

She decided to try some of the checked vests in sheer wool, same designer, along with a Soo Yung Lee white silk blouse in two sizes, a little sheer for any conceivable occasion, but sexy and a good buy. She really didn't need "sexy" in this desolate vacuum of her sex life as the good Lord knew but that could change as it had before. In the middle of the blouse inspection a stiff-coiffed saleswoman approached: "You can't try those on out here, lady. Take them into the dressing room!"

Disgruntled, Dolores gathered up her heavy coat, her eight vests, the two silk blouses and her purse, hating to be called "lady," which made her feel like an anonymous wreck, older than her thirty-two years. "Fuck it," she

---

8

moaned inwardly, a disconsolate, foul-mouthed, aging adolescent. The line to the dressing room was long, her arms overburdened with the garment-hanger-coat-purse pile; the pain of restless fury began to stiffen the small of her back. "Only four garments, please," the attendant warned each customer in an impersonal loudspeaker voice. "Four garments, please!"

Dolores began to scream and harangue and cry internally. She would have to make two trips, hang the extra vests back up outside, because the Bloomingdale's fascist motherfuckers would undoubtedly refuse to let her put them on the rack in front of the dressing room. This fury, a bitter taste and burning sensation on her skin, which made it impossible for her to breathe normally in bank lines, token lines, or any other symbolic organization of social restriction, seeped into her mouth and stung her eyes. Her control snapped; she threw the entire twisted mass of vests, blouses, and hangers on the chair and split, stomping, a parody of a stomp, an ineffectual, raging Jack-the-Giant-Killer stomp, for the escalator. "Let's buff out of here," she said, almost aloud, using another of Julio Bravo's expressions and adopting his heavy ghettoized Puerto Rican accent; it suited her.

Once outside, ashamed of her tantrum, over what? asinine trivia, she decided to case the big thrift shop on Fifty-ninth near First, where she would surely find a decent vest for a dollar fifty, fuck Kenzo, fuck designer snob appeal. The frigid drizzle had increased its momentum, wetting her hair through her sleazy scarf and moistening her forehead with icy drops. Her thin Kung Fu shoes were nearly soaked through; why hadn't she worn her boots? This little spree would undoubtedly result in pneumonia, she thought, dodging umbrella points; well, pneumonia wouldn't be half bad, she would lay up in a comfy hospital with *A la Recherche du Temps Perdu*, which she'd been meaning to read for years, and refuse all visitors, including Vasco. This was one of her favorite fantasies, succumbing to a nonfatal or not-too-painful illness, preferably in an exotic foreign land, reclining on an overstuffed mattress until she had finished Proust straight through instead of always quitting after *Swann's Way*, having to begin over again with it because she'd forgotten it altogether, rotten memory, when she vowed to read Proust again. Pneumonia would enable her to bag the makeup book for a while, render her incapable of normal existence, and in the long run prove far more constructive than compulsive shopping and/or involvements with criminal maniacs and warped souls who consumed all her spare psychic energy and time.

The thrift shop was more of a circus than Bloomingdale's, packed with careening women, beyond middle age, swathed in shapeless, bulging coats, ill-colored faces heavily pancaked, rouged cheeks inflamed, and shuffling, jobless, used-suit-hunting men. The vests were part of a mass of out-of-date women's pants, dresses, skirts, and blouses, all heaped together on a flat table. She burrowed into the soft, greasy pile of old clothes, stinking of kitchens and camphored closets, until she found, yes, a gold corduroy vest; but it was a man's vest, and when she tried it she saw that it gaped hugely at the sides and had a hole instead of a button, violently ripped from its moorings, plus a split up the back seam. She could repair it or take it to the tailor, but then it would only cost five bucks less than the beautiful new Kenzo vest; its price was three fifty. "Will you let me have this thing for two dollars?" she asked the matron in charge.

The matron looked through and beyond Dolores, transcending riffraff. "No reductions," she stated automatically.

"But look at this hole, and this one!"

The matron inspected the vest without interest, making Dolores, garment suspended from wrist, wait awkwardly. "You don't have to take it," she said at last.

Behind Dolores another customer waited to bargain for a pair of scuffed red suede pumps. "You can't charge ten dollars for a pair of used shoes," she wheezed.

The matron was fed up; a nerve in her powdered cheek trembled. "Just walk over to Bloomingdale's and see how much a pair of dress shoes will cost you there."

This remark infuriated Dolores. "Yeah, sure!" she said stridently. "But they're *new* shoes without the smell of some stranger's dirty old diseased feet in them! You can get a brand new pair of shoes on sale for twenty dollars— that's only double what you're charging for this crap."

"Not everybody who shops here can afford to buy new shoes like you can," the matron trebled haughtily.

"Sure they can!" Dolores said, her voice breaking into a fierce, high octave. "I bet everyone in here can afford new shoes. They're looking for bargains, just like I am, and these prices are no bargains! This is the most expensive thrift shop I've ever seen in my life. It's outrageous!"

The woman holding the shoes nodded vehemently. "That's right!" she said.

Dolores felt herself approach the invisible edge of a thrilling projection—protest, furious diatribe. In a minute she would begin raving, on and on. She could scream, kick, spit, a demonic succubus hoyden. An airborne vehicle was poised to take off; the motor hummed loudly. The matron turned her back pointedly. "What a rip-off these places are," Dolores continued loudly, angrily ad-

11

dressing the old woman with the shoes. "They want three dollars and fifty cents for this lousy vest full of holes. It's insane! They get this junk for free!"

"Oh yes," the shoe-woman quavered. A crushed hat topped her thin, yellowed hair. "Oh yes. Oh *yes*! They'll take you." She fixed Dolores with colorless pupils, mad, circuitous, split in the middle, creped lids tackily shadowed in blue, of course.

"I know. Outrageous." Dolores backed away from the woman's slanting body, her tubercular cheeks, wild eyes, a crazy woman, the brand of which she would soon be herself, was already, a younger version. Why had she lowered herself to create such a low-class scene in a thrift shop? There was no reason for her to be scrounging around these Godforsaken places. She was earning enough money on the makeup book, more than she ever had, to fritter away fifteen bucks at Bloomingdale's if she so desired.

She thought of the Kenzo vests, their ineffable, soft luxury; wanting one now created a palpable emptiness, a yearning hole for her other thoughts to march around. She ran through the rain back to the store, her head light, dizzy; she hadn't eaten since breakfast. The few blocks from the thrift shop seemed spaceless air miles. Perhaps the vests would all be gone. A sticky perspiration squeezed from between her breasts, despite the cold. She leaped up the escalator steps, deranged gazelle, to the third floor, panting, and found the vests, still in a pile on the chair. Without trying them on again, without debate, she selected two, the turquoise and the gold, and went looking for a salesgirl, who droned, "Cash or check?"

"Cash," said Dolores. Her hands were, could it be possible? shaking as she fumbled through her purse, past the wet silk garbage blouse for her wallet. She was inexplicably excited, eager to please the moronic salesgirl, slightly terrified, as always when she was about to waste money—fifteen dollars, thirty dollars, fifty dollars, no matter—she felt those dollars were her last in the world and she would transport herself to a different state of being by spending them.

On the subway Dolores began to shiver. She was cold and depressed. She had compared seven brands of translucent face powder on the main floor of Bloomingdale's, finally chosen one, then realized she didn't have enough money to pay for it—she had spent all but two dollars on the vests. She spotted the dials on the watch of the man next to her; it was almost four thirty. By the time she got home it would be five, late. She was bone weary, too exhausted, achy, to face a hoity-toity, pretentious dinner party at Vasco's. She hadn't done a stitch of work all day long or thought about anything but superficial nonsense. She hadn't gone to the Guggenheim; she hadn't taken a yoga class. She had more vests than she could wear as it was. Why had she bought two? She had already spent the extra money she allotted herself for compulsive shopping this month and it was only the seventh. She reached in the bag and felt the alluring texture of the fine corduroy with her hand, but now it inspired a sickening sense of guilt instead of pleasure, wretched overindulgence. She was becoming as materialistic as the people she despised, none of whom thought there was the slightest thing wrong with rampant materialism. It seemed she could no longer suffer one of these intense, irrational desires for petty goods for more than a couple of hours without at once rushing out to gratify it. A disturbing tendency. Soon she would want more, a cooperative apartment, a house in the country, like her friends had or were planning to buy, and then she would have to get a full-time job in some stifling office to pay the mortgage, a car to reach it, and she'd spend the greater part of her days worrying about leaking roofs, broken boilers, closing deals—subjects that would drag her mind into petty troughs. Her literary agent had warned her that poor writers needed more money as they grew older, and she had vowed she would vanquish the pattern of desire–gratification–new desire before it consumed her, made a sucking mouth out of her soul, like the undulating center of a feeding octopus. So far she had vanquished nothing, only wanted more, always. When she had finished adorning herself for the time being, she immediately desired utilitarian objects—towels, sheets, even potholders. She wondered if these piddling desires were substitutes for a greater desire she would never see satisfied. Perhaps she was shopping for Love or Renown.

Suddenly she remembered; she had a gold vest, not corduroy, gold wool, but it was gold, almost the exact shade of the new one, if not as well cut; no, no rationalizations. Disgusting! Maybe she could take it back and exchange it for the smoky blue; but then she would have two blue vests, if you could consider turquoise in the same category as blue. The receipt said "Final sale—no returns;" did that also mean "No exchanges"? She couldn't make her mind think about any of it anymore.

The subway stopped, metal screeching against metal, between stations for an unannounced reason. The perverse iron crawler had come to a dead, puffless halt, and to top off all the miserable phenomena of this dreary, wasted day she was stuck in the most nowhere middle of nowhere at the very moment she should have been washing her hair and dusting her face with the non-existent translucent powder she had gone to Bloomingdale's to buy for a decadent artist's dinner party she didn't wish to attend. The dark, featureless tunnel outside the window seemed an apt metaphor for the negative space that pressed around the few years she had left on this planet. She was wasting precious time. She didn't write enough poetry. If she died without publishing a book her life would have been wasted; she would leave nothing behind. She didn't read. She had managed to screw herself out of the only worthy career opportunity that had presented itself—thanks to her near fatal fling with Julio Bravo—and now she was forced to write shit again for money, better paid, but still shit. She was growing stupid and dull and unadventurous. No one loved her (certainly not Vasco) and she substituted self-pity for constructive action. The only accomplishment she could point to in the last few months was a dubious one—getting rid of Julio Bravo—and *accomplishment* was probably the wrong word for that.

CHAPTER

2

_D_OLORES arrived at the dinner party late, a major offense in her devotion to fleeting time, to be late for anything, or worse, to wait for anyone. Yet she'd needed time to pull herself together, internally, externally, with new red silk skirt, cashmere sweater, high-heeled gold snakeskin sandals, hairwash, makeup, an ideal look that obstinately finessed perfection, thanks to pale streaks in the skirt's sublime fabric, the payback for washing it with Woolite instead of taking it to the rip-off dry cleaner, and some ineffable principle of sabotage that mercilessly attacked any image she tried to construct that would portray her the way she wanted to be. She had chucked the garbage-can blouse away, moral compensation for the wasted afternoon. Finally launched, she balanced her way precariously to Vasco's on the slender heels; water from the sloppy street seeped in the toe hole and moistened her stockings.

Vasco accepted the three spidery chrysanthemums she handed him with the benevolent spirit of reception he reserved for things aesthetically correct. She had hoped he would focus on the Ikebana-like significance of the white buds instead of their chintzy quantity. He gave her the once-over, the obvious, appraising stare, emitted his usual approving "Hmmmmmmmmmmm," which did not necessarily represent approval. "You look gorgeous!" he exclaimed, yet she felt sure he'd registered the streaks in the skirt, her wet feet, the invisible, disintegrating principle; no flaw in any façade escaped him, despite his feeble vision, preserved with contact lenses.

Vasco had mastered the rebellious aspects of his own person and environment, cured or transformed the unlovely, and expected no less perfection from the rest of mankind. When he visited someone's dwelling for the first time, he snooped eagerly about, evincing flattering curiosity, lifting knickknacks from their shelves, inspecting titles in the library, and examining every artwork on the wall. Later, in private, he would make his unflattering pronouncements. "Such a tacky place! Did you notice those dreadful plants? Caladium," he'd state contemptuously in his articulated, resonant voice, as if *caladium* was the only word necessary to describe what was wrong with caladium. Then he'd add, "Did you notice that he's reading *Céline*?" by which emphasis she'd know Céline and caladium were in the same hopelessly unacceptable category of things God should never have made.

Vasco, of course, had not cluttered his own spacious loft with grubby weeds; only an elegant palm, no yellowing fronds, and one purposely stunted conifer conveyed an austere suggestion of nature and harmonized with every line and point in the scene. His library, too, was impeccable—all difficult hardcovers, no grimy paperback good reads—and each item on the walls, floors, and shelves had been chosen to complete the holistic design. Even his large, abstract paintings were so ferociously well-executed they cast the eye that dared to observe them scornfully away. Dolores had rapidly discovered that any words she chose to comment on these masterpieces were historically, aesthetically, and intellectually inaccurate, and had learned simply to gaze as if her rapt eyes were really seeing them instead of cowering in their sockets.

Vasco's physical presence, too, was perfectly contrived. Tonight his slim physique was encased in a black wool jump suit that the average male would never wear, almost effeminate or not quite aviator, designed by a "young lady" he knew. The satyrical black curls of his hair clung to the contours of his scalp and framed his smooth face, marred by neither blemish nor visible whisker; his ears, too, pierced along the rims and through the lobes by gold rings, emphasized his sensual, aristocratic features. Julio Bravo, who wore one simple ear stud, would have called him "stuff" or "faggot," and then discovering, as Dolores had, his vigorous amoral masculinity, would have said in the jocular voice he used to admit mistakes, "He ain't stuff!" True, she had seen Vasco kiss another man, a moist, intimate kiss, but she'd chalked that off to European custom. Once, he'd confided, he'd allowed an incomplete sex change to seduce him in a bar and spirit him off to "her" Lower East Side hotel. "He knew how to make his asshole seem exactly like a pussy," Vasco said, but complained the hormones the man had ingested

18

to increase the size of his breasts prevented him from getting an erection, so it was impossible to tell whether "she" had enjoyed the episode or not. "I'm afraid," Vasco had sighed, "I'm seventy-five percent heterosexual." He saw nothing unaesthetic about a roach-infested, undusted hotel room or the vaguely furred body of the Incomplete; in the name of perversity everything was beautiful.

The other guests at the party were women, predictably, except for one middle-aged Italian, a Gilbert Osmond *La Dolce Vita* type, and one forthright gay man, who discussed Off Broadway theater, with vivacious, stereotypical wrist action. It was impossible to determine who these women were, or their specific relationship to Vasco; they didn't let on, but seemed forlorn and hollow-eyed. They slouched about bonelessly, sipping cocktails, many cocktails, talking, not exactly to each other nor to themselves. Neither Vasco's estranged wife or present girl friend, a very young art student, was among them. The girl friend, Vasco constantly complained, was not intense, she'd been carrying *Pride and Prejudice* around for three months and the marker was still on page 40 ("Do you think she can read?"), she wasn't especially good in bed, couldn't deliver a halfway decent blow job, and worst of all, Dolores bet, she was a *bad* dresser. "Such youthful exuberance though," he would sigh in an unmistakably thirty-eight-year-old voice. He loved admiring her voluptuous young body, he said, a perfect form, tiny waist, firm thighs. She wasn't here; no, there were no bad dressers present besides Dolores herself, a secret bad dresser in her heart and soul.

Dolores made some attempt to be sociable, and approached a pale blonde, who revealed she had never recuperated from her mother's death, her mother had been her best friend, she was close to her father, too, who'd died of Hodgkin's disease shortly thereafter. Teutonic body, not Vasco's type, but you never knew. After her morbid recitation she pulsed down gin and tonic nervously, her white Adam's apple jumping, gulp, gulp, gulp; there was nothing more to say. Another floating female, wantonly curved, pouting mouth glossed, introduced as Sister of Girl Friend, lounged on her elbows on the kitchen butcher block, talking to Vasco while he cooked. Her theatrical voice intoned half-audible intimacies; Dolores strained to overhear. Why was the sister present and not the girl friend? The plot thickened. Vasco often said the young student was "not presentable." A mysterious blue-eyed redhead laughed and laughed.

Dolores gave up, wobbled on the uncomfortable shoes toward the safe leather boundaries of the Corbusier chair and ate many of the thin-sliced pale fennel sticks, looking, she hoped, as if she thought vital, poetic thoughts. She wondered what the others found to talk about, what words actually filled the heightened animated forms of strange dinner parties. She only enjoyed talking to people she already knew, who perversely bored her because she knew them, or to those rare souls, seldom encountered, she instantly understood on a level beyond superficial exchange. That was how she'd felt about Julio Bravo—a hazardous delusion. The next words she might be called upon to utter, the bright, boring, predictable question— What do you do? Do you live in Soho?—strained angrily against her gritted, half-smiling teeth. She could not be counted on to say the right thing, to be civil, she thought defiantly; but Vasco knew that and had invited her anyway. The truth was, admit it, she didn't feel comfortable here because so far she'd been ignored, barely acknowledged, then shoved to the sidelines. At the first offering of true attention she'd be panting and slurping like an ultracharming dog. These people must all know each other from art openings or previous parties.

She sat, continuing her systematic attack on the fennel, taking in the configurations of Vasco's perfect world—his antique silk muffler from Harriet Love, slung on a chairback, his superior paintings, plants, book titles, smooth body bent over the stove, even the invisible image of his elegant penis, despised by him for its smallness, admired by her for its simple, clear lines. He had held its indifferent head in his hand, eyed it with pretended wrath, and made his pious speech, "Whenever it looks like it could turn into something . . . blah, blah blah." Impossible to believe a man could suddenly go impotent; he'd been perfectly potent for quite a while, in fact, until the moment he'd decided not to be. Still, she could not remove her gaze from his smoothly muscled forearms, incongruously tough, like a sailor's, or his strong, blunt fingers. She continued to want him (because she couldn't have him, no doubt) and his flawless environment, because it, too, excluded her. She would always pursue the things she didn't have, couldn't have, or even logically want to have, like Julio Bravo; the question was *why*. Wasn't having better than wanting? No, it was better to want that which would destroy you or completely change you until you died.

She told herself this, but still felt a reprehensible, embittered yearning for what she now saw—beauty, in its most exalted, bourgeois, materialistic form. Flocks of thick-stemmed calla lilies flew above the long oak table, where excellent wine glowed in the candlelight and ironed linen napkins were precisely placed beside porcelain and silver. She again felt the perverse pleasure of deprivation, envisioning the ugly, chipped plates that occupied her own cupboard, those her mother had gotten

21

for free when she deposited money in a New Jersey bank. The same class of desire, felt then denied, applied to Vasco, by no means the sensible man she'd thought she was determined to find.

The first course was fresh ravioli, available at Raffetto's only, carefully steamed, accompanied by a brown butter sauce laced with chopped walnuts, a peculiarly subtle combination. The conversation on one side of her concerned mirrors. The gay man, revealing himself as the owner of a prestigious antique shop on Madison Avenue, remarked that people simply did not appreciate the value of mirrors and some, in their ignorance, actually removed fine, beveled glass from an antique frame and substituted inferior, modern junk. Dolores considered remarking that she loved mirrors, collected them in haphazard, cheapo style; her living room reflected her from every angle as well as her plants, including a shrinking caladium, and she kept an old hand-mirror in her desk drawer, examined her face every morning before starting to write, supposedly to check the progress of her skin, but actually to ascertain that some three-dimensional form of herself continued to exist. She shut herself up, afraid she would confess she'd found her favorite mirror in a garbage can, a statement that would undo her for all time with Vasco, seated on her right, enthusiastically discussing the divine properties of salted codfish with Gilbert Osmond, the Italian count.

"The Portuguese began eating bacalao during the war when it was impossible to get fresh fish," Vasco expostulated. She loved his careful voice no matter what it was saying. "Now they can't live without it; they actually prefer it to fresh fish. I have to beg my mother for fresh fish when I go to Lisbon."

"I *adore* bacalao," the throaty sister intoned. "It's so

completely yummy with olive oil and chopped dill. I had it the first time when I was in Barcelona with Felix." She looked meaningfully at Vasco, apparently privy to the extreme significance of Felix.

Dolores had nothing to say about vile bacalao. Moreover, she hated to discuss food, especially some titillating morsel no one was eating. It might have been reasonable, if dull, to talk about ravioli, but the too vivid thought of this obscure salted fish, which had stunk up the Puerto Rican bodegas in the bad, dynamic neighborhood she'd inhabited before moving to Soho, seemed to massacre the relatively pleasant taste of the pasta in her mouth. No one could possibly pretend to like bacalao; she was sure Julio Bravo, a true primitive, wouldn't touch it in a bomb shelter, much less any of these slightly paunchy, gourmand snobs. She considered an outrageous statement that would put an abrupt end to this pretentious discussion ("I once knew a Puerto Rican armed robber who ate bacalao sandwiches on Bond bread") but canceled it, fortunately. She imagined the throaty sister's dark eyes widening and Vasco's faggoty-voiced *Please*! or worse, no visible reaction. She was becoming hostile and for no good reason except no one had noticed she was alive, much less wonderful; thwarted ego. She took a gulp of wine.

Vasco left the table and returned with the main course. "Bollito Mixto," he announced in reply to the ensuing "Ahhs" and "Ooooohs."

"I'm glad you told me," Dolores thought sarcastically, eyeing with distaste the supposed *pièce de résistance*, an unimpressive assemblage of boiled trussed meat hunks, phallic sausages, pieces of chicken with unbrowned skin—the unabashed remnants of a slaughter—to be eaten, Vasco said, with *salsa verde* and a platter of vegetables steamed *al dente,* carrots, Italian squash, potatoes, and worst of all, cabbage.

"I love hearty food," the redhead said. "It brings out the peasant in me, the Tom Jones."

"That's just what I was hoping for," Vasco said salaciously, and everyone laughed.

"The last time I had a real Bollito Mixto I was a little boy in Naples," said the Italian count, pronouncing *Bollito Mixto* in unmistakably authentic tones.

"The sauce is exquisite," the pale orphan said.

"What's *in* it?" thrilled the voluptuous sister. "Vasco, you're a genius!"

"Hard-cooked egg white, basil, dill, parsley, watercress and shallots in oil and wine vinegar," Vasco recited, carving portions of the sausages and slices of meat with a well-honed Sabatier. This hearty pile of supposedly unpretentious flesh had probably cost poor Vasco a fortune, Dolores thought; she knew he lived well beyond his means and he thought she was cheap.

"The beef is *cured*!" announced the gay antique dealer in triumphant tones.

Around her the crowd belabored the joys and misconceptions of peasant fare: A simple cassoulet, for example, which took days to prepare ("Americans don't appreciate beans"); bouillabaisse, just a glamorized fishhead soup; truffles, underground mushrooms eaten by hogs, not as tasty as morels by any means; and pheasant, really only *game.* ("Did you ever have it at Le Plaisir?")

The eulogy to food continued. The sausages were divine. Had Vasco prepared them himself? Where on earth did he get the casings?

"At Mancello Brothers! Do you know one of the Mancellos, the old one with the long face, took out his cock and laid it on the chopping block right in front of Kathy?

Yes, he *did*! He did it to Kathy and to someone else she knows."

"The only place to buy good cabbage is at Balducci's."

"This taste is really special, Vasco; it's a *special* taste."

"I left out the turkey," Vasco declared. "I looked at the recipe and I said, 'Enough is enough!' "

"Thank God. I loathe turkey. Pure Thanksgiving."

"So much to do about a fucking boiled stew," Dolores muttered to herself. Her mind was rapidly slipping out of her restraining grasp, like a badly trained dog about to leap and bark and break its leash if she didn't guard it carefully. But when the plate was passed to her, alas, the plunging beast broke free and words, gritted down, bound the entire evening, no, the entire day, were on the rampage. "No thank you!" she said loudly.

"No thank you?" Vasco repeated. He shot her a questioning, not hurt, interested stare.

"I don't eat meat anymore," she declared defiantly, and though no one expressed the slightest desire to hear why not, she went on to denounce the consumption of animals in religious, political, and practical terms, her voice banging like a tom-tom in her own ears. "When you kill an animal you terrify it," she said intensely, false intensity, nothing to do with food. "And that fear sends certain dangerous hormones . . . like adrenaline, flooding through its body. Those substances stay in the meat and when you eat it you absorb them . . . they change your nature . . . make it fearful and aggressive. . . . And animals raised for slaughter are injected with hormones to begin with, probably carcinogens." This was a somewhat inaccurate version of an argument she had once heard a spaced-out Californian put forth in a cheap restaurant in Mexico and at the time she had continued chewing her way through a tough *filete* and thought, Bullshit! "Have you ever noticed the teeth on people who can't live without their meat?" she asked, a direct quote from the Californian. "Sharp and pointed and yellow—like dogs' teeth. Meat-eating makes you bellicose and aggressive," she repeated, noting, even in the midst of this diatribe, the sonorous beauty of the word *bellicose*, "which is why Buddhists don't eat it."

The rest of the party had receded into a silent blur, unfocused, except for the eyes of the orphan, which observed her with the lack of expression people reserved for the dangerously insane on the IRT. She ranted on, afraid to stop—the grains they fed pigs and cattle would feed starving people all over the world; in rural areas cattle farmers used all available land to graze cows and poor people had to pay outrageous prices for imported fruits and grains. She wasn't sure where she had acquired these facts or why she now remembered them. The blur receded and she realized her voice was lower than she'd thought, almost a growl; the company had eclipsed her, chatted on around her, and only Vasco was actually listening. Dolores felt sick; she knew Vasco knew she ate meat; she'd downed many a hapless poisoned creature in the restaurants he'd taken her to in the first days of their short affair before fake impotence had eliminated her. Before this very party, in fact, she'd paused long enough to gulp down half a raw burger at home to forestall the hypoglycemic starvation fit she'd been about to have all day. "If people stopped eating meat they could get rid of their doctors and their psychiatrists," she finished desperately, an eloquent conclusion for a lecture to the Hindu Vegetarian Society of Bombay, but here, the final ravings of an antisocial lunatic. Having vented her feeble hostility she sat, isolated and miserable, starving for a piece of the homemade sausage and cured beef.

Yet her speech had pricked Vasco's sensitive moral nerve, the hairline structure that occasionally led him to abandon his cultured poses and rise up screaming against repression and injustice, as when, for example, he heard some poverty-stricken young artist had been evicted from his co-opted loft by a rich insurance broker, though he would be the first to curl his refined lip at the poor artist's pitiful attempts to create art. It was this moral sensibility, which both heightened and diminished the impact of his perfect physical self and world, that she admired in him. "You're right," he sighed woefully. "In Portugal an entire family could live for a month on the money I spent on this dinner party." He was glumly sincere; always basically guilty, he was pleased to be called to task.

The sister, catching Vasco's interest in starvation, resonated, "I've always wanted to go to India, so I could see hunger firsthand!" A discussion of the fabulous temples of Madras followed and let Dolores off the hook. She sat in silence, condemned to her spare porcelain plate of bread and salad, ignominious in her own eyes, again bypassed by the conversation, wondering why she felt compelled to ruin the best moments of her social life, the very ones she was always hoping and shopping for. With a sneaking, fiercely gluttonous gesture, almost sexual in its impolite rapacity, Vasco scraped the last of the *salsa verde* into its silver serving spoon and gobbled it up. Only Dolores noticed and admired this magnificently ill-mannered move. Her feet, caged in their chic snakeskin sandals, were killing her, even sitting down.

．　　．　　．

Later she found herself alone with Vasco in a bar near his loft. The rest of the dinner party had drifted away, including the desirable sister. Vasco was drunk and morose. For some reason his nose was bleeding a little. He dabbed at the blood with furtive grace, seeming to decorate rather than soil his linen handkerchief with the brownish plasma. His entire body was extraordinarily sensitive, developed strange maladies and chills: his lower back often bothered him; boils surfaced on the soft insides of his thighs, due, he said, to the steam heating in winter. His eyes were so weak Dolores wondered how he could see to paint, much less scrutinize the ubiquitous imperfections around him. He suffered, too, from herpes simplex, which had afflicted him for the first time on his honeymoon and forever after when he fell simultaneously in and out of love. His mortal body, it seemed, was determined to give the lie to his perfection. "Oh, *God!*" he groaned, screwing his beautiful face into a desperate grimace. "I'm doomed!" He had just finished telling Dolores how hopelessly enraptured he was by the sister's charms, her gorgeous body, her fabulous tits. (He had once shown her naked photos of the important women in his life and evaluated the form and structure of each pair of nippled globes.) He desired the sister, he went on, though he knew she was brainless and irritating ("Can you imagine actually *saying* you want to go to India and see the starving firsthand!"); he didn't like her as much as his girl friend, basically better-natured, if also a little dumb, who would commit suicide if he fucked her sister. Maybe he should see a psychiatrist; no, he loathed psychiatrists and everything they stood for. He continued his list of grievances: He'd had everything a man could want in his marriage and had given it up; now his estranged wife was scheming to steal his loft; his paintings had been

28

passed over for an important European exhibition and his best friend's paintings, very superficial, had been selected for the same show; his debts were increasing; he was furious that no one at the dinner party had commented on his new painting, though he'd purposely turned out the light in his studio so no one would look; he probably wouldn't get a Guggenheim; he would only be able to leave New York for forty days next summer, thanks to the crummy trimester teaching job he'd taken, which he wouldn't have to have if his worthless dealer got busy and sold some of his work. His nose spurted a small cataract of blood and he moaned and dabbed at it.

"Don't forget to mention your tiny penis," Dolores reminded him.

"Oh *God!*" he groaned again. "It *is* tiny, isn't it?" He loved to talk about how tiny it was and how much trouble he had getting it up for undeserving women. "How about you?" he asked. "Have you got any gigantic black kidney-wipers lurking around your place these days?" Dolores had once confessed her dalliance with a black dancer and he'd never let her forget it. She was glad she hadn't told him about Julio Bravo.

"No," Dolores said. "No kidney-wipers at all these days." In fact, she was relieved, despite omnipresent isolation, to go to bed by herself and wake up in peace. Life was not stimulating, but it also lacked the possibility of catastrophe she both feared and craved. If she could summon the self-discipline to reverse her viewpoint, enjoy her solitude instead of regretting it, she could use it, use it now, to her advantage, shake herself out of her lethargy and write some decent poetry, apply for grants, for readings, send out her old work to literary magazines and publishing companies and calmly throw the rejection slips in the wastebasket instead of stamping on them or burning them with matches or sending them back to the editors with vitriolic comments typed on the back. She should stop her unproductive bitching about the makeup book (not the lives of the poets, God knew, but a timely source of income), finish it quickly, then move onto higher plateaus, professional, spiritual, or the actual snow-ridged peaks of the Bolivian Andes. He is happy who sees not his unhappiness, she thought. Who said that? Probably Gurdjieff. She repeated it aloud.

"Dolores," Vasco exclaimed gratuitously. "You're so wonderful! Why didn't I fall in love with you?" He'd made the same below-the-belt remark when he'd called to announce he was in love with the college girl; but it was all right—below-the-belt had played a certain cathartic role in their relationship from the moment it began, a month after Julio Bravo had disappeared.

She summoned an innocuous, abstract reply, a misquote from some poet whose name she'd forgotten. "The longer I live the more I think two people in love is a miracle," she said. Vasco looked baffled; he wasn't into poetry, though he, more than her other friends, who thought she'd gone insane, might understand the desire to throw one's life down the path of a bizarre romantic fantasy, provided the object was aesthetically acceptable, which Julio Bravo was not. She wished Vasco was in love with her. He was appropriate; he was not sensible enough to be deadly; he might save her from the dangerous excesses that would surely tempt her again. She believed that whether he knew it or not he *was* in love with her, that he had mistaken his love for friendship, or was it that he mistook dislike for sexual desire? He kissed her warmly and she went out into the night. She thought (Did he think so too? Probably not) that it might have been nice for them to pass the lonely, dissatisfied night together, but she was content to push that possibility into the safe arena of the future or wishful thinking.

To punish herself for her undisciplined outburst at dinner she walked home in the rain on her high gold heels. By now, at two in the morning, they had sprouted fangs and claws that tore mercilessly into the tender flesh of her metatarsal arch. Every step she took shot dribbling pains up her calves and pressed further agonies into her toes and heels. Her ability to balance on the narrow talons, rocking and skidding on the slippery sidewalk, had diminished with drink and exhaustion, and she felt as if her aching progress home should be applauded as an acrobatic act. The street was wet and insidious puddles penetrated the thin leather soles; the shoes would be ruined, she thought, a possible blessing.

The drizzle, now in earnest, soaked her hair and the soft blue wool of her decent coat, but she could not direct her mind to any locale but the terrible shoes; she might pass out from the pain, plunge forward onto her face and lie prostrate, unable to right herself until the police packed her frostbitten body off to Bellevue. She considered taking the shoes off, throwing them away, and slopping barefoot through the cold, wet streets; but she was afraid of glass and nails piercing her flesh, killing her with lockjaw, the disease she dreaded most because of its name. As she staggered, the simple agony of aching feet transcended less concrete miseries, leaped upward to become a dismal, vacant space in her perceptions, a blank in the mind's eye, like her appearance outside a mirror. Her heavy body, unseen, hurtled itself from block to block, a moth's body between disintegrating wings.

By the time she reached her apartment even her relief was demoralized. The beginnings of a hangover had already sucked the moisture from her mucous membranes and spread its fuzzy, disordered padding throughout her brain, obliterating her plans for the following day, plans she carefully constructed, actually written down on small slips of paper, inevitably lost or disobeyed, which nonetheless allowed her, in theory, not a single minute of idle, meaningless time, during which she became scared to the point of the shakes of a vague galaxy she could only define as "death," though it was probably something less dramatic—maybe the aura of her lonely life. Certainly she would lose another half day on *High Styling Your Face.* She was practically allergic to alcohol but kept drinking it, especially lately, because nothing in or around her was definite. Minus her shoes her feet still hurt; she felt the soft excrescences of new blisters with her fingers. Too exhausted to take a hot, purifying bath, or wash the makeup, now slick and garish, off her face, she went to bed, body cramped, and heard, just beneath her immediately blurred consciousness, the sound of a knock.

Startled to semiawareness, she yelled in a hoarse voice, "Just a minute!" The knocker remained silent. Who could it be at this Godforsaken hour? She fumbled in her closet for her pink silk kimono, couldn't find it, and without turning on the kitchen light looked out the peephole of the door.

"It's Julio," the voice, husky and scratched from endless unfiltered cigarettes, said. She spotted the edge of his brown Afro through the peephole and then, as he stepped closer, thrusting himself into its distorting range, his unmistakable face bulged into the small circle of glass.

Dolores swayed. Her first half-asleep thought was that she was naked; molecules of air brushed her skin, her pores.

"Listen, Dolores. It's Julio," he said, his staccato accent separating the syllables into singsong tones.

Dolores still didn't answer. Gradually her mind lost its involvement in the retreating labyrinth of dreams and began to focus on the fact that Julio Bravo was once again outside her door. Her body wanted to be elsewhere, away from the perverse temptation to answer, a temptation she'd sworn would never afflict her again. Could she actually not answer, even knowing he knew she was there?

"Dolores . . ." he said again, anxiously.

He had come for something, that was for sure. Basically he'd always come for something—because he wanted to "rap" to her, wanted to knock out one of his so-called poems on her extra portable typewriter, wanted a sandwich, a place to smoke a joint, wanted to fuck her instead of looking for a job, wanted to use her, wanted her to save him from himself, then not to save him, or to save him in spite of his desire not to be saved, which she had never managed to do. Now, maybe he wanted revenge. No, that was paranoid; his tone of voice told her that was untrue. Then she remembered the gun, or remembered she had never really forgotten it, taped, as it was, to the underside of the kitchen sink, where she never saw it, or had to touch its shape or evil metal texture. Of course. That was it. Whatever he would say had brought him back to her door, Julio Bravo had come for his gun.

CHAPTER

3

*D*OLORES first met Julio Bravo, otherwise known as "Julito" and "Duke," in jail. She'd had the good luck to get a job teaching in this prison in the fall of the preceding year, one course, "Introduction to the Arts," part of a community college extension program for inmates. She had decided to skip the rest of the arts, a bullshit idea, and transform the course into an inspired poetry workshop. It was clear from the way she was hired, sight unseen, that nobody at this college cared what was taught at the Godforsaken Briarstone Correctional Facility, or who taught it; but it was still fifty bucks a class, and more important, an unexpected opportunity to venture into unknown territory.

She imagined the squalid cellblocks, flickering twenty-watt bulbs illuminating strung-out, desperate eyes, lonely knuckled hands gripping bars, a highly charged atmosphere, the sudden flash of a homemade knife, all men, handsome, unjustly incarcerated, political prisoners, or imprisoned for quintessentially evil crimes, and herself, an important missionary of poetry, come to invoke the revelation of new emotions in poems so fine, so unique, many would be published in *Antaeus* and *The Paris Review*, catapulting the second-rate college to a vicarious academic renown. She would then be offered the reward of a full-time, tenured teaching job, far more lucrative than her free-lance project of that time, a dismal encyclopedia entry, "Fruits of the World," that paid only twenty-five dollars a page, or roughly twenty-five dollars a fruit, and she would reject it because college teaching was too secure to inspire a true poet.

With all this in mind she approached the fortress-like prison facility, the guntowers, the wall, not the least prepared for the drab, institutional plain that greeted her, or for Julio Bravo, who was into movies, "*mak*ing movies, man," which he announced at once from the file cabinet he was perched upon, like a king who had known better days.

The file cabinet was part of an abandoned flock of furniture, stored in the only part of the prison she was allowed to see—the room where her course was held, an incongruously large gymnasium of sorts, stacked with useless surplus desks, chairs, benches, and shelves, giving the impression of a bankrupt industry. The walls, painted with obvious tail ends of paint, originally intended, perhaps, for cheap dance halls or hospital operating rooms, were alternately a bilious flamingo pink with blinding yellow trim, and chalky pale green with flamingo pink trim, colors that inspired immediate depres-

35

sion. No twenty-watt bulbs, but overbright fluorescent lamps drained the natural lifeblood from every face, whatever its pigmentation, and bleached it a jaundiced sallow. Sounds echoed fearfully in this dismal room. Voices grew and hollowed, distorted by the tunnel-like space, so words were hard to distinguish, tones impossible to gauge. A loud train roared by on a track, inexplicably present outside the window, every few minutes, filling the room with mechanized thunder that hovered and bounced off the walls, obliterating all other sounds, until the next train passed and refreshed its noise. A weary, heavy-jowled guard, not a vicious sadist, just mildly mean and dumb, sent, she presumed, to make sure none of the inmates escaped or attacked her, snoozed on one of the irrelevant benches, his portable radio playing loud, echoing Muzak.

Yet, the entire east wall of the room was composed of tiny panes of glass, which looked out over the distant river and cliffs beyond. Dolores's course ran until early evening, and the sun set while she was there. At times she tuned out the sounds of the class, even the monotonous ramblings of her own voice, and turned toward the plaintive, fading glow of the sun, dazzling the glass into an infernal, sparkling shine, an abstract, ignited reference to desolation. "A hundred-dollar-a-night-hotel view," the jovial guard, who transported her to the classroom in a type of armored van, called it.

At first Dolores had no idea what to do with Julio Bravo. Unlike the other inmates, who sat bitterly in their chairs, chewing their cud of chained passive resistance, he had enthusiastically bought the entire idea of "Introduction to the Arts." From his file cabinet he proclaimed the virtues of "Art!"in his throaty, staccato prison lingo, as if Art were a banner of war, and he the corporal privileged to carry it. "Dig it, Art! I *need* to instruct myself about *art*, my man, because art is one of the ways we can bring the message to the people!" He thought, moreover, that movies were the most important form of art because, "If we be making movies we can show the people on the streets what is happening behind the walls." He questioned Dolores minutely about movies she had seen on the "outside," how much she thought movie equipment cost, whether she could pressure the warden to supply the class with cameras and shit, could she get some books on moviemaking, and so on. For the first couple of weeks, Dolores, determined to be accommodating, devoted part of each class to heming and hawing about movies, and then moved hastily to the intricacies of verse, rhymed and free, the demanding writing process. Finally, in response to his surprisingly technical question about Super 8, defiantly following her reading of Yeats's "The Second Coming," one of her all-time favorites, she looked Julio Bravo straight in the eye and stated, "To tell the truth I don't know jackshit about movies."

Julio respected the direct statement. His imperturbable brown eyes narrowed for his strange laugh, which always arrived at the moment Dolores had braced herself for hostility, argument, or criticism. When he understood that poetry gave him opportunities to spin endless yarns about himself, his inner and outer world, he submitted to it gracefully. "My *po*etry," he called it, with the tone of modest pride he might have used to refer to a millionaire offspring. His poetry wasn't half bad—temperamental, emphatic, narrative, rhythmic. If devoid of true English spelling or abstract imagery, it always had an authentic, personal tone. It was actually quite original, more than you could say for the work of most poets published by important literary magazines, Dolores thought, original, as she believed hers to be original, in a different way, of course. He read his poems loudly, combatively, defying the echoes in the room to take it away from him, perspiring nervously at first, and then, with increasing assurance. After almost every class he reminded Dolores and the other men that he had only completed the third grade; sometimes he changed his story and made it the seventh.

Dolores praised him extravagantly, as a missionary muse should. He did have undeveloped talent, if not quite as much as she indicated. She kind of got a kick out of him; he was the most vital and interesting of her students, and for that alone he deserved a little praise. She liked to look at him, to analyze his fascinating physical duality. On one hand he seemed a caricature of a prisoner, pure Jean Genet, complete with shaved head, right ear pierced with a gold stud, powerful body, a black, prison-done tattoo of a squat, expressionless tarantula on the tendons of his muscular wrist. On the other hand, he looked almost old-world, faintly conquistador, handsome aquiline features and bones, full, carved lips, smooth, tawny skin, carefully trimmed goatee. One impression cast the other in the shadow of its opposite— genetically refined, then tough and sinister.

Jail was Julio Bravo's world, a planet to which he'd been banished and whose geography he knew. He loved jail. He complained about it constantly but his brown eyes were gay and his voice relished the taste of his complaints. Though he'd spent fifteen of his twenty-nine years in various prisons and reform schools, he could still speak about being "locked up" as a continual drama in which he played the hero's part. He claimed, for example, to be personally responsible for forcing the prison administration to reinstate the Puerto Rico Discovery Day picnic, after it had been senselessly canceled in response to an escape attempt by an inmate in another institution, hundreds of miles away. Leaning forward on the file cabinet, hands clasped beneath his knees, he told the story sotto voce, so the half-snoozing guard wouldn't hear. "I said, 'Listen, my man, you have *got* to give us our day. You take away our day and I can not be responsible for what might jump off in here.' 'Why are you talking about violence?' they asked me. I said, 'I ain't necessarily talking about *vi*-olence, my man, I am talking about the way the brothers will feel when you take away their day. You can not be asking a man to give up the one day in the year when he is allowed to see his mother, his kids, his woman, eat his food, play his music, talk his language, the one time when he be greeting his family like a man, instead of like an animal in a cage, without asking for some bad shit to come down. We ain't asking you for no special favors, my man. The blacks had their day, the Irish had their day, now the Borrinqueños want our day, too. Dig it, we are only asking you for what is *correct*!' "

Correct was one of Julio Bravo's favorite words. He pronounced it with a special emphasis on the final syllable that seemed to give the simple word a host of meanings and imply a fearful, moral contingency, enforced with lethal weapons, if denied. Many of the words in his vocabulary bore this weighty, accented syllable, which redefined the word it hit, giving it an extra aura of significance. He spoke in a staccato, chanting singsong, biting some words hard, letting others float huskily into shallow holes. He separated words from each other with visible spaces, making each word, even minute ones, equal and important. He severed apostrophe forms of

---

pronouns and verbs, split contractions, transforming the formal, "we are," "you are," and "can not" into drumbeating iambic dimeters. His verbal rhythms were mesmerizing; Dolores was often conscious of focusing more on his sharp emphases, than on the sense of what he was saying. His vocabulary was a mix of street and prison jargon, Spanish expressions, selected for exclamatory value, and occasionally a pedantic phrase he must have picked up from his lawyers or the books he read in his cell. He always addressed someone called "My Man." Dolores was never sure who "My Man" was, since it wasn't her, or the other men (plural) in the workshop. She sometimes thought "My Man" was an invisible higher power—Julio Bravo's personal God.

In such emphatic monologues he often spoke of the state's renowned prison riot, six years before. He had been, to hear him tell it, an important leader in this event, a "security guard." He had given the negotiators "safe passage," and had subsequently been indicted on forty-seven counts of murder and kidnapping before all participants in the politically inflammable holocaust had been pardoned by the governor. One of his most effective poems, in fact, was called "Forty-Seven Counts." ("Forty-seven counts/ you gave me forty-seven counts/ me/ your Carib brother . . .") Yet, he spoke of this prison riot in the convivial, nostalgic tones a Yale alumnus adopts to describe his freshman fraternity hazing, though the scenes—dying inmates, helicopters, machine guns, tear gas—were catastrophic. Dolores only vaguely remembered the prison riot. She had been in graduate school at the time, studying the labored intricacies of metaphysical poetry, and writing worthless papers about it. She had always only thought of herself and stuck to the narrow borders of her selfish preoccupations, too trivial to admit the terror or beauty of anything in the real world.

"I did not know there could *be* fear like that!" said Julio, in an intimate, rough voice, walking her to the door after the class. His tones, suddenly close to her ear, were devoid of jocularity. "I was lying in the mud, dig it, face-down, and the state trooper has his gun barrel in my ear. 'Keep your nigger nose down,' he said to me. In one second I *knew* that motherfucker was going to pull the trigger and blow me away. Around me I be hearing the sound of clubs hitting on flesh and bone. *Coño,* I did not think I was going to die, I *knew* I was going to die! You know how they be talking about death, the poets, like it was an a-*byss,* or some shit like that. I know that a-*byss,* my man, that a-*byss* is a friend of mine. Yeah. . . . I was looking into its face, I was looking down *into* it. I could not breathe because of the tear gas, Dolores; I thought I was already iced. Then one of the other hacks comes running up and says, 'Cool it, man, there has been enough killing here,' and the *po*-lice takes his piece out of my ear and walks away. Just walks away. Man, I was fucking dead, I was al-ready dead." He shook his head as if disengaging it from a clamp. "I can't even write no poems about that. After that I could never be scared of nothing, Dolores, nothing in life."

Dolores was shaking when she left the jail. She only had to be reminded of the a-*byss* to feel it, frantically ever-present in her own queasy innards. It was easy for her to understand how Julio Bravo felt with a gun barrel in his ear; she could empathize with that resigned terror. She often felt it herself for less concrete reasons; she knew airplanes would crash, or cars would swerve off bridges, crashing through guardrails, or run her down on the street. In bed, alone at night, she lay on the barely tangible edge of something about to metamorphose into a formless something else, characterized by a total absence of familiar qualities.

She went to the library and read a back issue of *Newsweek* on the riot; she even looked it up in *The New York Times*, squinting at the hazy microfilm. She found a photograph in a book, taken after the riot, of the prison inmates, their hands over their heads, stripped naked in the litter and rubbish of the yard they had seized, while a guard in an old-fashioned uniform waistcoat and gas mask inspected them for weapons. The photograph was blurred and the figures in it out of focus; this technical deficiency, plus the almost ungraspable nature of the subject matter, made the scene appear to have been photographed in the long past, during an early world war, before the invention of the modern camera. Dolores inspected the naked figures in the photographs carefully, buttocks, shoulders, legs, genitals, then realized she was looking for one she could recognize as Julio Bravo. That made her slightly uncomfortable.

Though most of Julio's stories made him the champion of anti-establishment forces, he was capable of switching sides if the situation warranted. When one of the participants in the Alcoholics Anonymous meeting, held the same hour as Dolores's class, sneaked into the parole board review room and was apprehended sawing the bars, Julio Bravo claimed to have drawn him aside on his way to the "box." "*Coño!*" he said. "What you did was not cor-*rect*. Nobody likes being locked down, my man" (he always spoke the words *locked down* or *locked up* with special pejorative emphasis, as if to punish them for inflicting their outrageous ordeal) "but, dig it, when something like this goes down you are putting *my* privileges in jeopardy." He was right. The next Arts class was suspended until the prison administration made "special security arrangements." The following week it took the officials in charge nearly an hour to locate a "secure" room for the class, which turned out to be the same old pink and green room, chaperoned by the same snoozing hack. Dolores learned later that her students had been strip-frisked before they could return to their cells, even though none of them had sawed the bars. "That dude who be sawing the bars, man . . ." reflected Julio Bravo, "he shot his own wife with a .45!" He shook his head, exasperated with the frailties of mankind.

It was considered poor prison etiquette to ask an inmate what crime he'd committed, and most kept this information to themselves, because, as one of the men in her class attested, the majority were "down" for such "petty shit," they didn't want to acknowledge it. "If we was to tell you why we was locked up, you'd laugh," he said. "You'd say, 'You did *that*? Ha *Ha*! You're down for *that*!' " Julio Bravo, however, doing the tail end of a fourteen-year bid for armed robbery and grand larceny, was more than willing to own up to his crimes. He extolled them like a deacon, used them as fables to illustrate the sins of his past compared to his total reform, the difference between what he had been, what he was now, and what he was going to be. The character in his war stories was not really himself, but a much-beloved, basically noble, errant knight, whose slightly misguided desire for profit, adventure, and righteous action had led him willy-nilly into the quicksands of shit creek. At age ten he had robbed a *blanco* kid selling ice cream in the park at knife point, and the fucking judge had sent him upstate for a whole year for that, even though the victim had protested, "I know this guy, your honor; he's a nice guy, honest, even though he did that thing to me." By the time he was sixteen he was a stoned junkie, shooting heroin and cocaine. He woke up on Christmas morning, eighteen years old, handcuffed to a hospital bed, shot during the holdup of a service station. He wrote an ironic lyric about this misadventure called, "Merry Christmas, Asshole!"

When he got out of jail he couldn't stay out of the "nightlife," he said. He was still strung-out, *embaldo,* my man. Every morning his two partners would pick him up in their red Thunderbird, paid for in cash, no time, the trunk loaded with guns—a Thompson submachine gun, a .38 special, a .45 automatic, and a .357 Smith & Wesson magnum—and they rode out to pull a sting. One morning they smashed into a discount electronics store in the South Bronx, faces masked, guns smoking. A little old lady, "like my own grandmother, man," started to cry piteously. Julio took her by the shoulders and sat her down on a carton: "You just sit right here, *abuelita,*" he said softly, "we ain't going to take nothing of yours."

"Please, mister, just let me go home," she'd begged.

One partner had the store owner covered with the automatic, and the other was emptying the cash register; Julio stood guard at the door. The tension was like a stretched thread. Suddenly they heard the wail of the police sirens; they were surrounded.

Handcuffed in the paddy wagon Julio began to laugh. He couldn't stop. That laughter was *loco,* man, he couldn't keep it in his mouth, no way. "What are you laughing for, you dumb spic?" the pig said to him. "Don't you know what kind of trouble you're in?" Julio kept laughing and laughing; *coño,* he could not stop. When he finally stopped, he said, it was a month later; he looked around and saw he was in the Tombs. Later that day they called him down; he thought he'd made bail. "We have been looking for you for a long time, motherfucker," they told him. "We have you down for eighty-two armed robberies in the South Bronx alone."

"Was it really that many?" Dolores asked, amazed.

"I figure it was about sixty-seven," Julio said.

After he did that bid Julio Bravo got out, then went back to jail on a parole violation, his present term. He'd been doing good, he said, *real* good, and then he let some cocksucker talk him into holding up a small-time dope dealer in The Bronx. It was a little job, no one was there, the lock broke easy, but they found only four hundred dollars in the stash and argued who should get the lion's share. Julio was disgusted. *"Vaya, hombre,* you want to give me only two yards? I am risking my parole for this chickenshit!" Then the familiar siren sounded.

The police asked Julio to inform on the dealer, whose headquarters was a small fruit and vegetable store. "Shit, man, you know this dude ain't making no fifteen hundred dollars a day selling lettuce and papayas," Julio said. "Why are you asking me? I ain't no snitch." He got sent up longer for his scruples. He wrote a poem, inspired by this recollection, called "My Gun," which sarcastically rendered the passionate feelings of a convict for his favorite weapon, his "machismo," as Julio called it, the same weapon that put him in the joint, took away his family, his children, left him lonely in a "bed of steel," without love.

Many of the poems written in "Introduction to the Arts" were about love, unrequited love, lost love, and Julio Bravo, too, waxed eloquent on this subject. "Love, my man. Do I know what love is? Do I *feel* love? Have I *ever* felt love? This is something I be always asking myself. I don't know no more. Dig it, sometimes I am not even sure if I love my own children. I do know I can't live wit' their mothers." Dolores wondered how many mothers and children there were; he made them sound like a large, screeching army. He gazed into the glow of the setting sun, his narrowed eyes honestly befuddled. "When a man is locked down, what can love mean to him, man? Love don't mean shit! . . . *Love* is this feeling that is driving him crazy, some feeling I have for a nice soft thing that don't even remember I ex-ist right now. Any love I am able to feel in here has got to be a spiritual love, and *spir*-itual means no touching, no kissing, no talking, no nothing that signifies love to me, man. Letters don't mean shit when it comes to love. *Coño,* maybe it is easier for me to feel this kind of no-love than to feel real love. My mother said to me one time, when she was alive, 'Julito, you don't love nobody, you selfish moth-erfucker,' he concluded, laughing. Dolores found all this quite interesting, quite intense; she had seldom heard a man philosophize about love before; either they loved, didn't love, were loved or weren't loved, and that was as far as they went. Incarceration, she thought, might well lead all men to discover new sides of themselves, as the Quakers had thought, if not in quite the same sense.

Some of the inmates wrote glorious eulogies to her sex, especially Sam Evans, whose women were electrified, their hair dissolving into sparks, their skin melting in transparent blue flames. She complimented him on his subtle imagery, wondering, with doubts, if any of her lovers would have described her as such a sublime fire. "If I can write about 'em so good, how come I can't get along with 'em?" he muttered.

Julio Bravo, still leading the flag up the hill, inter-rupted. "Listen, my man, getting along wit' a woman ain't easy. Maybe these fe-males you be writing about don't give you no room to be yourself! I have had this *problema! Vaya,* if I was playin' chess or solitaire, my woman, La Flaca, she be coming over and putting her arms around me, sayin', 'Julito, are you mad at me?' and when I was telling her, 'No, I ain't mad wit' you, woman, I am only trying to *think!*' right away she be starting to cry and says, 'How come you don't love me no more?' When I was wanting to go up on the roof and fuck around wit' my pigeons she be asking me, 'Why don't you ever do nothing with me?' " "Now what would you want to be doing on the *roof*?" he'd answered.

La Flaca, the thin one, thought Dolores, intrigued. This unique name, more than any of Julio's stories about his abstract "wives," transmitted an immediate image of his life.

Julio went on to discuss women's inability to understand men. One time he had gone out for a pack of cigarettes and hadn't come home for three months. When he did his woman told him she could not be with him no more. "Why didn't you call?" she'd demanded.

"I *couldn't* call," he'd replied.

"Why didn't you write?" she'd asked.

"I *couldn't* write!" he'd said.

"I'm on her side," Dolores said smugly, and tried to turn the discussion back to poetry, how to transform your real life into cosmic images, with specific, yet universal, importance. This was a bit beyond the class, she thought, but Julio nodded with eager understanding. Later she recalled the "I couldn't call" story with particular vividness.

It surprised her when she began to dream about Julio Bravo. One morning, the day after her class, she woke up and remembered with a sense of shock, that Julio Bravo had come up to her as she was leaving and taken her hand, as if to shake it. Then, instead of releasing her hand, he had lifted it to his mouth and licked it. At the time she had barely noticed this unseemly gesture, but now it struck her as a preposterous and disrespectful act. Why hadn't the guard said something? Perhaps he hadn't noticed. The other men deliberately looked away. Afterward he'd kept his eyes fastened on hers and she hadn't been able to avoid them. He must think she was coming on to him because she gave him so much attention, so much praise; the other men must think so too. How embarrassing. So far she had prided herself on her impeccable professional behavior; there was no way, she had thought, that even these deprived males could think of her as a "fe-male." She had presented herself as a poet and a teacher, through and through, a denatured muse. She had probably been gazing at Julio with far too much interest as he told his stories (she was admittedly fascinated with his voice, his weird sinister-prince face). Then, as morning confronted her half-asleep mind, she realized she'd only dreamed Julio Bravo had licked her hand. Of course she'd only dreamed it! she thought, enormously relieved; nobody licked a teacher's hand, anyone's hand. When he'd raised her hand to his lips in the dream she was sure he intended to kiss it, like an old-world Spanish courtier, and then the kiss had become a more-than-sensual, grossly intimate gesture.

Once she'd digested her relief that the image was a dream she felt uneasy; she had dreamed this, after all. Dreams were not innocuous. If she was going to start having iffy dreams about convicts the least she could do was pick the most eligible, like Harold "Flash" Gordon, a slender, light-skinned black, who'd tailored his prison greens to fit his well-muscled body, gloved his small feet in fine black alligator shoes, undoubtedly left over from some profitable pimpdom, and read his well-constructed but uninspired poems in a confident near-Oxford diction.

An enjoyable repercussion of her prison teaching job was the impact it made on her friends. They were impressed, Dolores realized, and more than anything she loved to impress. They asked her if she was afraid. "You always do things I never could do," her former college roommate said enviously. "Those guys aren't in there for drinking too many milkshakes, after all," a male friend commented. Dolores, who thought of herself as the world's most frightened person, again understood she was not afraid of the same things other people were.

The truth was, after the initial disillusionment of finding the prison a less inspiring place than expected, she felt oddly comfortable there, more than she did in fancy restaurants, or at parties where she didn't know a soul, or other poets' poetry readings. First of all, she was in charge. Second, the inmates she taught liked her, respected her for the right reasons, her talents, and on the whole seemed more self-aware, more introspective, more sensitive than the men she knew on the outside, which she greatly enjoyed telling those men.

The worst part of the job was riding home with the "Reverend" Albert Johnson, not exactly an ordained minister, but a retired dock worker, who played an important role in some obscure church, and conducted a Bible-study group for prisoners that ended the same time as her class. The Reverend was a tall, powerfully built older man, fifty-nine, he proudly told her, whose placid face was still relatively smooth, except for a sprinkling of small brown age warts on his cheeks. He wore a cowboy hat and dark suit and drove a large gray car, at least ten years old. When Dolores saw him in the prison's reception area he would always greet her enthusiastically: "Hello! How was your week?" then add, as if she'd demanded an appraisal of his car's condition, "It's running just fine today," or "I had to put in a new distributor coil. I heard the motor going pap, pap, pap and I said to myself, 'You'd better take care of that right away.' " Nothing bored Dolores more completely than any conversation dealing with the insides of a motor vehicle. The Reverend Johnson was black, which should in itself, she thought, make him mildly interesting, but he was not at all, ever, the slightest bit interesting.

As they drove toward the city along the tree-lined highway, he conducted a nonstop monologue of colorless, imageless, unimpassioned virtuosity. He seemed to regard her as an anonymous sounding board, someone he could talk to in his soft, righteous voice instead of himself. "I am so proud of that girl," he said of his teenage granddaughter who recently won an award for sports participation in her high school. "Do you know she's only fifteen years old and she's five feet eight and a half inches tall! I'm six feet two myself, and both my sons are over six feet. The forty-year-old is six three and the other's six four. I have another granddaughter who's five ten and a half."

The Reverend had been married for forty-two years. "Can you imagine that?" he said. "I got married when I was eighteen years old, and my mother lived in the same house and made sure I was in by midnight, even after I was twenty-one and had two children of my own. She said, 'A married man hasn't got no *business* being out after midnight,' and do you know, she was right. The Bible says, 'Honor your father and your mother,' Dolores, and I've always abided by that law and it's made me happy to do it. I raised my children the same way," he continued. "My oldest boy is raising his children that way too. I never let my children go idle. Every week I'd put each child's name on a bulletin board and his chore for the week after it. So and so had to do the dishes, so and so had to help with the cleaning and so and so had to take out the garbage. When my wife and I go to visit my son he's got the same bulletin in his house." The Reverend's six children had produced uncountable grandchildren. "If the Good Lord lets me and my wife stay around until our Golden Year we intend to renew our vows," he stated.

After his family the Reverend's favorite topic was the weather ("They said it was going to rain tonight," he'd observe carefully. "I hope it waits until we get back to the city. I thought it would rain yesterday, but it stayed sunny the entire afternoon. My wife said she was sure it would rain too. It is a little chilly though") and his meals ("My wife said to me, 'Do you want to eat before you go up there?' I said, 'No, I think I'll eat when I get home' "). He had been a vegetarian since childhood, he told her, and had never touched meat, coffee, tea, whiskey, or cigarettes. He went to bed every night at ten o'clock. "Past ten my eyes just automatically start to close," he said. "I've been like that my whole life. I never was a wild one."

The Reverend's boring monologues drove Dolores crazy. Since he never asked her what she did, or anything about her life, and didn't seem to care if she listened to him or not, she sat, looking angrily out the window into the peaceful woods, trying her best to obliterate the constant interference of his voice from her thoughts. It infuriated her to be talked at when she wanted to think over the night's class, rehash it in her own mind. She mumbled, "uh hum, uh hum," at what she hoped were appropriate intervals in the pious sermon, realizing that, try as she might, she could not totally eliminate its droning homage to dull normality. She did find the Reverend's vegetarianism somewhat interesting, and questioned him about his diet. His answer, however, was predictably uninteresting. "I eat pea beans, lima beans, navy beans, pink beans, black-eyed peas, kidney beans, mung beans, and soybeans," he said. "My wife boils them with onion and flavors them with Mazola oil. I don't like heavily spiced food because I know it's bad for my system, and I have to have my beans—that's how I get my protein." Every week he announced, "My wife made her home-made rolls on Sunday! I am poor, Dolores, but I eat like a king."

He seemed to think his minute habits were the stuff of real conversation, and after several trips home, Dolores could envision his day like a film she'd seen many times: his morning walk, his drive to New Jersey, where he chauffered his daughter, mother of five, to a shopping center for cheaper groceries, his bland bean dinner, his early bedtime. He drove her as far as the subway in The Bronx, and she gave him a dollar for gas. "Where's your gas kitty?" she asked every week, though she well knew it was his car's ashtray, never sullied, of course, with the foul remnants of cigarettes. "Put it there if you like," he'd say, "but you don't have to unless you want to," which made her feel she was not contributing quite enough to a worthwhile African mission.

Often she sat in the car debating whether the two bucks she saved by not taking the train, a dollar seventy-five actually, was worth riding with the Reverend Boredom, as she called him. Between her preparation time, travel time, train and subway fares, not to mention the books

52

she ended up buying for the students, without which she couldn't teach them much, her profits from this job were minimal. Vicious dogs also patrolled the street leading from the prison to the railroad station, and the train didn't arrive until an hour after her class ended. So she continued with the Reverend, amusing herself by imagining his sex life (he was still a vigorous man, not bad looking for his age) and then, as her bored fury increased, herself and her inmate students stoning him, and finally binding him to a post and setting thousands of armed sodomists to raping him—his just deserts for remarking, as he did one night, that he'd advised a confessed homosexual in his study group, "The Bible says you people will not be saved!"

When these fantasies failed to amuse her she sat in silence, glaring straight ahead, silently begging this tedious blabbermouth to shut up, omitting her acknowledging "uh hums." But the Reverend remained as pleasant, cheerful, and talkative as ever, asked her considerately, three times per trip, if she was chilly, should he close the vent, should he turn on the heat, and did not seem to notice her stiffened silence. He made her feel peculiarly nonexistent, like an image blipped on a television screen.

One evening, however, after blabbing away about his wife's wonderful cornbread and his youngest grandchild, he suddenly turned to Dolores as if registering her flesh and blood presence for the first time. "Tell me, Dolores," he asked, "are you married?"

Dolores's imprisoned fury pushed her voice out of her mouth, already angry. "No! I don't believe in marriage," she said abruptly.

The Reverend looked at her curiously. She wondered if he was trying to ascertain her age, or whether she was human. "Well, I'll tell you," he said, "my marriage has been a good one. I was darned lucky because I found the right woman. Forty-two years, Dolores, and if we make fifty we intend to renew our vows." He didn't seem to want to know *why* she didn't believe in marriage.

The truth was Dolores had no idea if she believed in marriage or not. At thirty-one she had never managed to think about it seriously, except as one of society's vague requirements for success, as she had thought about college when she was a child, without really knowing what "college" was. She had expected her thirtieth birthday to grant her immediate insight into the nature of marriage, but no such knowledge arrived, and this famous *rite de passage* remained an abstract concept, comprehensible to others, but not to her. She noticed that other women did not regard marriage as an elusive abstraction, had definite requirements for men, definite expectations of them, kept an ideal situation they hoped to achieve with them in mind, rightfully theirs by decree, and she did not. "It's not what I want," they would say firmly about an unsatisfactory relationship. Dolores sometimes heard herself use the same expression, "It's not what I want," to reject a lover who was giving her a hard time or to describe what was wrong with him; but unlike her friends, she had no concrete notion what it was she did want, if anything, from these lovers. What she really wanted, she suspected, was just another lover, someone new, different, more exciting. She was sure not having a positive vision of domestic bliss, or a good "relationship" (a term she scorned because it seemed to describe some commodity you got because you paid for it) was a sign of mental illness. Yet, when she tried to imagine her future, she envisioned herself living in her same small apartment alone, exactly as she lived at the moment, with male creatures fluttering in and out like ephemeral butterflies. The future she dwelled on, tried to concretize, was the afterlife. She tried her best to believe in reincarnation, read the *Tibetan Book of the Dead*, and worked to imagine a future in which she would be dead but her poems would live on in anthologies and high school English textbooks. When she was twenty-eight a man had asked her to marry him, a nice architect she had been living with for three years, she then realized, and she'd felt inexplicably terrified, as if a complete stranger had threatened to expatriate her to an uncharted island.

The Reverend now took note of her statement. "Don't you want to have children?" he asked. It was a moment before she realized he had voiced a new question instead of continuing his dreary, self-defining monologue.

"No," she replied defiantly. "Definitely not," and then, unable to check her bitter furies, raced into one of her terrible verbal rampages, out of control from the moment it began. "Look at the population crisis, for God's sake," she boomed, watching the Reverend shrink in size beneath the sonic pressures of her loud voice, like the bad witch in the Wizard of Oz. "If everyone in the entire world keeps on having six or eight children" (an oblique reference to the Reverend's massive family) "none of us will have anything to eat soon! For every irresponsible woman indulging her selfish maternal whims and bringing too many kids into the world, at least one of us has to abstain. It's not that I don't like children," she roared. "I *love* children!" (one hundred percent untrue) "but I'm performing a necessary social action by not having them. People who have more than one child are pigs!" she went on, unable to believe her own ears. "Thieves, in a way.

55

No one can give five, six, eight kids what they need in a world like this. Look at the price of gasoline!" she shouted irrelevantly, and concluded, "I believe in mandatory abortion!" shaking with the stunning force of her attack, with joy, with guilt; she had finally stoned the Reverend.

He reacted with calm, injured dignity. "I didn't ask you to have eight children, Dolores," he said quietly. "I want to see you happy, that's all." The sincerity of his tone made Dolores feel miserable. He meant it; though he knew nothing about her, he assumed her wishes and dreams were normal ones; he assumed motherhood was happiness; he cared if she was happy. She considered apologizing, but that desire perversely made her feel angry again, if only for her inability to apologize. She had stated her true opinion, more or less. She had revealed herself. Should she apologize for that? The car was silent for the first time, wretchedly silent. Why did she hate this perfectly nice man, who did her such a big favor every week, with such ferocity?

After that the Reverend didn't wait for her in the reception area and she deliberately ran her class overtime to avoid meeting him. She took the train, braving the dogs, waiting a restless hour on the sub-zero platform, and remembered her rides with the Reverend with guilty nostalgia. Having insulted him beyond repair she thought of him fondly, like her dead grandfather, and despised herself for venting her perpetual bad temper against a man unworthy of it. Look how he'd achieved stability, raised a good, hardworking family despite his age, his race; he'd grown up in hard times, fought prejudice, a depression, a rough neighborhood, and he'd survived. She hadn't liked him for the most trivial, superficial reasons. He was boring, so what? She was arrogantly obsessed with her snobbish, limited world; she prided herself on tolerance, yet lacked it completely. The Reverend was a fine man and she was a nasty, bourgeois, egocentric, white bitch.

CHAPTER

4

WHEN Dolores began teaching at the prison she was "in love," or at least felt the vague drafts of jealousy, dependence, and desire she assumed represented the onslaught of this elusive state, which, like Julio Bravo, she was not sure she had ever experienced or defined. Two months later, however, this "love" had been emphatically displaced by an icy climate she defined as "hatred," accurately, she suspected, though she wished to believe herself incapable of such a base emotion. Irrational; how could she hate a man who appeared to love her devotedly, without reservations, whatever she did, or said? Nevertheless, crass disillusionment overwhelmed her, and one Monday morning she left the fruit assignment to molder in her typewriter and rushed to her journal to vent her agitation and analyze the pros and cons, mostly cons, of one tall, thin, bedroom-eyed Don Mansion, an unemployed jazz musician (specialty bass and sitar), who made his living working in a chic men's boutique in her Soho neighborhood. She wrote:

. . . feel emotionally chaotic, in tormented flux. Everything I originally felt about Don Mansion has reversed itself, and I am afflicted with enraged feelings that expand far beyond their justification, terrifying, because they seem to issue from some nasty demon nestled in my guts that makes me say and do the most debasing things to him, self-debasing, because if I don't like him I should simply get rid of him, but then I will be alone again, and for better or worse, I have become accustomed to his constant telephone calls, however much they annoy me at eleven in the morning and three in the afternoon (as Sylvia Plath said, "No day goes by without news of you"), and his warm, skinny body in bed at night. I also know that any normal female would be delighted with this guy, who adores me, and wants nothing more than to be with only me for time immemorial, though it's abundantly clear he hasn't the slightest idea who I am, and it's obvious that the reason I loathe him so much (at the moment anyway) is because he likes me beyond what the quality of our "relationship" dictates he should and because I am *not* a normal female. A normal woman would snap Don Mansion up like a shark, especially in New York, where we statistically outnumber sane, heterosexual male specimens thousands to one. Perversely, if he stayed away for a while, expressed doubts about me, let me imagine there was another woman, a rival, I would probably agonize over him twenty-four hours a day and treat him like The Hero of Our Time.

Abnormal or not, D.M. is driving me crazy. When he comes at me for the forty-second time in a single hour, his slightly sweaty palms outstretched, crooning, calling me his "sweetness" and grabbing my tits, which he calls "his nimmy-nims," flapping his ever-kissing lips at me like an overstimulated goldfish, I feel like I am choking to death and I literally cannot breathe. Once he even followed me into the toilet to embrace me. Could it be that I am not especially affectionate, i.e., not a "normal" woman, in this department either, a rude awakening, considering my biggest complaint about P.K. was that he was cold and unaffectionate? Well, what's "normal" in this day and age? Nobody knows, do they? Just two months ago I was rejoicing to have found a really warm, gentle man. What happened?

Anyway, I try to reverse my negative feelings toward D.M. with positive actions that demonstrate affection—like whipping him up a nice little dinner, his favorite strawberry pie, a smelly bluefish stuffed with crab meat (I like eating fish but I hate cooking it), while he waits, lounging in my living room, listening to the tapes of Indian music he has given me, smoking joint after joint until his eyes are more glassy and noncomprehending than those of the long-dead fish I am crouched over in the kitchen.

Last night, so engaged, I roused D.M. from his narcoleptic trance and sent him out to get some heavy cream for the pie, rushing to turn down the blaring raga the minute he was out the door. The telephone rang and it was Gregory, inviting me to a spur of the moment glamorous dinner party uptown—maybe it wasn't so glamorous, but at least I wouldn't be the one cooking it—and I had to say no, because I was entertaining and the fish was in the pan. Thus, when D.M. returned with the cream, giving me a husbandly little kiss as he handed me the bag, I found myself even more irrationally furious with him than I'd been all evening and shrieked, dodging his pursed lips, "Can you please just leave me alone for one second!"

"Okay, okay," he said with an injured look, making me feel instantly guilty, but the damage was done and what could I say? I followed him into the living room, where he'd already turned RAGA back up to its full earsplitting volume and lit another joint, no, maybe this time it was a cigarette, and said, "Look, I'm sorry, but if you want to get to know me why don't you try reading some of my poems." He hasn't shown more than the most perfunctory interest in my poetry, my reason for living, though I don't write as much as I should, as much as I want to.

He looked up and smiled soporifically, forgiving me at once for my previous outburst. "I can know you best by your hugs," he said in a saccharine voice, telling me by his tone and salacious eyes that by "hugs" he meant "cunt" or "box," as he calls the poor benighted thing! I trust my look, which could have withered a redwood, said all.

Evidently I made my point. During dinner (I could barely eat I was so enraged), he said yes, he *would* like to see my poetry. I should select one poem and he'd read it as soon as we finished eating. One entire lyric poem! Thanks a lot, pal; I only have a book-length manuscript of unsung masterpieces waiting to see the light of day! Anyway, after dinner I brought

61

out *the* poem, selecting, of course, the one that recently appeared in *The Mississippi Review*. I am proud of that poem and thought D.M. would pay more attention to anything he saw on the printed page, like most people. Besides, springing a published poem on him implied all my poems get published in fancy literary magazines—scarcely the case. The real question is: Why am I still trying to impress this man I secretly think is a jerk?

The raga was still blasting away and the TV, by then, was also projecting its frenetic football game, though the sound was almost inaudible. D.M., lying on the couch, lifted my poem to his face and scanned what must have amounted to one line before his droopy eyes closed and the *Review* dropped back to his scrawny chest. I was sitting across the room, pretending to read the Sunday *Times*, but actually scrutinizing D.M.'s face for reactions. It is always a heavy moment for me when someone I'm close to reads my poetry for the first time. I waited a moment before D.M. picked up "Tallulah Head" and attempted to read it again. His eyes closed once more for what seemed to me five or ten minutes. Finally, I couldn't contain myself any longer. "If you're too tired you should wait until you feel like it," I said in a tight, but civil voice. "I don't want to force you."

"I was just listening to the music," he replied defensively. "That sitar riff, right after the tablas, is one of my favorite sitar riffs in the entire world. There's some really nice imagery in the first couple lines," he added after a pause, referring to my poem. "I dig it."

At that point I completely lost my temper. I snatched *The Mississippi Review* out of his hands and screamed, "Just forget it! I'll never ask you to read another thing of mine again," and stormed away.

He followed me into the bedroom where I was sulking like a two-year-old, practically in tears. "I'm sorry," he said gently, putting his unwelcome arms around me, "please give me your poem back. I didn't know I was supposed to read it that very minute" (a hint of whine expanding in his voice) "I was really into that raga." Then he earnestly explained more about the stupendous genius of Indian music, about which I give less of a shit.

"I don't think it takes much sensitivity to realize you don't treat someone's art so casually when the artist is right there in front of you," I sniffed. I refused to stay in the same room with him for the rest of the evening and lay on the bed in an immobile rage. Now I think I should have kicked him out; but I guess something in me wanted to smooth things over, make it all right, like it was only a few weeks ago. At the same time I was secretly glad that D.M. had committed a truly serious offense, one anyone could identify as a major crime, so if I do decide to dump him and Joanna says, "Well, what was wrong with *this* one?" I'll have a story to tell that will get her just as angry and indignant as I am.

It is ironic that the men in my Arts class at Briarstone all listen with the most flattering attention when I read them one of my poems, despite the train noise, despite the fact that I am white and educated and they are black and Puerto Rican and supposedly ignorant criminals to boot. Their praise is enthusiastic and their critical analyses quite perceptive. Naturally I couldn't restrain myself from mentioning that to D.M., and added, "If you don't like poetry you don't have to be afraid to tell me." He's never talked about a book he's enjoyed and I don't believe he went to the Manhattan School of Music like he said. He may not really know *how* to read for all I know; his grammar isn't very good.

Well, to continue a long story, which Posterity will no doubt find incredibly boring and trivial (except for the good evidence it provides of the old maid poet's neurotic inability to get along with men), this morning D.M. arose, rather late (Monday is his day off), and finally did the dishes which I'd asked him to do the night before. I hate waking up to find yesterday's dishes dragging the dirt and muck of the past into the present. After he finished he asked me to fix him some eggs (as a reward, no doubt). I was immediately inclined to snap, "What do you think I am, a short order cook?"; but for some reason (probably misplaced guilt for treating him rottenly the night before—though he was definitely in the wrong, I could have spoken to him about it in a controlled and reasonable manner instead of screaming and sulking and comparing his intellect to that of the thieves and murderers in my Arts class) I fixed the fucking eggs and even sat at the table while he ate them instead of working on Fruit, which is due any day now. The eggs, needless to say, dirtied up more dishes and though I don't mind washing my own eggy dish I just can't bear washing someone else's—there's something about another person's slimy, congealed yolk that has always made me instantaneously nauseous. Right after egg and toast consumption and two cups of coffee, D.M. again came for me, having forgiven me and assuming I had forgiven him. I tried to push him away, but somehow, though I only wanted him to get out of my place so I could settle down at the typewriter to expound the true grit about Pineapples and collect another measly twenty-five bucks, my arms would not perform the necessary pushing action. Maybe I simply didn't have the time or wherewithal to connect all my current negative feelings for him with my former feelings of desire. Maybe I want to love him, even though I do not.

He dragged me onto the couch, his lips, his eggy breath all over me. The last thing in the whole world I wanted to do at the moment was fuck the insensitive bastard, but my body behaved as it always does, like an electrical appliance—push the right button and it whirs into action—even though afterward I lay there like a zombie, even during more or less, hating D.M. and hating myself for being such a pushover. Then I said, "I feel just like I did when I was raped," thinking at the same time, Oh Lord, here I go dredging *that* up again. D.M., however, did not seem especially shocked or even take instant offense. "Raped?" he asked casually.

"Yes!" I exclaimed in a melodramatic voice, mustering as much intensity for this event as I could, seeing as how it happened more than three years ago, and I've repressed its emotional impact (maybe there never was a great emotional impact) or simply forgotten it. Though he didn't ask for details and probably did not want to hear them, I recited my traditional "rape saga": The walk along the beach in Mexico, the sudden encounter with a tall, leering peasant who said, "I want to marry a *gringita*," smiling at him like the dumb get-to-know-the-Third-World tourist I was, thinking he was only a mildly pesky macho, never dreaming he harbored thoughts of rape, that such a montrous thing could happen to me, realizing everyone else on the beach had disappeared, running, running, him behind me, running the wrong way, finding myself in a cowfield, fighting him off, afraid to kick or bite too hard for fear he might kill me, succumbing at last, looking up in the middle and seeing all the cows had gathered in a circle to observe my downfall with sad, disturbed eyes. D.M. listened. Sensing my story had not made much of an impression I went on to describe my visit to the Mexican doctor for a clap test, who assured me Mexican men did not rape women, that their pleasure lay in convincing the girl, hearing him ask, "Were you raped or were you convinced?"

After this woeful tale I waited, with the usual curiosity, for D.M.'s definitive comment. Why do I insist on telling this tale to lovers? Perhaps I'm testing them with it, hoping to discover one who will come up with what I consider an appropriate reaction, though I'm not sure I know what that would be. In my mind I've catalogued the reactions and once suggested a story to a woman's magazine, "What Men Say to Raped Women" (fortunately the magazine folded before I could write it). D.M. seemed to be struggling to mold his features into what he considered the proper expression—some brand of horrified sympathy he obviously didn't feel—and which emerged, as a result, resembling an advanced case of motion sickness. He then said reflectively, "I don't think I could rape a woman. I just don't think I could get it up at the crucial moment." I've heard that one before! At least he didn't ask me if I'd come, like J.D. did, or inform me what a fool I'd been to meander down a beach in broad daylight alone, like P.K. did, or advise me how to put out rapists' eyes with my fingers, like P.R. did. D.M. did not seem to recall I'd announced I'd felt the same way during sex with him—like I'd been raped—or demand to know why I had said such a despicable thing. (It really was despicable. I simply should have refused if I didn't want to have sex with him.) I think I said it because I felt on my own couch as I had in the cowfield, that I was floating above this undesired copulation, watching my own body and his sadly, as the cows had watched me. During the rape I suppose I protected myself from its traumatic effects with this feeling of detachment, aided by the dreamlike foreign setting and my inability to believe this terrible thing could be happening to me. Today I felt removed, detached, alone, to protect myself from the self-destructive knowledge that I was indulging in sex I didn't want to have. Come to think of it, I've almost always felt removed from my so-called acts of passion since Mexico.

D.M. finally left and here I am, miserable, yet overjoyed to be alone, to have him *out*, wondering, as I have for weeks, if I have amassed enough evidence to justifiably give him the shaft. Perhaps I should make a list of his good and bad points, evaluate them on a scale of one to ten, add up the total, and make my decision on a mathematical basis.

Good points: Good lover (objectively)
              Loves me

Bad points: Insensitive
              Not as smart as I am
              Arrives late

Calls all day then doesn't call when
    he said he would
Won't read my poetry
Doesn't know who I am
Doesn't share my interests
Doesn't want to take me anywhere
    interesting
Smokes too much dope
Too materialistic
Talks about boring things and only
    boring things

But don't the good points deserve ten each and the bad points only one to three each?—giving him a total of twenty for honestly earned good points and a maximum of thirty for trumped-up bad points. Aren't a lot of the bad points really the same point? Aren't some of them too subjective or unfair? For example, though he doesn't share my interests I don't share his either. This exercise was useless and idiotic like almost everything else I do lately, and hasn't begun to answer the fundamental question I've wasted this entire morning trying to resolve, i.e., What to do about Don Mansion, about men, about love, about my entire self-defeating life? I close with the usual scream of total confusion.

CHAPTER
5

*T*HE community college informed Dolores, in an anonymous, near-form letter, that it would be unable to finance the prison extension program for the spring semester, thanks to city budget cuts, and thus, her "Introduction to the Arts" class ground to a premature halt at Christmastime. Alone, having dumped Don Mansion, finished at long last with Fruits, almost finished with a tedious article on mattresses for *Apartment Life* magazine, and now, with no course to teach, she would be free—completely liberated to write her own poetry. If she cracked down on her compulsive spending, the money she'd earned would hold out until spring, or almost, and then she would worry about looking for more. This promised state of freedom, however, loomed ahead remotely, an empty glass jar waiting to be filled, a cold, plain little glass, by no means the inspirational flame she had expected to find burning in her brain like an image-packed hallucinatory fever. In fact, she hadn't the slightest idea what poem would emerge when the moment came to sit at her clean desk with her own notebook. Though she'd scribbled down countless ideas for poems, even random first lines, almost grasped the shadows of their rhythms, while she'd slaved over the monotonous passages of Fruits and Mattresses, now that the time to execute them moved closer they had mysteriously disappeared. The notes she'd made about them had no meaning; her mind was an obstinate blank. Not only poems but important thoughts were absent from its vapid cavity. In any case, she would soon have nothing to do but write poetry, and that suddenly seemed like not very much to do. She wanted to split for the wilderness of a foreign country (it seemed a lifetime since she'd laid eyes on a tree), but she didn't have enough money for that. She wanted to keep teaching at Briarstone; that class was the one obligation in her mundane life that offered content for speculation, tension, a not easily analyzed spectrum of emotions.

Her final walk through the prison gate and the screeching metal detector, her last greeting to the old arthritic guard, who regaled her with tales of his tour of duty in the South Seas, was sentimental. ("They have pits fulla alligators and snakes to throw you in if you try to mess with their women. Do you know we gave them soap and they ate it! Ate it! And that stuff had lye in it, too.") What's more, she felt deprived, a victim of bureaucratic injustice. Why should she have to give up the only thing she had to do that she also liked to do, a worthwhile thing, because of money.

Julio Bravo, too, seemed depressed. He had abandoned his file cabinet throne for an ordinary folding chair and ostentatiously abstained from the class. He slammed the last poetry book she had given him on a chair in front of him and sat hunched over its pages, sulkily pretending to read. When he lifted his strained face she saw it was pale, and marked with red, hive-type blotches, like mosquito bites. Without Julio to carry the flag the workshop lost its direction. She could only get a limping discussion going, and the men seemed apathetic, uninterested. Perhaps it was because it was the last class—why bother?—perhaps because it was the holiday season and they were stuck in jail. Personally she would rather be locked up than headed to her parents' home in Jersey for the same old holiday routine—the eggnog, the tree, the formal dinner, opening the small presents they put in the same red felt stocking with her name on it she'd had as a child. Christmas made her feel jaded, old, and alone.

She tried to read an obscure medieval lyric about the Christ child that no one understood. She gave up, said it had been a good class, there was a lot of talent here, and they should all continue writing on their own. Mutually they condemned the shitty college, the city; of course the establishment screwed the men behind the walls first; why couldn't the prison finance her class, or at least pay for her transportation? She gave them her address and told them they could send her their poems in the mail if they wanted. She briefly wondered if it was dangerous to give her address to prison inmates; other people would certainly think so. Finally, she asked Julio if something was wrong.

Yes, there was. He had been denied parole because the board claimed he had not participated in enough prison activities. "That is their ex*cuse*, my man," he said angrily. "They know I have been in this arts class, that I have worked with the Jaycees. They know I took that pottery class with What's-his-name, that Eye-talian dude, last fall."

"Did you remind them of that?" Dolores asked.

Julio rallied a bit as he "ran down" the story of his visit to the parole board. To his surprise he had found that one of the three members was a little old lady, "wit' gray hair and them strong blue eyes," he said, "them eyes that be looking right through a dude. I couldn't talk right with that lady there. Dig it, I sat in my chair feelin' like I was shrinking up . . . you know, getting smaller and smaller. She says to me, 'Son, do you really want to do all this time?' " He imitated himself, a small and diminishing mouse before the piercing gaze of the ancient lady parole board officer. " *'No Ma'am,'* I says, and then she goes, 'Well, son, you had better get involved in more of the excellent rehabilitative programs we are offering here at Briarstone,' " gathered up her briefcase, took off her spectacles, and walked out the door. According to Julio Bravo, his tongue turned to stone before he could defend himself. "I never expected no lady, my man," he said. *"Vaya,* wit' a dude on a dude everything is cool; I can talk to another dude straight on, but this lady, my man, she made me feel like some little kid who stole a nickel out of his mama's pocketbook! Now I am locked down for another Christmas. Shee-it! My sisters and my father, man, there ain't no way they can get up here to visit me neither." He said he only had a few months to go before he maxed out anyway, so what difference did it make if he went to more classes and shit now? What that lady said was coming out the side of her neck, man; they just wanted to keep him locked up as long as possible. But he had counted on going home for Christmas; they wouldn't even give him a fucking furlough! Dolores felt sorry for him. She asked if it would help if she wrote a letter to the parole board, saying he had participated in her class. Julio looked up, surprised; his eyes were warm, openly grateful. "Thanks a lot!" he said eagerly. "*Gracia!*"

The warden had refused permission for the class to have a Christmas party, because the package room was not open after three in the afternoon, and food and drink could not be inspected for contraband. Still, the guard was conspicuously absent. With a furtive glance around the room Strike Watkins reached into his pocket, brought out some tightly rolled joints, and threw them quickly to the other men. Dolores wondered if it was up to her to put a stop to this illegal activity. Well, they couldn't fire her now. She didn't want to seem uncool.

In fact, when it came to dope she wasn't very cool, not cool at all. She secretly believed all drugs were harmful, addictive, and unhealthy, and that those who took them regularly were either much cooler than she was, on a higher plane, or complete morons with addictive personalities. Perversely, this basically negative stand made her pretend to admire drug-taking, smoking, snorting, shooting, hallucinogenic trips, et al, and to try as many different kinds of drugs as possible, provided people gave them to her and she didn't have to plunk down good money for them. She thought she was the sort of person who should like drugs, and wondered why she didn't. She especially hated marijuana—it made her enormously self-conscious and paranoid, and she refused to believe it made anyone else feel better.

When the joint was passed to her, however, Dolores took it; they were all waiting to see if she would, she knew that. It was, in a sense, her final examination. Besides, the opportunity to tell her friends she had smoked dope behind the walls of a maximum security prison, a crime punishable by electrocution, no doubt, with the guard footsteps away, was too tempting an anecdote to pass by. It was probably oregano, she thought. No, it was strong, she could tell right away. She almost choked, which would have revealed her inexperience with this drug and embarrassed her to death. Actually, she always choked; she hated the taste and the smell. She could feel her lung cells disintegrating. Already wandering in her thoughts, she heard Julio Bravo say in his rough, jocular voice, "You know . . . Dolores . . . She has *heart!*"

Under the influence of the drug she deemed this the most magnificent compliment she had ever been paid. She giggled incongruously, how idiotic it sounded, but Julio laughed too. So did the other men, a kind of laughing gasp of pent-up relief. Other people had said she was "brave," "had guts," and often that she was "strong"; yet she always imagined these terms were not really compliments, meant she was selfish, hard, and mean-spirited in her dogged pursuit of independence. "To have heart," however, bore an entirely different connotation, especially in the emphatic singsong of Julio Bravo. His brief look of recognition stuck before her eyes, like a slide of the landscape of her own soul. "A woman with heart" described her exactly as she wanted to be— not only brave and noble, but vulnerable in the right places as well.

She looked at the convicts sitting in the circle of chairs. They were all quiet and relaxed. Strike rested his cheek in his hand; his thoughts, easily visualized as shiny blue bottles, were delicately reflected in his gentle black eyes. Sam drew a small, intense sketch with his felt-tipped pen, humming almost inaudibly to himself. Mohammed, the

Black Muslim, grinned toothlessly and announced in his soft, velvet voice, "This was a *bad* class. Yeah, man, *bad!*" Bad meant good. Dolores remembered that she had refused point-blank to ever smoke dope with Don Mansion.

Julio Bravo tilted back on two chair legs, his hands planted in his green pockets, heels digging into the worn concrete floor. He smiled benignly, his pupils alight with some interior glowing coal. He'd obviously forgotten how much he wanted to go home for Christmas and remembered how much he liked jail. She heard little birds whistling their blurred chirrups in the banyan tree around her head, then realized she was hearing the steam hissing through the nearby radiator. She laughed out loud, felt foolishly uncool. "The radiator . . ." she started to explain, and everyone laughed knowingly, kindly. They had all heard the same birds. This is what is meant by *mellow*, she thought, feeling total comprehension of an expression she'd detested before. Finally, Julio grew bored with the calm silence. "Nobody brought no poems down?" he asked, a statement more than a question. There were no poems. "Okay," he said. "*Vaya*. Let's rap!" He began the rap session himself, of course, by again telling the story of his Christmas gas station holdup, embellishing the details, and adding a description of his first dismal holiday season behind the walls.

At the end of the class Julio escorted her to the door as usual. She had noticed he seemed to regard this escort service as his special assignment. Although the other men hovered around, waiting to say their good-byes, and the guard had returned, for a space of several moments she felt that she and Julio were alone. For the first time she noticed he was a good deal shorter than she was, two, three inches perhaps. He looked up; the greenish fluorescent light threw the red sores on his smooth face into bas-relief. "What happened to your face?" she asked. She was still stoned. The red blotches ballooned to a major leprous affliction, and filled her with a maudlin, piteous sympathy she relished for its definite visceral sensation. She realized that she had almost touched his face; her hand had jumped perceptibly up from her side.

"Oh," he said, reaching self-consciously for his cheek, "I get this from the strong soap they be giving us."

"Maybe it's got lye in it," Dolores suggested nervously.

"Listen!" he said again. "Dolores . . . if someone was to do something to you . . . if some freak was to hurt you . . . rape you . . . God forbid . . . You let me know about it, all right? I know someone in every joint in this state. . . . You know what I am saying? If the dude that did that to you was to end up in jail, any jail . . . I would have him taken off the count."

Dolores rode home on the train, still stoned. She was astonished and moved. She hadn't known how to reply and finally said, in somber, formal tones, "Thank you," probably not the cor-*rect* response. Did Julio Bravo intuitively know or sense she had been raped? Was there something about her, an injured sadness, a leftover victim quality in her movements and eyes, that had telegraphed this historical fact to a special sensibility that he, as a criminal, surely possessed? It was incredible to think he would have a man who raped her murdered in her behalf, simply because she had offered to write a letter to the parole board, or because he considered her a good teacher, or even a sympathetic friend. She wasn't sure she would have wanted her rapist, just a dumb peasant, to die because of what he had done to her. Prison or mild torture would be punishment enough. He hadn't hurt her, or sodomized her; no, it had probably been a picnic as far as rapes went. Even at the time she told herself that if she could imagine she had seduced the creep the experience would not have differed greatly from some legitimate versions of the same kind. It would have been just another penis, and who cared about that? It was she who had given the event the melodramatic designation *rape*—possibly so she could get some literary mileage out of it. For the Mexican peasant it had appeared to represent a crude act of courtship; afterward he had picked her up off the ground, helped her brush off her clothes, and offered to walk her back to her hotel. Imagine! She had lectured him in her feeble high school Spanish, "That is no way to know the pleasures of love," and he had replied, *"No! Buen gusto."* Did that mean "good taste" or "good pleasure"? How ludicrous, she'd thought, they were discussing their sex life. She was so stoned.

Even now, as she once again tried to dismiss the importance of this rape, she saw a helpless, boneless long body, her own, lying on the ground, a pathetic, devastated image of herself and felt a deep, retracted pity for that vision. God, she was stoned! Somehow Julio Bravo's passionate offer to avenge her injury had brought it back in some morose new perspective, stripped away the defenses she had instantly erected around it, kept trying to resurrect, even as they crumbled down. She tried to summon back the anger she'd felt for months after the rape, fury at the doctor, fury at other men for not responding appropriately, inexplicable fury at salesmen, bus drivers, anonymous men, and felt her throat dry up and squeeze together; in a minute she would actually be weeping on the Conrail local. At the time she hadn't cried, or even considered crying. It was impossible to feel this miserable about an event in her remote past; she must be sad because she was leaving her prison job, because she had no idea what she was going to write, because she was alone again, because it was Christmas, or just because she was stoned. Julio Bravo didn't know she'd been raped; he couldn't know.

When she got home she sat down at her typewriter to write the letter to the parole board. If she didn't take care of small chores like this immediately she never did them at all. She was tired, but her mood had improved and her thoughts were clear. Julio had given her his identification number and the address. She wrote that he had participated in her class, showed an aptitude for writing, and demonstrated unusual leadership abilities. "The nature of the class enabled me to get to know the inmates in it better than the average teacher knows her students," she added, for the final paragraph. "Therefore, I talked at length with Mr. Bravo about his future plans and learned that he intends to continue his education on the outside. Because I feel well acquainted with his character and aspirations, I can say with confidence that Mr. Bravo is now ready, willing, and able to renounce the activities that have brought him repeatedly to prison and give legitimate society the benefit of his remarkable intelligence and new ambitions." She was pleased with the letter, a minor masterpiece; *ready, willing, and able* was a nice touch, emphatic. She had always been able to write an excellent business letter, first draft. She put the letter and the carbon she'd made for Julio Bravo (it would improve his self-esteem to know she thought highly of him) into two envelopes, addressed and stamped them before going to bed.

On the verge of sleep she felt nagged by an uncomfortable awareness that signified an unresolved thought or emotion. She had learned it was important to identify the source of this kind of anxiety before it magnified into an inhibiting depression. Finally she discovered what it was. For some reason she had knowingly lied to the parole board; no, not lied, but distorted her impression of Julio Bravo. She had never talked to him about his future plans, and was only acquainted with his character as he portrayed it. He had not mentioned continuing his education on the outside, or the job he was planning to get, if any. She didn't have a clue what Julio Bravo intended to do when he got out of jail. He hadn't told her and she'd never asked.

CHAPTER
6

WHEN Julio Bravo got out of jail he called Dolores, whose number was listed in the Manhattan directory. "I want to show you a poem I wrote," he said, his voice carefully testing new ground. Without hesitation Dolores invited him for lunch in the enthusiastic tones of society welcoming a new member, a Living Statue of Liberty, she thought. Perhaps she should have thought twice; who knew, after all, what this ex-con would act like out of jail or what he would do when the two of them were alone in her apartment? She rejected these uneasy suspicions, paranoid thoughts she might be expected to think but wasn't seriously thinking at all.

At two o'clock on the appointed Saturday, Dolores posted herself at the exit of the Lexington Avenue subway, and waited for Julio Bravo to emerge. She had told him she would meet him there, assuming he wouldn't have the slightest idea how to navigate the unfamiliar streets of her neighborhood. He'd said he was living in the South Bronx with his sister. She felt distinctly foolish sitting by the curb; he wasn't a retarded child, after all; he would have been able to ask directions if he got lost.

She had used his visit as a good excuse to fritter away half the morning, cleaning up a bit, buying groceries, a pound of ground sirloin instead of the usual chuck, walking eight blocks for special pignoli cookies. She'd considered making a soup from Julia Child, but that would have been too fancy, too deliberately complex; hamburger had the right thrown-together casual quality, and he was sure to prefer solid macho meat to chilled vichyssoise. Should she dash down Mulberry Street and pick up some lettuce from the vegetable stand? He could probably use a decent salad after three, or was it four? years of prison food, a starchy, devitamized mixture of "snot and pus," as he himself had eloquently described it in one of his poems. No, it was already two fifteen; if she left now she might miss him. This anguishing over what to serve for lunch was absurd, she thought, worthy of her suburban mother; any lunch would do, really.

By two thirty Dolores wondered if Julio had taken a different subway. She paced around the exit in restless, dancing steps; she hated waiting for people, hated it. "Hate it" provided a rhythm for her nervous dance. Why were people, in general, never on time? Well, God knows how many transfers were involved to get here from the South Bronx, wherever that might be. He could have landed at the wrong stop, and when he didn't see her there, asked directions and gone straight to her apartment.

With this in mind she hurried back home, running down Spring Street, her breath hurtling in her chest, recklessly dodging the over-chic weekend art gallery strollers on West Broadway. But there was no sign of Julio at her place. He might have called when she was out to tell her he would be late, or couldn't make it. When her ship came in the first thing she would buy was an answering machine; she could buy one now if she stopped spending every compulsive penny on clothes she didn't need. She collapsed on the couch, wondering what to do—go back to the subway? Then she remembered he had given her his sister's telephone number. She dialed and a man's blurred, accented voice answered immediately.

"Julito?" he said. "He ain't here." The Hispanic accent, the muffled baby's cry beneath an insistent salsa beat in the background, intoned the presence of an unfamiliar world.

"Do you know if he went downtown?" Dolores asked.

"Is dis the parole?"

"No . . . I'm his poetry teacher," she said feebly, feeling white and ridiculous.

"I don't know where he's at," the anonymous voice replied, and the receiver fell impatiently.

I should have asked to speak to his sister, Dolores thought. She scribbled a hasty note on a piece of envelope: "Julio, I'm at the subway looking for you. Be back in a minute," and stuck it to the door with masking tape. She hurried back down Spring Street again. She was sweating; it was warm for early April. Julio was not waiting by the exit now either. Ludicrous; she couldn't keep galloping back and forth from her apartment to the subway all afternoon; she had already wasted the entire day with this Statue of Liberty luncheon project. She waited five minutes, just five more, stretched it to ten, then started back; undoubtedly he wasn't coming. Stood up again! She had a talent for befriending unconscionable morons who arrived late or never showed at all; she could dig a late arriver out of the most remote corner of the universe. Ironic, since the one thing in the world she could not bear was waiting for anything or anyone, that she always found herself shuffling on street corners, pacing the floor of her apartment, glancing nervously at the clock in the lobby of movie theaters, learning or not learning some cosmic lesson of patience designed for her by the punitive powers that be. Even her women friends were always late, and it had come to the point where she didn't expect any appointment she made with a male to transpire at all. She was still hurrying frenetically, trying to calm herself down, slow her steps to a normal pace.

As she ran home for the second time her own anxious breath reinstated the physiological memory of other times she had waited, specifically for the Czechoslovakian maniac, who had once kept her pacing and dialing and wailing for thirty-seven hours, finally appearing, leaving blue iris at her door, just when she'd given up and gone to a Kung Fu movie, too tearful and enraged to focus on the kicks and punches on the screen. She could never again, under any circumstances, tolerate this brand of inconsiderate behavior. The first thing she would tell Mr. Bravo, if he deigned to show at all, was that lateness is unacceptable, not only to her, but to everyone in the world "outside the walls." Then she recalled through her swelling agitation that Julio Bravo was no tardy lover, but a bare acquaintance; why was she so overwrought? What difference did it make if this former student came to lunch or not? She could eat the hamburger herself. If she didn't eat something in two minutes she was going to pass out; a vague hunger headache pressed its muffled layer of pain over her eyes.

Back on West Broadway, still hurrying, she ran into Gregory. He fixed her with his round blue eyes, faintly bewildered, possibly hostile, since she'd rejected him for reasons she could now judge "self-destructive." He was rich, a well-known interior designer, smart, witty, even handsome, if you liked red hair, and treated women well. "Hi, Greg," she panted, and when he halted his collected gait, rushed by him like a horse late for the finish line. "I'm in a hurry," she gasped. "I've lost this criminal friend of mine!" She took pleasure (and simultaneous chagrin) in his obliquely amazed stare, indicating he understood he was lucky to have been spared this careening madwoman.

As she turned the corner she saw Julio Bravo lounging against a parked car in front of her building. She clapped her hand to her forehead to signal from afar her angry frustration, the long wait, the mix-up. The first words she planned to say were reproachful ("I've been waiting for you all afternoon. What the hell happened to you? Why weren't you at the subway?"), but they vanished from her mind as she drew closer. She had unconsciously expected to greet the Julio she knew in jail, complete with prison greens and shaved head. She had never imagined the version of him facing her now. His shaved eagle's scalp had sprouted a massive round walnut-colored Afro, which seemed to live an electrified life of its own in the air around his head. His face had shed its blotches and was brown and smooth, still distinguished by the neatly trimmed pirate's goatee. He wore a loose-fitting black leather jacket, rather elegantly styled, over faded blue baggy overalls, with no shirt underneath. The slightly adipose paunch she had detected under his prison uniform had vanished and a lean, narrow abdomen replaced it. Through the short, curled dark hair on his naked chest, Dolores spotted another tattoo, its crude, prison-done black letters spelling the name "Graciela." His gold earring remained. As she stared, Julio grinned, revealing even white teeth and the gap where one was missing near the back. This ecstatic smile narrowed his eyes to small, crushed brown lighted slits, rapturous eyes that left no doubt about what he felt, the visceral sensation of freedom in the hot, dynamic city of New York, freedom in the newly born, balmy spring. He was obviously overjoyed to see her. It was impossible to cherish her outraged feelings in the presence of this smile; quickly they trickled down to a mere iota of resentment. She extended her hand, preparing to deliver him a warm, teacherly handshake. "Welcome back to the real world!" she said.

He pulled her toward him by her extended arm as if she were a mere fifty pounds of boneless fluff, hugged her briefly and easily kissed her on the corner of the mouth. *"Vaya!"* he said. "It feels good, my man! It feels real good! It feels cor-*rect!*" He pushed her away from him, holding her at arm's length with both hands, making her feel helplessly small, like a child about to be examined by a long lost uncle. "Hey, you be looking good, girl," he said huskily. *"Linda!* Real good!" and still smiling at her, he commented, "The grins . . ." which made her conscious she was smiling too, smiling so hard the skin around her lips almost hurt.

Settled in her spindly kitchen chair, which he tilted back onto two legs, Julio shook a Camel out of its pack and proceeded to make oral history of their first post-prison encounter. "When I seen that note on the door, man, I figured you was planning to take me *out* to lunch because you did not want me up here," he said, "that you did not want me in your place. I could dig it. I thought, 'That's how come she has gone to the subway.' Then, when I seen you coming down the street and the grins started . . . I knew it was cool!" He smiled languidly and stretched out a sneakered foot to rest on the other chair. "Yeah . . ." he said again, ". . . the *grins!*"

"You were late," Dolores said sternly, recalling her agitation. She was self-consciously bustling around the kitchen like her mother would, removing the hamburger from the refrigerator, the buns from their plastic bag. She should have bought at least one tomato. "Besides, I told you I would meet you at the subway on the telephone, when I invited you." Suddenly her voice sounded matronly, authoritative, unfamiliar to her, the voice of an indignant middle-aged librarian who has discovered gum between the pages of a classic.

Julio obviously considered his lateness far too trivial to waste words on. He focused on Dolores with his still delighted gaze. "You know," he said, "one of the things I was missing most in the joint was watching women do their thing around the kitchen . . . opening the icebox, putting food on a plate . . . stirring." He laughed. "All that little shit they be doing. It is beautiful to watch that, man," he said. "The way they move . . ."

"Don't Puerto Rican men ever help in the kitchen?" Dolores asked, taking refuge behind women's liberation's most bitter, if flimsy, barricade. She felt confused, disoriented by this unexpected, outrageously masculine presence in her kitchen. She did not know exactly what to say, or what tone to adopt. His new, hairy, half-naked self, his simple and direct placement of her into a category something other than "teacher" unnerved her, left her stranded from the stand she had expected to take. She had planned to serve him a pleasant lunch, then escort him to her office, where she would go over his latest masterpiece (nowhere in evidence), criticizing the diction, the structure, but praising the direct language and imagery, as she had in jail, encouraging him to continue his writing on the outside and bring it to her when he had enough to make it worthwhile. She let the whir of the blender blot him out, then plunked a brandy Alexander, too strong, maybe, in front of him; the baffling nature of this occasion called for a little booze. She was still not sorry, she thought, taking the first sip of hers, that she had invited him. So far, it was not a mistake.

Julio set about to answer her question. "I am a macho," he said, "a *bad* macho! This is one of the things I be working to change in myself, Dolores. I believe in freedom for the woman. . . . I believe every person should be free . . . man, woman, *niño*. I have been locked down too long to think anything different, my man." (Dolores noticed he used a present tense, *have been locked down*.) He cocked his head slightly, his eyes glazed with a memory. "The last time I was on the street I was working, working hard, my man. One day I be coming home and I was *hun*-gry. I had not eaten nothing since lunch. I come into the house and my mother and my sister and my second wife are in the kitchen, cooking and gossiping. They was really getting down . . . like a bunch of monkeys, man. My mother, she yells to me, 'Food in five minutes, Julito . . .' so I go into my room and five minutes passes . . . then half an hour passes. I can still hear them out there." He made a duck's bill out of his hand and opened and shut it rapidly. "Yakety yakety." Then he took a long swig out of his brandy Alexander. "Hey, this shit is all right," he interrupted himself. *"Muy rico, nene!"*

"It's a brandy Alexander," Dolores said. What did *nene* mean?

"Anyhow, pretty soon I be so hungry . . . starved, my man . . . I couldn't stand it no more," he continued. "I started slamming my dresser with my hand . . . *bam, bam, bam.*" (He pounded her round maple table, causing the saltcellar and sugar bowl to jump precariously.) "My second wife, she be coming in to see what is making all that racket. 'Julito,' she says. *'Cabrón! Calmate! Por Dios, hombre! Qué pasa* wit' you?' Dig it, I was so hungry and frus-trated, my man, that I picked her right up off the ground, dumped her in a closet, and locked the door. She was screaming and carrying on in there like a crazy bitch . . . *loca*! Then my sister be coming in to find out what was happening to my wife. I put her in the closet too. Finally, my mother come in to find out where was the both of them. 'I am hungry, *Mamí*,' I said. 'Just because you are hungry, Julito, don't mean you have to go carrying on like this,' she said to me. 'If you be so motherfucking hungry you cannot wait for your dinner, you take your ass into the kitchen and cook it yourself.' " He laughed. "Dolores, I wish you could have met my mother. She was something, man. The first thing I did when they let me out was go to visit her at her grave."

"You're still married?" Dolores asked. She had been totally mesmerized by that story, she realized, that blatantly chauvinistic tale, or if not by the story itself, the way he'd told it, his gestures and energized voice. She didn't even feel compelled to deliver her usual lecture on the destructive nature of male chauvinism to the male himself.

88

"Nunca!" he answered. "That was Carmen. She is the mother of one of my sons, but we was never married. I don't believe in marriage, my man," he added. He yawned noisily, fingered one of his nipples, small, erect, a warm, tawny color, encircled by hair. He opened and closed his fingers into and out of a fist. The sinister tarantula tattoo flexed its crudely drawn mandibles.

"I love women!" Julio went on. "I won't do no cooking or wash no dishes yet, but I *love* women, man. You know how they be saying that when a man is down he turns into a sissy, right off? That is bullshit, my man! No way! When I am locked up I can be waking up at four in the morning in a cold sweat and pounding the wall before I kiss no neck wit' stubble on it." He talked on, chewing his burger at the same time, letting the juice run out of the bun over his strong hands. He looked up reflectively. "Yeahhh . . ." he said. "There was this one Costa Rican dude . . . a real young brother they put in my cube when I was up in Corsica. We got tight, me and this dude, yeah, real tight. There was not nothing he wouldn't do for me, *nada,* man. I was sharing all of my things with him and pulling his coat to some of the shit that goes down in jail. Finally I says to him, 'Listen, Iguanito' (that was what I be calling him), 'you and me . . . we are both down where there ain't no fe-males, *tú saba?* You are locked up for two years and I am doing a fourteen-year bid for armed robbery. We are sharing a cell . . . we are speaking the same language . . . we are coming from the same neighborhood . . . We are *hermanos, hombre* . . .' " (He let the implication of the thought go unsaid, as he probably had when talking to Iguanito.) "You know, Dolores, when that little brother went home, I cried like a baby! And I *know* I ain't stuff.

". . . This burger is good, my man. You don't get no

meat like this in the joint," he continued. "Man, I love food. Dig it, I could never have got down with no Mahatma Gandhi, my man. That dude did not eat nothing. He was going into one of his visions and when he be coming out of it there was not hardly nothing left of the cat. He was just in them visions all the time . . . them visions was his food. Sometimes he be eating a little fruit, maybe sipping a little wine . . . but he didn't even smoke nothing, and they got some good shit over there, that gan-ja shit. Dig it, that man was *clean*! His people, they be telling him, 'Mahatma, my man, *vaya*, what is happening to you,' because it got so he was nothing but bones. But he didn't pay them no mind, no way, because he was digging that vision he had. I could not get behind that shit. He didn't take no fish, no meat, no smokes. Man, I would have had to have me a little fish, or at least some *crab* meat. I was at this girl's place, Dolores, and she be finding me in the kitchen at three in the morning, opening a can of shrimp. 'You eating again?' she asked me. 'Julito, that shrimp is for my *cats*!' " He laughed. "Shit, I love to eat!"

"Were you reading Gandhi's autobiography?" Dolores asked, the wrong question, unmistakably schoolteacher. It felt weird to sit like a stupefied audience in her own kitchen, giggling foolishly at these nonstop monologues, a little off-the-wall, but fascinating somehow. Usually she was the one who talked on and on, told stories, while other people listened.

Julio got up and stretched with a loud exhalation. "No," he said. "Sam Evans was talking to me about that." He went into the small bathroom just off the kitchen, leaving the door open at least a foot. She heard the sounds of his overalls unsnapping and then his urine striking the water in the bowl, but he continued to talk loudly to her, something about prison food, she couldn't quite hear, then emerged, buttoning the overalls up over his smooth pectorals.

"You look thinner than you did in jail," Dolores commented cautiously. It was still not the right voice, and she didn't want him to think she was ogling his muscular body, which, in fact, she was, she reminded herself. She'd better stop. Actually, there was no way to avoid looking at him when he was talking to her.

"Before I got out I was working out with weights again," he said, flexing his arm in an extended position, so the triceps bulged. The skin was shiny, as if it had been polished. "When I was up at Corsica, man, I got up to one hundred and eighty pounds and I am only five feet six inches tall. I was one bad motherfucker. But, dig it, they put me into one of them small planes after the riot to transfer me to Greenhill, and there I be, almost two hundred pounds of solid muscle and pure *punk*, my man. I was never in no airplane before." He grabbed the back of Dolores's chair with his hands, as if it were a plane seat, and vibrated in mock terror.

Dolores made more brandy Alexanders. After that she ran out of cream and Julio began drinking Blansac Finest French Brandy out of the bottle. She was already half bombed herself; her glassy eyes felt weighted in her head. It took maximum effort to focus on what they were talking about, or rather, what he was talking about. He returned, via circuitous routes, to the subject of women. "Dolores," he said, "I want to write a poem about this chick I met while I was in the joint."

"Uh huh . . ." she said. It was easier to let him talk on than to try to talk herself. In his presence she felt peculiarly devoid of anything to say; her usual modes of expression had faded, like the markings on a worn map,

91

and whenever she opened her mouth her voice was still groping, too formal, teacherly, not right. Or maybe this was her real voice she now heard, a droning record, played on the wrong speed.

"Yeah . . ." he said, massaging his bearded chin reflectively. "This girl got my name from my sister, Rosa, and started writing me these letters, man. First thing she asked me was how big was my dick. I wrote back and said I did not have no tape measure in my cell, but it was a nice dick, man, *real* nice, and not to worry because I was going to let her see it and hold it in her hand and play with it too, if she wanted."

He began discussing his private parts with the same nonchalance he discussed food and his mother, with no noticeable change of emphasis or tone. He said that the girl, whose name was Alicia, had written back that she was sure his dick would turn out to be one of the nicest ones she had ever seen and she could hardly wait to play with it or show him her size 40D titties and let him suck on them and squeeze them. She told him her pussy was nice too, and it got wet when she thought about him. "We was writing this shit back and forth for a couple of months," he said. "I did not even know the girl, my man. Finally, she comes up to Briarstone to visit me, and I seen right away that she had big tits like she said, but her *ass* is also as big as the middle of next week. I like slender women, but I said to myself, 'Julito, don't look a horse in the teeth.'

"She was telling me how rotten she thinks it is that they lock human beings up like animals . . . it turns out she was in the joint once herself, taking the rap for her old man—the Detention Center up in The Bronx—and she had to leave her little boy wit' her sister, who was strung out on coke, for a year, my man, and when she was coming out of jail her kid did not even know her no more, and like that. So we was hitting it off, and before you know it we got to kissing and touching each other and shit. . . . Them big tits was nice, my man. I put my jacket over our legs so we could really get down with it." He put his fingers up her pussy, which was juicy, real juicy; it was a *good* pussy, and she put her hand on his dick which was as hard as Bethlehem steel, and believe me, that is *hard*. The hack in charge knew Julio—he had done him a favor once—so he walked out and left the two of them alone. She put her mouth on his dick and she was sucking it, making her lips flash down on it real fast like, and playing with his balls with her other hand, flicking her tongue around the top, man, a little hot flame, and he felt it building up, twitching in his thighs, his toes were curling under, and just as he was about to ex-*plode* the fleabag came back in and said, "Okay, Mister Bravo, time to let the people go home!" The cocksucker!

"*Coño*, my *cujones* wasn't blue, my man, they was aquamarine for the next week and a half! There wasn't no *way* I could get that one off! Ordinarily I do not believe in getting down with that kind of shit in the visiting room. I will play chickie for another dude and his woman in the john, but it does not give me no satisfaction to get off that way myself. No matter how long I have been without no kind of sex, I do not just want to get my shit off. I want to hold a woman in my arms and kiss her and play with her hair. I want to *love* her, my man."

When they had the Puerto Rico Day picnic, he went on, all the dudes were under the tables, or wrapped up in blankets with their women, but he did not dig that shit. "Man, to me that do not show no respect for a woman. Dig it, it does not show no respect for yourself." Julio and his "wife" were at the annual picnic and she was burning. *"Vaya, Papí,"* she said, and Julio said to her, "No, *nene,* that is not cor-*rect.* Now get up off the ground and give me your hand, and let's walk over to where the band is at and do some dancing, *niña.* I did not want to degrade her like that, my man. I will get off myself wit' my mattress or my hand before I will insult a woman I have feeling for by dicking her in front of the entire population of a maximum security prison.

"But this was a different thing with Alicia, with them letters she was writing and all, and I did not even know her from the street. I wrote to her and told her we would have to cool it until I got out of jail, because I know you now, and I like you, and it is something else. I want to show you some respect just like I would show to a woman I know from outside the walls. She wrote back and said, 'Julito, I can understand what you are feeling, but believe me, it was still good,' and she told me how I had made her come right there in the visiting room, and how much she liked sucking on my nice hard dick and what a big dick it was and how she only wished the hack had stayed in the other room for one more minute. I got hard all over again just reading her letter."

Dolores listened, half embarrassed, half amused, wondering what risk, if any, was involved in her amusement. In her mind she was constantly preparing to interrupt, to ask, "Julio, why are you telling me all this?" but the stream of his voice allowed no interruptions, and besides, to stop him would be prudish in the extreme. In her heart of hearts she was a terrible prude, due, no doubt, to the way she had been raised by her mother, who had indicated sex was a slightly medicinal, corporeal trial one could avoid until marriage. She had first discovered the facts of life in their cold New Jersey backyard. Her mother, colossal in a plaid lumber jacket and woodsman's hat, was chopping logs for the fireplace. Dolores sat on a freezing stump, waiting for a pause in the ax swings. "How do babies begin in the mother's womb?" she had phrased the essential question. Her mother laid down the ax, and looked toward the heavens for aid. "The man inserts his penis in the woman's vagina and a discharge called *sperm* comes out of it," she'd stated.

Whatever she had expected to discuss with Julio Bravo, it was not sex. But why not? Just a week ago a hopelessly platonic male friend, the one who had gotten her the job at Briarstone, had asked her over dinner if penis size made a difference to women; leaning forward with ill-concealed anxiety to catch the first syllables of her reply, he'd knocked an entire glass of Burgundy onto her pale lavender pants. But this sensitive, intelligent, nonchauvinistic professor had soft, hairy arms, not polished, tattooed biceps, which along with the question he'd felt compelled to ask, made the real image of sex impossible.

She had smiled (or grimaced) through Julio's graphic story, but her attitude had not been correct—neither stern nor casually bawdy. What would the correct attitude be? As a secret prude she could not really know, so she had concentrated on keeping the Victorian prune-lipped creature inside her under wraps. (Thanks to some miraculous adjustment to modern mores, it never surfaced in her own sexual escapades, but raised its purdahed head in response to pictures or tales the remnants of its antiquated viewpoint could unabashedly term *filthy*.) Besides, there was no indication that Julio told her this tale to shock or seduce her. He never once shot her a telltale, underlidded glance, or knocked liquids into her lap, indicating he measured her reaction for his own advantage.

In fact, despite confused censorship from her interior prude, a large, round, air-filled sack was in the process of inflating itself in her pelvis; "lust" she labeled the troublesome pressure. This secret basketball, smooth, heavy, swelling desire, weighted her reluctant abdomen. No wonder; she hadn't had any sex at all for a couple of months; she shouldn't be surprised to find occasionally she was a healthy thirty-one-year-old "fe-male" with normal synapse connections. "Lust" was isolation's unavoidable offshoot. She should never have had the second brandy Alexander, much less the third. Drinking diminished her stoic reserves, fuzzed up the clean, sensible space she put between most people and herself. Drunk, she unconsciously leaned in the direction of whatever human being happened to be next to her, almost felt the warm pores, the textured construction of his, even her, skin. No, lust was not discriminating or even totally heterosexual, though she herself appeared to be. The smooth undersides of arms, the down on cheeks, the even curve, attracted her whomever it was attached to, whatever the gender. Now Julio's warm, polished, inappropriate skin drew her into its tingling vortex; it was imperative to maintain her distance, to keep in mind who he was, who she was, or should be in relation to him, if no longer his teacher.

He continued his tale. "So when they let me out I could not wait to see this chick. My collar was so tight I felt like I was choking to death, my man. She came down to the city on the train and I went to the station to pick her up. I took her to The Bronx, to my sister's place. We go into my room. Man, she looked good to me! We was sitting on my bed, rapping and shit, and then I started to stroke her, real gentle like, and I was kissing her and touching her and playing wit' her, soft, man, because this time it was real." He undressed her and started to suck her pussy and all of a sudden she sat up with a real mad face and said, "Just fuck me! Get on top of me and fuck me and get it over with!" "She just lay there, stiff and cold, man, like a dead person. Afterward I said to her, 'Girl, I don't think you and me can make it together.' She begins to cry, 'Please, Julito, give me another chance! I don't know what came over me. I was thinking about something bad that happened to me once. I really want to do it with you. I do!' Then she told me she wanted to pull a job with me, help me knock off this store she was working at." Julio shook his head. "Dolores, now you are a fe-male. Can you run that down for me?"

Dolores loved giving her opinion. The lives of other people, if not her own, were easy for her to analyze. She always knew what they should do, what motivated them, saw the mistakes that would mow them down while they still reeled in confusion. Lately she had vowed to stop delivering her clairvoyant pronouncements; friends, she had discovered, disliked her for them in the end, did not see her advice as money they could stop wasting on their stupid psychiatrists, but as unsympathetic meddling. The people whose problems she solved avoided her. But now she couldn't resist. He had asked, after all. "I think what she really likes is tantalizing men," she told him. "Not the real thing. When she wrote to you and visited you she could have the kind of sex she likes. She never really had to go through it. As soon as you were available you didn't interest her anymore. Maybe something bad did happen to her—"

Julio Bravo cut her off midstream. "Yeah . . ." he said. "I don't know, my man. I just wanted to hold her in my arms and stroke her hair and kiss her," he said again, and kept talking, his voice rumbling on with the methodic click of a well-oiled machine. Dolores, now groggy with alcohol, rode the humming vehicle of his voice and let her own brain grow silent. She had been going to say, "Maybe she was raped," but it was lucky she hadn't. She didn't want to remind him of the offer he'd made the last time she'd seen him in jail, too intense for the real world of her own kitchen, or find an excuse to discuss her own sexual history.

When he was strung out on drugs he went into a hospital to kick the habit, Julio said. He fell for a young girl who was having a tumor removed from her neck. Her name was Violet. She was small and helpless, but strong, my man, *fuerte,* the way some small girls be strong, inside themselves. After a while he ran away from the hospital and went home, but he could never forget that girl. He came back to the hospital and went into the coffee shop there to get him a milkshake. "Man, I was so strung out I was nodding into the fucking milkshake," he said. "My forehead was dropping into that chocolate foam. Then this nurse, this nurse who loved me, was loving me like a son, and was always trying to help me out and talk to me about drugs and my responsibility to myself and my family, like that, was coming into the place and seeing me there. 'You are back on narcotics again, aren't you, Julio?' she said. She called me 'Jew-li-o' instead of "Who-li-o.' 'Go home now. They won't let you up on the floor like that. You can't see Violet, Ju-li-o.' " Instead, he went outside and stood on the grass, calling up twenty floors, yelling his brains out . . . "Viiiiiiii-olet. Viiiiiiii-olet!" He sneaked up to visit her when the nurse was off duty. *"Yo te adoro, niña,"* he said, and as he spoke, he leaned back in his chair and five bags of heroin fell out of his hip pocket. "You are back on drugs, Julito," she said. "I can't see you no more."

"I am going to prove to you that I love you," Julio told her. "I am going to go into the toilet and flush this shit down." He went into the bathroom, combined the five bags into two, stuck them in his sock, and flushed the toilet noisily. When he came back into the room Violet said, "I have a cousin who is a dope fiend and I know if those bags of heroin ain't in your shoe they are in your crotch or your ass. I can't see you no more, Julio. Don't come back here no more."

"That's a sad story," Dolores said, her voice quavering. A lump had unexpectedly risen in her throat, as it did in response to the most maudlin scenes in the worst movies as well as to Shakespearean tragedies.

"*Sí. . . .*" Julio said. He looked at her acutely, moved by the fact she was moved. He sat quietly for an instant, reflecting, wobbling on the chair legs.

"She was right though; you would have ruined her life." The pontificating teacher again. She liked herself better with him when she was silent.

"But maybe she could have saved me," Julio said. His eyes dimmed momentarily, as if acknowledging some lost, corrupt, never-to-return part of himself, co-opted by that past, eaten away. Then, as if to reestablish his solid reality in the present, he stretched his muscles vigorously. "Dolores," he said, "I have been clean for nine years now. I will never go back on narcotics, my man, because there is no worse death than that. That is a death in life, Dolores. If I OD on some rooftop it will be the Man who has killed me and me who let him kill me without putting up no righteous form of self-defense. Dig it, the white man keeps the black people, the Hispanic people, in chains. They give us their drugs and their wine to keep us down. The first thing we got to do before we can get our armed struggle together is to get our people off the narcotics. That is what my man Malcolm was trying to do, and they killed him for it. *Oye,* his own people killed him for it, because the Man had already killed them."

As he spoke an early spring fly, cumbersome in its heavy new birth, flew in the window and buzzed around the crumbs on the plates. Julio watched it intently as it left the table and gallivanted in an aimless, humming circle in the air. He poised on the edge of his chair, stopped talking, and at an instinctively given moment, jumped up, grabbed it in his fist with fluid, accurate ferocity, smashed it between his palms, and dropped the dead black morsel to the floor. Afterward, his face was a deep, high-blood-pressure red, though his expression registered no visible emotion. He sat back down and took another gulp of brandy.

"Who's Graciela?" Dolores asked.

She had obviously put forth an important question. Julio did not answer for a moment; his body was still poised alertly, as if gathering impetus for another rapid movement. He touched the tattooed letters on his chest and looked out the window. Graciela, he said, was an eighteen-year-old Puerto Rican girl, eighteen now, he guessed; *sí*, eighteen. She was only fourteen when he had met her, before he went back to jail. She lived in the same building as his sister in The Bronx. He was meant to fall in love with her older sister, but instead he fell for the Baby. He laughed. Her father did not dig that, my man, not at all. Her older sister, sometimes her *abuela*, always went with them when they was going someplace. He had started fucking around in the nightlife again, but he went to her house every afternoon. "I could not take her virginity," he said. "That would have been disrespectful to her and to her mother." One night they snuck away from her sister and went out to Coney Island. They were lying under the boardwalk on the sand. "I will tell

100

you that she almost lost her virginity that night," he said. When they got home his *cujones* was killing him, and he said, *"Nene,* I have to leave you now." "Why?" she wanted to know. "I want to be with you, Julito. I want to stay with you." He explained his pain, his temptation; she told him to be careful if he went with other women, because she had heard about these women and knew sometimes they were sick down there. She did not know that he went to women he knew, not to whores.

One night they left a party together. He put his arm around her waist. He asked her to be his, *quiero que tú sea mío,* and she said, *"Sí,* Julito." He would have given up the nightlife for her. He was off drugs a long time. Things was going good; he had a job. But then they pulled that sting with the dope dealer and he went back to jail. He was in his cell and the hack gave him the letter from her. It said she could not see him again and not to write her or nothing. "You have your way of life, Julito, and I have mine." She signed it, "Love, Gracie."

"I cried, man," Julio said. "I cried like a little baby. I went to the artist in the joint and told him, 'Listen, my man, I want you to put someone's name on my body— over my heart.' Dolores, this is the only woman's name I will ever wear on my body." Dolores had already noticed another small tattoo on his left biceps, sprawling, half-legible letters, which seemed to spell the word *Ellie.* Sure, she thought.

There was a pause. "She won't talk to me now," he said. "She be going to school. She has a job. Her mama makes sure she don't even run into me in the building." Sometimes he saw her dark braid turning a landing, or saw her walking with her sister a block away, but then she hurried on, avoiding him. If she really didn't love him no more, he reasoned, why would she be so scared to meet him, run away like that? Why would she have signed her letter "love" if she did not love him? "If I could just talk to her, my man, I know I could make her see that I have changed. I can wait, and then I will tell her, 'I want to talk to you, *nene*. You name the time and the place.' "

Dolores felt unreasonably annoyed by this unsophisticated revelation of true love, this display of latino chevalier morality, this virgin-whore complex. None of it really meshed with her evolving image of Julio Bravo, or the other stories he'd told, the inseparable bogus wives, the sexual adventures, romantic infatuations, most of which, she realized must have occurred simultaneously in the brief spaces when he'd been out of jail, or before he was twenty.

"Maybe she's not a virgin anymore," she said with spontaneous wickedness. "She might be engaged to someone else." She was startled by the angry tone of her voice and the tight, constricted feeling in her chest. She should be glad that he trusted her enough to confide this truly deep emotion, one that took place in the present; it proved he still thought of her as his teacher, or at least, some kind of friend.

"No," Julio said positively. He had not caught her evil tone. "She is still a virgin. She ain't with nobody."

Then the inexplicable anger reversed itself, and Dolores felt sorry for him, this tragic little man. He loved a girl forbidden to see him with the same naïve gallantry he'd expressed when he'd vowed to kill her rapist. In her semidrunken state she could feel his sadness, the pathos of his criminal life. Beneath all his poses and staccato rhetoric he was just a pitiful, ignorant, well-meaning macho with a sixteenth-century Catholic mentality, half-transported from the primitive island world where he'd been born to a confused, violent life in a miserable slum that had given him nothing, really, but imprisonment and pain. This was the real Julio Bravo. She was glad to have received this unerring perception. It had freed her from uncertainty, put her back in control of the fact that she was his teacher, former teacher, and would continue to be so by natural decree. She saw him clearly from the distant pinnacle where fate had placed her and where she would remain. She felt sorry she'd been mean. The best thing she could be to him, for him, was kind. She searched her brain for something kind to say that would emphasize the warm but vast distance between them. "Julio," she finally remarked, her voice slightly slurred, "you're a true poet. . . . When you talk, you sing like a bird."

CHAPTER
7

WHEN the brandy ran out they took to the streets. A sporadic, chilly wind, left over from March, ruffled stray sheets of newspaper, skidded tapping metallic objects down the pavement, and made clattering cymbals of the lids of garbage cans. It was early evening; dusk sank its dense, grit-textured cloud around the remote peaks of the World Trade Center. The "Real Julio Bravo" had forgotten his spiritual pain and walked energetically on the balls of his feet. Each rocking step propelled him upward with an elastic bounce. Between the moment his right foot hit the concrete and the left floated up, there was a minute suspension of movement, a near pause in midair, like the graceful rest in a piece of music. It was a typical Newyorican tough salsa streetwalk swagger, and Julio performed it with relish, though somewhat self-consciously, Dolores thought, as if he were not sure he remembered the exact choreography. She found herself imitating this walk, a walk meant for cleated rubber soles, not boots, a walk that led to running, dancing; flutes and congas played behind it. "Man, I like to get high and walk," Julio said, ". . . keep on walking, walk through the barrio, checking it out . . . but cool . . . very cool. When I am high I see what is happening. *Mira*, I see what is going to happen. I smell the smells, feel the vibes, hear the little sounds. Dig it, I am paranoid when I walk. Dolores, I want to get high and walk with you through the South Bronx. I want to show you the place where I came up.

"When I be strapped down," he continued in a lower, secretive voice, "I walk different." Dolores remembered that "strapped down" meant "with gun." Julio's walk changed to illustrate his point, slunk lower to the ground, a soundless, stiff-kneed step. His eyes narrowed, surveyed the target. "Fuck," he said, straightening up again. "I don't even have a *fingernail* clipper on me now." He said he wondered if people could tell by the way he walked that he'd been to jail. He demonstrated the prison walk, a close-stepped, wary, flat-footed pacing, eyes coolly appraising the right, the left, though barely moving in their sockets. Dolores imitated these walks, the baleful stares, too, exaggerating them, laughing, still loaded. Now that she had defined the Real Julio Bravo, the unbreachable distance that separated them, she felt comfortable and relaxed.

"Why are you grinning like that, *niña*?" Julio asked fondly. He had registered her change of mood.

She was leading him toward Chinatown, and they arrived on its vivid streets as darkness blotted up the last ribbons of gray dusk. The streetlights lit tunneling pathways through the black night air, illuminating red-painted storefronts, splashes of neon characters, piles of garbage, discarded fruit baskets and metal tins. Chinatown was Dolores's favorite place, a microcosm of a foreign land, enabling her to temporarily eclipse the familiar existence that clung tediously to her, even in dreams.

Julio said he had never gone to Chinatown after dark. "All them chimes, weird smells. The slants make me paranoid, my man, *too* paranoid," he said enthusiastically. *Paranoid,* for him, was something like a positive term, Dolores observed. They went to her favorite tea shop, scuffed linoleum floor, fluorescent lights, and plasticized chairs. Julio sat facing the door; he had to see everyone who came in and went out, he said. His shoulders hunched into the protective barricade of his leather jacket; his eyes stared straight ahead with the intense, expressionless gaze of a cat seeing all. He cracked his knuckles and stirred five teaspoons of sugar into his coffee.

"One . . . two . . . three . . . four . . . five!" Dolores counted for him loudly. "Too much sugar, Julio. Do you know what sugar does to your adrenal glands?"

"We hit this Chinaman once," Julio said, his eyes fading to focus on a time, which like his grammar, was not consistently in the past. "He was running this clothes store up in The Bronx. He was one of them Chinamen from Cuba, *tú saba*? He spoke Spanish, like one of us. *'Qué tal, amigo?'* he would ask you when you be coming into his place; but then, when he did not want no one to know what he was saying, he would start this moaning and singing, my man—that was his language. He was no fucking good, that slant; he would give the people credit, but then he would add his interest and charge them more for the same shit on top of that. So the people who be needing clothes was thinking that this chink was doing them a favor, but they was getting burned.

"We came in and my partner said, 'Okay, sucker. Just give us the money and nobody will get hurt.' He did not want to give us nothing, my man. I had a .38 and my partner had a .45. We stood so that we had him between two streams of fire. I said, '*Oye, maricón.* I have nine bullets in this gun and you know that it is an automatic. Once I squeeze the trigger it will just keep on firing. I am aiming right below your heart because this gun will jump and fire higher. Even if it *mis*-fires, *hombre,* you are going down somehow.' The Chino looks the other way wit' them eyes of his and sees my partner's gun on him too. 'Take the money, *cabrón,*' he says. 'It is under the counter in a brown paper bag.' "

"Just keep your hands right where they are now," Julio said, moving slowly and evenly toward the counter, "up in the air. I am bound to hit you no matter how fast you move, *hombre,* and if by some miracle you get away, there will be another time."

"You know, Dolores," he said, "that Chino did not even call the po-*lice* on us, and I know he knew who we was."

"Why not?" Dolores asked. He was speaking so softly she had to lean forward to hear him. Now that he was out of jail his crime stories, told in settings that evoked the original scene, had a new, potent impact. This one inspired a sensation she could not quite label, not outright fear, but a definite chill she was conscious she enjoyed, like the grisly murder in a movie, deliciously terrifying because one knows it isn't real. Real fear, she thought, the presence of a real gun in your face, or even in your hand, would not inspire the vicarious, abandoned thrill of secondhand fear; real fear would be felt cautiously, with suspended belief.

"Because he knew we was getting revenge for the people," Julio replied. "Later, I ran into my cousin. 'Don't you owe that Chinaman on 138th Street some money?' I asked her. '*Sí*, Julito,' she said. 'I owe him twenty-five pesos and two interest.' 'Take it!' I told her, and I gave her twenty-seven dollars from that paper bag. 'You give this to the Chino, *niña*,' I told her, 'and don't buy nothing there no more.' "

"Robin Hood," Dolores commented. No, it wasn't exactly Robin Hood, perhaps more, or less.

"Dolores," Julio said, "we have got to teach the people. They have got to learn there is another way. If this was a righteous so-ciety there would not be no Chinaman; the people would get their clothes at the people's store, my man, and the price would be right. There would not be no credit or interest. We have got to teach the people about social-ism, my man, about how it be leading to commun-ism, about the governments that be working for the people. In China the people ain't ripping each other off. They ain't buying no fancy clothes, or fancy cars neither. They are all wearing the same blue uniform—it don't even fit good—and that is all right."

When he went on about politics, Dolores thought, he was almost boring. All naïve cliché. His heart was in the right place, but he didn't know shit about China. A Chinese friend had told her that when he went to visit his cousins in Peking, they barely spoke to him because he hadn't brought them a tape deck or stereo.

.   .   .

On the way back from Chinatown they stopped in the neighborhood bar on Dolores's block. Janice, the radical feminist who lived in her building, wandered in, lugging her usual weighty stack of propaganda; she located Dolores's face with her vague stare, and dropped bonelessly into the extra chair at their table. Julio immediately perused one of the leaflets, advertising a benefit at the Marxist School for an obscure Caribbean revolution, and scenting a kindred spirit, informed Janice he'd just gotten out of jail and was an enemy of capitalism himself. "Dig it, I am one week out of the joint, and I want things already. Al-ready, my man! I want a car, I want some nice threads. I want to own things, *muchas cosas*. I want to party! I feel this need inside of me and I know it is bad. I know this fucking capitalism is putting it inside of me, man. I have got to continue my education outside the walls. I have got to keep learning what the brothers was teaching us. I want to learn more about the politics, about the revolution. I want to write about that. I want to teach what I be learning to the people!"

Janice was enchanted. It wasn't every day, Dolores thought, that she got to meet an authentic victim of the penal system, and prison reform was among the many fervent causes smoldering in her pot. She approached these causes with faithful urgency, and though she could not summon the wherewithal to look for a job, remember to pay her rent, or clean her stuffy studio apartment—an unventilated jumble of dirty dishes, musty, holey sweaters, and unmade bed—she always found the energy to march and leaflet anywhere. Wherever Dolores went she inevitably ran into Janice, sometimes standing, usually leaning against a wall, other times collapsed on a stoop, current pamphlet in limp hand, her blue eyes caught in some middle ground between ardent mission and nameless fear. She claimed to be "mainly lesbian," yet her wild, sloven beauty and vacillating smile seemed to compel neither women nor men. Though she borrowed money and clothes and forgot to return them, Dolores still liked her, if only because she had more important things on her mind than money and clothes. Moreover, she rarely talked about romance or her personal ambitions, the two favorite topics of every other woman Dolores knew.

When Janice spoke in her flickering, incandescent style about her vital causes, the indignities inflicted upon women, the Third World, and the poor, Dolores keenly felt the absence of a cause of her own (poetry, after all, could not really be termed a "cause"), a place for her own furies and sense of injustice to reside. Now, as Julio and Janice discussed the evils of prisons and the death penalty, discovering they had both worked with the same radical lawyer, Julio's attorney for the Corsica defense, she felt her mind struggle to leap up and claim interest in these noble subjects, and then fall down. It was impossible for her to focus long on information outside an imagistic or dramatic context—a sign of her basic stupidity, no doubt. Still it pleased her to see Janice and Julio chatting like old friends, calling their mutual lawyer pal "Charlie," and discussing common areas of knowledge. Janice's respectful attention to Julio's points proved his ideas were intelligently formed; Janice was no fool. Dolores hadn't listened carefully to what he'd been saying about politics, possibly because his crude rhetoric had convinced her he couldn't know much, which only indicated she was a snob, despite her best intentions, and ignorant of these matters herself.

Julio was now describing the final scene of the Corsica riot to the spellbound Janice. "I felt it coming, man," he said. "It was quiet, all of a sudden like. I saw the lights go out when they cut the power. Then there was them loud, whirring sounds—the choppers. I saw the tear-gas bomb hit even before I felt that shit in my throat. I did not hear the machine guns until I seen one of the brothers go down. It was after that I knew what that *ratatattatttt* was meaning. We was guarding the hostages, man. We had treated them good, real good, giving them the best food that was there, giving them the blankets so they did not get cold. We was cold ourselves, but we was giving them the blankets. We did not treat them like no animals, like they had been treating us. That was political though. We did not want them to go back out there and say we treated them bad, because that would mean that bad shit would come down on us, so we treated them good. We talked to them. They be telling us about their old ladies . . . their kids. That tear gas chokes you, man. . . . You feel like you are al-ready dead. You can't see nothing. You be wishing you was dead. There was no time to be thinking of nothing. We shoved them down into the trenches and we hit the dirt. The brothers was falling around me. I was crawling, crawling blind, man, looking for cover wit' my hands. Later, they said they found the hostages with their throats cut." He looked down at his clenched fingers. "But there was not no knife wounds on those dudes. No way. The National Guard motherfuckers shot them; the pigs shot their own brothers, man. Then they said we slit their throats and cut off their dicks."

At the final words of the story, Dolores felt Julio's palm encircle her knee and grip it under the table. Her body stiffened and blood ran to her face. So everything was different than she'd supposed.

Janice, unaware that any change in undertable dynamics had taken place, was still shaking her head over the

Corsica riot, muttering, "My God . . . how can a man survive an experience like that?

"After that I could never be scared of nothing in life," Julio said.

"Did it change anything, Julio?" Janice asked earnestly. "I mean . . . did it *really* change anything?"

"Yeah . . ." Julio said. "They gave us some bullshit like snacks and telephone calls. . . . They put in some programs. They stopped fucking wit' our mail. But you cannot change nothing behind the walls until you change the so-ciety that is putting the people there. You have got to get *rid* of the penitentiary to change the penitentiary, my man. Corsica ain't so bad no more, but Greenhill is a fucking pit. Greenhill is fucked up bad. The brothers up there are just waiting for something big to jump off. . . . They have got a lot of patience, but it has got to happen, my man, and when it blows it is going to make Corsica look like a kid's birthday party."

All three of them were silent for a moment. Janice was contemplating the horrors of Corsica, Dolores, the significance of Julio's hand on her knee, and Julio, staring moodily at his ever-fuming cigarette, indicated no thoughts, no emotions at all. Finally, Janice asked Julio what he planned to do now that he was free. It was a logical question, Dolores realized, a necessary question, one she herself had planned to ask, and somehow neglected to do so, though the answer was obviously more important than any of these jolly reminiscences about his past.

Julio had several answers. He said a friend of his from the joint had put in a word with his uncle who owned a trucking firm, a big Mafia cat, and the uncle had written a letter to the parole board, saying he would give Julio a job as a driver. That had helped to get him out. If he could get his license he could work as a trucker for almost three hundred a week, but the fucking parole did not want to give permission for a license; they thought he would use it to drive to another state and commit crimes. A second possibility was construction work; he had done a lot of painting and plastering jobs the last time he was out. He thought he might go to school. He knew this place where they had courses for ex-offenders, fixing boilers, plumbing, like that. When you finish they give you a license. "I know that I am ready, willing, and able to enter society, man," he said, his first tribute to the letter Dolores had written in his behalf. "What I really want to do," he continued, "is to work wit' the gangs, teaching the young brothers what is needed." That is what he had been doing the last time he was out of jail, helping the jitterbuggers get off narcotics, giving them political training. "The mayor asked me and two of my partners to meet with him," he said, "and two days before the meeting I went back to jail. *Coño,*" he reflected, "I wonder if it is possible for a man to make a *con*-scious error?"

He then launched his favorite monologue, the never-ending tale of his knight errant adventures, beginning with the bodega shoot-out that landed him in the Tombs. Janice, hearing it all for the first time, was captivated. Then he went on to new stories, in which he still played the role of Robin Hood. "Once me and my partner busted into this place," he said. "We stood in the hall working on the lock for two hours. Finally, I seen the door was so thin I could kick it down with my little toe. We get in and there ain't nothing there. No Tee Vee, no radio. There was not even no food in the refrigerator. The clothes in the closet was looking like rags. I put down my last four dollars on the table and I said to my partner,

'*Vaya*, let's buff; these people are doing bad, my man.' Later I spread the word around, 'Don't crack on so and so in such and such a place, because them people are doing *bad*!' "

As he talked he kept his hand on Dolores's knee, gripping it tighter when his sentences needed periods or exclamation points. What should she do with this hand, mesmerizing her entire body, sending nervous crawls up her thigh? Her knee seemed to burn underneath it, like the round coils of an electric stove. That hand told her whatever Julio was saying, whatever attention he focused on the enthralled Janice, his thoughts were really with her, his intimate considerations with the knee he caressed. It should be easy to remove the hand, as she had removed many an unwanted hand; she could simply get up, go to the ladies' room, return, and sit farther away, or on the other side of the table. But to remove the hand would be to acknowledge its importance in a negative way. Besides, it was not necessarily a sexual overture, more likely a warm, friendly gesture. No, that was bullshit, or it might not be. She was always so uptight; a simple, earthy caress automatically telegraphed "sexual come-on" to her.

Janice began scribbling on her cocktail napkin the names and phone numbers of contacts who might help Julio get a job—friends who worked in hospitals, for radical organizations, and youth groups; her political activities had made her a number of influential pals, none of whom, Dolores noted, she had managed to contact about a job for herself. She knew this one really great guy who worked with kids up in Harlem, she said, and when she mentioned his name Julio's eyes lit up and he said, "*Vaya*, that is Sharif. That is my man!" Sharif, it turned out, was a brother who had stood with him on the Corsica ramparts. He removed his hand from Dolores's knee long enough to light a Camel, then put it back.

"You smoke too much," Dolores said. Overcome by cigarette fumes, the unprecedented amount of booze she had been swilling since early afternoon, and the confusing probabilities put into play by Julio's hand, she had begun to feel irritated. It was later than two. Suddenly she wanted to be home and in bed; she wanted to be alone. She lurched to her feet. Julio stood up too. She had more or less hoped he would stay and continue his nonstop rap with Janice, who was plainly entranced by him, and relieve her of the embarrassing necessity of dumping him coldly at her door. She was tired of it all, of Julio, his constant voice. It wasn't that easy for her to spend more than a few hours in the company of anyone, much less someone who never shut up or let her get a word in edgewise. She began to imagine what she would say to him at the door of her building, how she could politely relay him back to Janice in the bar and climb the stairs to her apartment alone. Janice and he were clearly meant for one another; maybe they would go off to some flaming battlefield together, and Janice would renounce the daughters of Lesbos for him.

Instead, she delayed the inevitable confrontation and suggested Julio walk to the park with her for a breath of fresh air. She was a total coward when it came to difficult male-female moments. She shivered and Julio stripped off his leather jacket and put it around her shoulders, which left him topless, except for his overall bib. "You'll freeze to death," Dolores protested. Next he'd be spreading his jacket over mud puddles so she wouldn't soil her shoes.

Julio laughed. "Listen, Dolores. I am seventy-five percent Carib. We Caribes don't feel no kind of weather.

115

My *antepasados*, my ancestors was running naked through the jungles of Puerto Rico, man, before Puerto Rico was Puerto Rico, before it got ripped off by the conquistadores, shooting birds with blowguns, eating raw meat, human flesh." Her knee still stung from the pressure of his hand.

He talked on as he had for the past umpteen hours (Would he ever run out of stories?), in no way acknowledging the new dialogue he had introduced by touching her; but something had changed. She thought she was walking closer to him than she intended; maybe she imagined that. Washington Square Park was a bleak place in the early hours, empty and dark.

"I like that Janice girl," Julio said. "She has a good head." He went on to say that for years he had been prejudiced toward white people, and it was white women who had first indicated their possible virtues. I said to myself, "*Coño,* Julito! You like their women. Now maybe you should take a second look at the *dudes*!"

"Janice is gay," Dolores announced, apropos of nothing. Immediately she felt disgusted with herself. Why was she betraying a friend's most private confidence to this man? To turn him off, she realized, quick to ferret out and condemn her real motives, because she was jealous, jealous that he had been so eager to establish the same rapport with Janice that he had with her. Only a thoroughly dishonest bitch, she thought, could drum up possessive feelings for a man she didn't want, disillusion him with the very woman to whom she had been willing, a minute before, to relinquish him. She had once told Janice she considered it a miracle she was not a lesbian herself.

Julio shook his head. "That is too bad," he said. "A beautiful girl like that! Man, there ain't nothing a woman can do for another woman that a dude can't do." He laughed. "Once I was at this girl's place and this dyke who was having a thing for her comes into the bedroom and says to me, 'What the fuck are you doing here, *hijo la gran puta?*' That means 'son of a whore,' Dolores.

" 'What do you mean what am I doing here?' I asked her. 'And don't call me no bastard because you *know* my mother ain't no whore!' Then I slapped her upside the face a few times. 'You want to be a man,' I told her, 'you can take a man's punishment.' She was crying and begging, 'Duke, man, we know each other. We went to school with each other.'

" 'I know that,' I says, 'but don't you ever call my mother no whore.' "

"I'm wiped out," Dolores announced firmly. "I want to go home." They were seated on a bench that felt damp and cold beneath her thighs. That last anecdote opened yet another revealing window on the Real Julio Bravo— a crude, violent man with a nitwit latino slum morality, completely beyond her capacity to understand. Janice should hear the revolutionary hero now! She stood up definitively. The jungle gym bars traced their phantom outlines against the black sky.

"This park . . ." Julio said. "I had to fuck some dude up in this park one time."

"Why?" She asked the expected question in a sullen voice.

"Because the nigger tried to put his hands on my wife!" Julio exclaimed, still indignant.

"Oh, Julio," Dolores said wearily.

As they walked back down her block toward her building, his arm encircled her waist. Here we go again, she thought. She wanted to be home, in bed, this minute, without further hassles, verbal, physical, any kind at all.

She was too exhausted to cope with anything more than dragging her body up three flights of stairs. Julio Bravo was silent for once, as if contemplating himself the significance of his embrace. His strong arm gripped her side like a vise from which there was no escape. She made some faint, wriggling motions to extricate herself, without making it too obvious she was trying. She didn't want to deal with a thwarted macho ego at this hour of the night—who knew what form it might take—but her feeble struggles only seemed to tighten the pressure of his arm. There could be no question of romance between them; that was abundantly clear. Yet at the moment she felt physically incapable of eluding this hot, solid arm, which drew her waist, her entire enervated body, into dependent contact with him. She really wanted him to disappear, yet some wishy-washy, lonely, overtired need wanted him to keep touching her.

"Dolores," Julio said, "I am going to tell you something I don't want you to tell nobody." There was a pause. He tightened his hold. "I did have to shoot somebody once, some dude who was fucking with my partner, holding him a hostage. I waited outside the window, man. I had my .45, a beautiful piece, chrome, with wooden grips. The dude was sitting there, cleaning his fingernails with a knife. My partner was tied to a chair in the middle of the room. They had him gagged so he could not make no noise. When the dude went to answer the telephone I came right through the screen. He turned. He had his gun in his hand and it was loaded, so I did not have no choice. The bullets went in right below the heart, and he jumped. I untied my man and we went out the way I had come in. I ran into the house, up to his woman, and I gave her my gun. 'Your husband is going to come up here and he is going to die,' I said. 'He is not dead yet, but he will be. And you will be dead too, if you open your mouth. You will leave that little baby an orphan.' Then I went back to the stoop and sat there. The po-lice came by and said, 'Did you hear any gunshots?' 'All I heard was some firecrackers,' I told them."

"Did he die?" Dolores asked, feeling the tremulous pe-culiarity of this question, the fearful compulsion to know the answer, and the absence of the proper emotions, dis-gust, outrage, she should feel as she asked. Some last muscle of resistance gave way and her side, independent of her will, surrendered to the confines of Julio Bravo's arm. He now seemed to support her entire weary, help-less weight; his grip collapsed the vast distance she felt expanding in an abstract plane between them.

"I did not wait to find out," Julio said hoarsely. "I split for Boston the next day. I don't think so though. I am sure I seen that dude in the mess hall at Briarstone."

When they arrived at the door of her building Janice was standing in the vestibule. It wasn't clear if she'd just arrived, or if she'd been waiting there for a while. Julio greeted her enthusiastically. "*Hola, niña*! Ain't you in bed yet?" He flashed his pirate's smile, letting go of Dolores's waist, which retained the tactile impression of his em-brace like a plaster cast.

"I saw you coming," Janice said self-consciously. "I thought I'd wait for you and say good night." Her deter-mined manner indicated she'd been waiting for a reason.

"Well. . . good night, Julio," Dolores said, resurrecting her formal, schoolteacher voice from she didn't know where. She was actually relieved to find Janice there. Her final moment alone with Julio would have been problem-atic; it wouldn't have been easy to get rid of him at all.

"Good luck with the job," Janice said. "Don't forget to give those people a call."

Julio did not reply to these gratuitous remarks. He looked bewildered as he grasped the fact that the two of them, these two white women, were dismissing him for the night. He stared almost desperately at Dolores, swaying a bit on his feet; his bloodshot eyes were fixed on hers, compelling her to admit something he knew she knew, that the rhetoric of the entire day, the false, superficial chitchat, was only the external trappings of their real intimacy, a fated intimacy that smoked through social forms like a locomotive on a track. His eyes attracted hers as they had in their last meeting in jail, when he had sworn he would kill for her. Dolores felt Janice's hand on her arm and realized she was swaying in the direction of Julio Bravo like a tree that had been sawed through and would momentarily topple and fall. She had thought she was looking elsewhere, but she had been staring back at him, riveted into his eyes.

"Good night, Julio," Janice said again. Now her voice was the prim teacher's. Julio still gazed at Dolores; she had to look away, at her boots, at the wall. "It was great meeting you," Janice said. She was pulling on Dolores's arm, practically yanking her into the hall. "Keep in touch."

"Lots of luck," Dolores blurted stupidly.

They left Julio standing there, rooted to the spot, eyes suddenly dazed, bereft. He did manage a version of his spirited voice and a *"Gracias,* good night!" but he didn't move or turn to go. It was unnerving to see him standing there forlornly, his arms dangling at his sides. Every muscle pulled Dolores back to something she'd left unsaid. How unforgivable to dump him flat, after the long afternoon, the intense night, without saying what was on her mind, though she was not sure exactly what it was, something that ought to be acknowledged now, and simultaneously denied. It was hard to force her drunken body up the stairs. Her legs felt heavy, unwilling, as if they were slowed, not by drink, but by a spell.

Janice lived on the second floor. When they reached her landing Dolores said in a voice that emerged half grateful, half peeved, "Thanks for rescuing me."

"Dolores," Janice said urgently. "He's wonderful! He's beautiful! But he's for real!"

Dolores was surprised to hear her verbalize the merits of Julio Bravo in such extravagant terms; Janice, the radical, feminist lesbian, who claimed to despise the majority of men. Yet her sincerity shone in the dim hall, making Dolores feel doubly guilty for betraying her.

"You don't think I should be his friend?" she asked.

Janice sought her with her blue stare, which, at this moment, refused to waver, held firm, nothing to do with nameless fears, undone laundry, unpaid rent. She was in a territory she understood and could defend—sisterhood. "Of course you should be his friend," she said. "He needs all the friends he can get. Just don't get too involved! Dolores . . . I'm afraid for him!"

"Don't worry," Dolores answered, startled by her own grim tone. (It struck her odd this sister hadn't said, "Dolores . . . I'm afraid for *you*.") "I have no intention of getting involved with him."

CHAPTER

8

*I*T was nearly dawn when Dolores collapsed in bed and had her recurring dream about the mysterious island. She arrived, as she always did, by an ordinary subway, which changed into a transgalactic express, zipped non-stop through New York City, sped past the United States altogether, crossed a tumultuous flooding river, and smoked through a mountain-sided valley before becoming the interior of a small plane. When the pilot circled over the archipelago, she saw the familiar configuration of small islets, curved harbors, and the jagged washboard of inland mountains before landing on the island itself.

When she disembarked Dolores discovered, as usual, that she had landed far from the particular place she was supposed to go. Someone was expecting her on another part of the balmy, tropical island, or perhaps she had a mission to accomplish there. She was not sure what obligation drew her to this specific destination, but she knew that was where she belonged and she was already late.

She began the usual frustrating ordeal with the local transportation. First she waited for the bus, napping on the uncomfortable floor of the station with the other travelers, faceless phantoms, who never spoke or removed their woolen overcoats; the bus did not come for hours, and when it did, it was jammed with passengers and she couldn't squeeze on. At long last another bus arrived; she managed to get a seat, after creating a furious scene that no one seemed to hear, but the dilapidated vehicle broke down a few blocks from the station. She had to transfer to a small rowboat, impossible to row, since it hadn't any oars. As she sat bewildered in the prow, the powerless boat bobbed on a sea that visibly expanded until the distant shore disappeared.

Without knowing how she arrived Dolores soon found herself sunbathing on a crowded beach on exceptionally uncomfortable gritty sand. She did not think a beach was her final destination, and if it was, this beach was not the right one. The water was not blue, did not roll and pitch with waves; its dank, bad-smelling ripples sloshed listlessly at the shore, leaving a scummy residue behind. She was afraid to set foot in this murky pond, clearly polluted with poisonous wastes.

As she watched the water it began to swell, inflate beyond its boundaries, changing rapidly from a stagnant pond to a giant tidal wave, which swept violently toward the beach; the sun vanished and torrential rain fell. Dolores fled inland, running, running, her feet barely moving, though she willed them to go as fast as they could. The other people on the beach had disappeared, and she was alone. At last she reached a pier, breathing hard, clung to its warped post with all her panicked strength, and watched the wave, now metallic gray and miles high, descend upon her. She was terrified, although she'd seen this wave in other dreams, and knew she would escape it, as she had before. The water engulfed her, collapsing her skeleton with its force, filling her lungs and ears, and just as it was about to pull her from her post and drag her into the endless sea, she was miraculously transferred to a mountain, awesome in its breadth and height, sure the place she belonged was on the other side.

Dolores had often attempted to analyze this dream, which repeated itself in varying forms, and had ransacked it for mythic images for her poems. It seemed she always voyaged to the island dream world when she was about to fall in love, or felt a new, erotic presence in her life. One time the candidate himself appeared, rushing down the beach with a cigar-shaped pole balanced on his nose. Nothing subtle about that symbol! Apparently her unconscious had chosen the image of water to represent sexual desire, perhaps because she had almost drowned at Montauk when she was fourteen, and had begun to experience erotic sensations for a certain lifeguard. Obviously she was subconsciously afraid desire would "drown" her. She also thought the water might symbolize intimacy, and she was afraid of that, as one friend, a longtime survivor of the Freudian couch, had suggested. None of this brand of analysis, however, rang true; even if it was accurate, it was also irrelevant. It did not explain the most significant aspect of the dream—her definite feeling that she belonged on this island and knew it well, her certainty that once she bypassed the obstacles, she would be exactly where she belonged.

She had come to believe the island was her homeland in a previous incarnation. It possessed that truly vivid, attached familiarity, like the view of the crossroad in New Jersey where she had waited for the school bus during the childhood of this life. Her "real destination" in the dream, she felt, was either the house she'd lived in before she was born, or, another possibility, the place she was going after she died. Perhaps future and unremembered past lives were one and the same in an individual's over-all destiny; perhaps time, out of this earthly plane, did not divide itself distinctly into future and past. The reason she could never reach the place she belonged was because she was not dead yet. The consuming waves and polluted waters were instruments of death, and her escape symbolized fate's current unwillingness to let her die or wake up anew in its timeless continuum. Why, then, did she always enter the dream when a new lover was on the horizon? The dream itself, in fact, often alerted her to the erotic possibilities of someone she'd ignored before meeting him on the island. Perhaps love and death were connected in her fate. Someone she was destined to love would be the person who caused her to die, the human embodiment of the expanding sea. The dream was warning her.

In this version of the dream she struggled back down the mountain without reaching the top, knowing she had little time to catch the boat or train that would take her back to New York. She would not make it to her destination this time either. She hurried along an asphalt road, lined by groves of diseased palms. The airport was still far away and so was the train station. She only had an hour, a half hour, a few minutes left. Time was always nebulous in dreams, an inhibiting weight instead of clearly transversible spaces. She was moving as fast as she could, but the more energized her exertions the less distance they carried her. For a while she was on her bicycle, but as her own speed increased, so did the size of the road, until it became a vast freeway, rushing with traffic, no end in sight. She knew the approximate location of the airport, but she couldn't reach it.

Then she was walking again on the asphalt road, tired, nervous, sweating in the humid climate. A narrow, polluted stream ran beside it, trickling slimily, a runoff from the poisoned pond. From a distance she saw a small figure kneeling by the stream, attempting to scoop water from it into his cupped hands. She tried to walk faster, to warn this foolish soul that the stream was lethal sewage, or laced with chemical waste. He would contract hepatitis, at the very least, if he drank that filthy water.

As she drew closer, she was sure the shrunken, old-looking man was her grandfather, who had died several years before. She realized then that she'd missed him, though at the time of his death she hadn't seen him for several years. It was her grandfather! She felt a surprisingly ecstatic joy at the prospect of seeing him again, forgot the waiting boat or train. "Grandpa!" she tried to call, but the inexplicable powers of dreams silenced her voice. As she drew closer, however, she saw the small, old figure had become, or always had been, Julio Bravo.

CHAPTER
9

*T*HE telephone rang, lifting Dolores from her island dream; it was Joanna. Sometimes, when she took stock of the people in her life, she categorized Joanna as her "best" friend, because they treated each other with the casual, constant concern of family members. Joanna described the details of her daily life to her, right down to every last moan and heave of her sex life, relegated, as it was, to her husband, Tom, with whom she'd lived for nine and a half years. Dolores, in turn, regaled Joanna with equivalent trivia, mundane inanities that cluttered her mind, too dull to foist on other people, from the attentuated ghosts of her past lovers to the sums of dry cleaning bills. Their relationship was comfortable; only with Joanna was she assured she did not have to present an interesting façade to be loved.

"Were you sleeping?" Joanna asked her. "For Chrissakes, it's after eleven! Are you sick?" She well knew Dolores regarded sleeping past nine as extreme moral failure.

"Not sick, hung over," Dolores said. "I was out until dawn." Her veins had a constricted, achy feeling, too much booze and smoke. "I was having the island dream again." That dream still wafted its dissolving terrors through her consciousness.

"You want me to call you back?"

"No, it's okay. I have to get up anyway. I have work to do." Dolores was far less diligent than Joanna, who hurried home from her full-time job teaching high school students, "little buggers," as she called them, and immediately installed herself among the poisonous fumes of her plastic resin sculptures. The very sound of her voice reminded Dolores that an unfinished poem, unfinished for days, waited on her desk.

"Hey, guess what I got?" Joanna could scarcely wait to tell her. "An Anne Klein silk paisley jacket, reduced from two hundred and seventy-five smackeroos to only sixty bucks!"

"Yeah . . . !" said Dolores. The thought of Anne Klein vanquished the last meanderings of the subconscious. She was immediately envious. At the moment there was no way on earth she could shell out sixty bucks for a silk jacket . . . maybe she could. "Where was it?" she asked.

"Place Elégante at Bloomingdale's. I saw that jacket and I said, 'Boy, this is just too spiffy to pass up!' It is *gorgeous,* especially with my brown leather pants. I got a pink chenille sweater, too, reduced from forty down to twenty-five." That made roughly Joanna's fifth or sixth chenille sweater this season. She bought things in cycles with a compulsive mania that made Dolores's seem a tiny tic by comparison. One year it was silk blouses, maroon, gray-striped, navy blue; the next year boots and raw silk pants in pastel shades. She favored silk because, she said, of the way it slid against her skin when Tommy took it off her. Her vast wardrobe had long since flowed out of the closet in her loft, bigger than Dolores's entire bedroom, and onto racks appropriated from the garment district. Dolores rarely saw her in anything, however, but her resin-smeared ancient jeans. Even when dressed to the nines, she shunned makeup and high heels and let her thin, unkempt hair float freely over her pale face like the dark silk of a windblown milkweed.

Joanna went on to fill Dolores in on her life in the last two days: how much work she'd done on her new piece, a life-size tree, the gallery she'd approached, what she'd said to that half-blind jerk, the dealer, other tempting morsels she'd spotted at Bloomingdale's, and finally, the latest on her sex life. "Boy oh boy," she said, "Tommy and I sure had one terrific fuck last night. He started by taking off my clothes, real slow, the way I like him to. Then I told him to begin by kissing at the top of my head and cover every single inch until he got to my feet. He did it, too. About halfway down he wanted to dive right in there with his enormous hard-on, but I said, 'Just a minute, buster, you aren't quite finished yet!' Was I wet, let me tell you! Then we fucked like bunnies until three in the morning."

Dolores had never managed to connect the round-shouldered, plump Tommy, who did the bulk of the shopping, cooking, and cleaning, with the incredible tales Joanna related about her well-hung superstud of a husband. She knew the exact length and circumference of his mammoth penis, as if she'd measured it herself; she had been privy to its every virile stir, and the entire history of its forceful thrust vis-à-vis Joanna. ("When I first saw it I said to myself, 'This little beauty is never gonna fit!' ") She also knew how Tom's melancholies affected the moody creature, making it go sullenly limp for weeks, and the various tactics Joanna had developed to inspire it to leap up again. This morning, however, the details of Tommy's latest sexual gymnastics made her feel irritated and deprived.

"Well," she said, "I'm still celibate, despite an entire evening and night in the company of Julio Bravo." She dropped that small bomb and let it smolder. Joanna knew about Julio Bravo, and had been duly impressed when Dolores told her of his vow to kill anyone who injured her. She waited for Joanna's expectant "Oh yeah . . . ?" the usual invitation to tempt her imagination with the succulent details of a new conquest or promise of one. She obviously envied the continual process of sexual discovery in Dolores's traumatic love life, if not the traumas themselves; she had even confessed to longings for an extramarital peccadillo of her own, but with the wistful, uncertain yearning of one who firmly fears what she desires. This time, however, there was an uncomfortable silence then an easy, "So he's out of the slammer, huh? Is he homesick yet?"

"He's out," Dolores said. "He's definitely out."

"So . . . what happened?" Joanna's voice was still uneasy, as if she expected to hear news of a disaster.

"Nothing happened. We hung around here talking. I made him lunch." (She deliberately omitted mention of Julio's late arrival. She knew what Joanna would say about that. She jokingly referred to Dolores's lovers as "The Tardy Boys.") "We walked to Chinatown. Then we went to a bar and talked to Janice for a while. Then he took me home." She went on to say that Julio Bravo was truly an interesting man, alive, enthusiastic, sensitive, and that she'd seldom met any middle-class, college-educated men with his intelligence and vitality. Dolores had a tendency to eulogize men who interested her, and then, when disillusionment struck, to condemn them in equally potent superlatives.

"Uh huh . . ." Joanna said, making her dubious suspicion clear.

"Of course I can't get involved with him," Dolores continued quickly. "He's just out of jail. He has to get his shit together . . . find a job and report to the parole. I got the impression it's not going to be easy for him to figure out exactly who he is out here. Besides, I'm in a completely different social class than he is."

"I'll say," Joanna said emphatically.

Dolores realized this conversation was taking a surprisingly negative turn. She had thought Joanna would find her encounter with Julio Bravo fascinating, and want to hear every detail about this interesting character. Instead, she now found herself defending him and her "innocence" stridently, as if she were on trial for wrongdoing. Joanna sounded almost hostile. "Not only does he have a lot of shit to get together," she said, "but if he got involved with you, it might keep him from doing it."

"I don't know why," Dolores said. "Maybe I could help him."

"Bullshit!" Joanna exclaimed. "Don't start playing social worker. This guy is a repeat offender. He's been in and out of jail most of his life. He keeps committing the same crimes, over and over. Are you gonna let him hang around your place, eating up the contents of your refrigerator, until he gets it up to rob some bank again? You've got a classical criminal personality there."

"He never robbed a bank," Dolores said. "He specialized in discount electronic stores." She waited for Joanna's chortle, which never came. "His robbery stories are actually very interesting," she added lamely. "He sees himself as a kind of Robin Hood."

"I bet he does," she said loudly and sarcastically.

"It's amazing he survived," Dolores continued. "He was a dope addict for years. He was a leader in the Corsica riot. Can you imagine living through that? He even had to shoot somebody once," she added, remembering Julio told her never to tell anyone that.

"Dolores . . . !" Joanna said, in the incredulous, horrified tones of one who sees a friend about to plunge headlong into a burning building.

"That's all in the past now," Dolores said quickly. "He's looking for a job."

Joanna was silent.

"You might not believe this, but he has a strange, uninhibited kind of honesty. He's an ex-con, but somehow he's a totally honest man."

"He's not honest!" Joanna snorted. "He's a criminal . . . a convicted felon. He couldn't be honest. He's probably conning you with his fake honesty just like he's conned everyone his whole life. No one who was ever a junkie could ever be honest. Ask Tommy about junkies! He worked with them."

"Janice liked him," Dolores said, invoking, as she often did in arguments, the supportive opinion of an invisible third party. "She thought he was terrific. 'Beautiful and wonderful,' she said. They had a mutual friend . . . some well-known radical lawyer."

"Sure," Joanna said, "go ahead. Fuck a repeat offender. She thinks it's cute. What the hell does she care? I'm concerned for your welfare."

"I'm sure he has a gigantic cock," Dolores said. This was the kind of salacious repartee they usually exchanged, but as soon as the vulgar comment left her mouth, she realized it undermined her sincerity in the context of the present discussion. In fact, she had scrupulously avoided envisioning the dimensions of Julio Bravo's member, not easy to do when he himself portrayed it constantly.

"I'm sure he does, too," Joanna said. "Almost as big as the .45 he's packing in his belt."

"Joanna!" Dolores exclaimed indignantly. "How do you know he's a criminal personality? You never met him! Don't you think it's possible he could have changed? Would you always want to be judged as the person you were ten years ago?"

"I'm not saying I don't think he could change," she replied, "but if I were you I'd wait until he *does* change before you start spending too much time with him. Think what might happen if you get involved with this guy and he starts fooling around with heroin again. How do you know he wouldn't rob you blind? What if you fall in love with him and then they stick him back in jail? I can just see the police bursting down your door and pumping a few hundred bullets into your apartment right in the middle of your next *Family Circle* article."

Dolores didn't laugh. Among other things she didn't like to be reminded of *Family Circle*. "He would never steal from me," she declared. "And he won't go back on drugs. You forget that I've known him for months already. We have a certain understanding. I'm his teacher. I consider him a friend. I can spend time with him without fucking him. I'm not an animal! I never said I was going to get involved with him. I said I wasn't. Besides, what's involvement? You can be *un*involved and have sex too. Why are you being so . . . ? I doubt if he wants to get involved with me either. He said he's in love with some eighteen-year-old virgin. He put his arm around me for a minute. Big deal! Besides, he could stay straight for five years and then go back on drugs or shoot a cop. You don't have any guarantee that Tommy won't shoot a cop someday either. Suppose I did want to fuck him; how long am I supposed to wait? Until we're both seventy?"

"How about five years?" Joanna suggested. "By then you might be involved with someone else. Besides being an ex-con he's a spic. That should make you stop and think for a minute too. Do you want to be waiting hand and foot on some macho who wishes you were a teen-age virgin?"

"Please," Dolores said angrily. "I haven't even kissed him and you already have me waiting on him." Joanna had said *spic*; though she had probably used the term facetiously, with no more rancor than she'd say "bugger" or "buster," the racist word registered with acerbic negativity. Why did nice, liberal people, who wouldn't dream of saying *nigger* even in jest, feel comfortable with the term *spic*? "Give me a break," Dolores said.

"I am giving you a break. I'm advising you to stay away from the creep."

Dolores was finally infuriated. "How can you call a friend of mine those names?" she demanded, and hopped snarling onto her podium. "You're reflecting the ignorant attitude of this entire white, racist, middle-class society toward people who've been in jail, mostly because they had the bad luck to be born poor, or black, or Puerto Rican. It's your kind of stupidity that forces people like Julio to become repeat offenders, because you won't give them jobs or trust them for a single minute. Just because

134

a guy commits some crime when he's twenty years old doesn't mean he has to go on committing the same crime for the rest of his life!" As she shouted these words, fully awake, she felt buoyant, high, as if her own voice had burned away the miasmas of other people's wrong thoughts from her mind.

There was an awkward silence as they both digested the significance of the first real quarrel they'd ever had. Dolores had always ignored the differences between them, thought them superficial; but now it was apparent that below the similar stratum of life they occupied, life in the same class, the same artsy-fartsy neighborhood, lay a real disparity, ready to cut them apart like a knife—different basic values. No, they were not intrinsically alike beneath their constant exchange of trivial news, compulsive shopping binges, and upward grovel toward career success. Racist, Dolores thought, relishing the definitive epithet. Poor conservative Joanna, cowering behind the fangs of her ungainly, vicious Doberman, half protected from the criminal-personality *spics* that climbed through the windows of her imagination day and night to slit her throat and remove the plethora of belongings from her narrow, constricted world! She would never be able to approach anyone different than she was herself; it was a good thing she preferred stinking polyresins to inspired words. At exactly the moment she knew she should clamp her twitching lips shut Dolores predictably uttered the coup de grâce. "If you weren't so hopelessly wedlocked to blubbery old Tom, you might get a chance to fuck someone sexy yourself," she said, and instantly regretted it.

Fortunately, Joanna, inclined to utter unforgivable statements herself, was capable of finessing below-the-belt blows. "I'm not saying I wouldn't like him," she replied calmly. "Probably I'd want to fuck him too. I already do like him from some of the things you told me about him when he was in your class. But that's all beside the point. It doesn't matter if he's interesting, or cute, or any of that. It would be better for you if he wasn't, so you wouldn't be tempted."

"That's easy for you to say," Dolores protested, knowing Julio would never tempt Joanna. "You've got a warm body in bed with you every night. You haven't spent a minute alone in your entire adult life. You told me yourself you can't sleep when Tommy goes to visit his parents. You can't begin to imagine how it feels to be alone night after night, with no one to touch or talk to." As she described this tragic plight, she heard her voice break and approach a whimper. "Now I finally meet one of the most attractive, interesting men I've come across in years, and I'm not supposed to go to bed with him because my hypocritical society thinks that robbing grocery stores is an abominable criminal act and killing Vietnamese women and children in the name of democracy is noble."

"What do the Vietnamese have to do with it?" Joanna asked.

"I doubt you'd understand," Dolores answered coldly.

Superficially they mended the rift. They both apologized. Joanna said she was sorry Dolores felt lonely. Dolores said she really thought Tom had quite a good body, and knew Joanna was giving her sensible advice, not even necessary, because she didn't intend to get involved with Julio Bravo anyway. Then they hung up.

Dolores felt uncomfortable after the quarrel. It was painful to fight with her closest friend; no apologies would restore their easy rapport. Joanna had refused to believe she would not get involved with Julio Bravo the instant she'd mentioned his name. She'd said she would not, and yet, she had pulled out the one argument in favor of that involvement, her wretched loneliness, that she knew would enlist Joanna's sympathy. In fact, she was not certain she felt so lonely anymore. Only a short time ago she had felt emphatically lonely all the time; when the ultimate intimacy of true love failed or was not available, she had desperately sought any kind of companionship, met anyone for lunch, talked to anyone on the phone. She had regarded her solitary state as a satanic affliction and began to believe she had made an unwitting pact with the devil to sacrifice love for eventual renown. But then the plague of constant desolation passed, as if she had struggled through its clutching swamps and emerged on dry but placid ground. Every day at sunset an intense feeling of forsakenness would overtake her, then abruptly subside. Perhaps by now she was either numb to loneliness or had invested it in deeper vaults— nightmares, fears of death and the unknown.

Lately, she almost relished solitude. Sometimes she considered calling a friend, and then, because she was able to imagine the exact content of their conversation, decided to stay home and read. It was impossible to extract the grist from most people. They gossiped and chatted, saved the essence up for their psychiatrists, it seemed, and looked at her queasily when she tried to hand them hers.

Not that sex, she thought, represented the deepest possible exchange between human beings. Sex, as a unifying force, was overrated. During sex the subtle aspects of her communication with a man escaped in a combustive vapor and she was thrown entirely back upon herself. She tried to keep a close watch on her thoughts in sex to discover what psychic event occurred during this rather simple physiological act that made it so important to everyone, so much the subject of conversation, books, and the media. Whether the particular sex that engaged her was inspired or ordinary she always tracked the same irrelevant thoughts through her mind. Sometimes she sank rapidly into a half somnambulism, and the jumbled images of her uneasy dream world made their first chaotic appearance. More often, her mind dwelled obstinately on trivia while her body thundered away—what she needed from the Grand Union (Clorox, garlic, Colombo yogurt), she'd better call her agent, whether she should go to her yoga class today or postpone it until Saturday. Whatever she thought of during sex, it was rarely sex itself, unless it was to wonder what she looked like while having it. She tried to remember if this peculiar detachment, which never prevented sex from being enjoyable (any more than other thoughts sabotaged the taste of a fine meal) had begun with her rape or if she'd always been detached. She wondered if the man involved also felt removed, if he was thinking about sex, or her, or what he would have for lunch, like she was. Sometimes when she met the eyes of her fellow copulator, they seemed to be staring at a disturbing or unreasonably beatific vision that did not include either her face or any object in the room.

How strange, she thought, that this physical act, which had an uncertain psychic impact while it occurred, caused the gate of intimacy to creak on its hinges and reluctantly swing open. Yet, the intimacy that galloped in with sex was rarely pleasurable for long; it inevitably dragged along its parasites—hostility, insecurity, psychic aberrations she thought existed only in textbooks, and an immediate betrayal of the elementary courtesies that made less intimate friendships persevere. Why had Joanna assumed, why did she assume herself, that an expanding contact with Julio Bravo must necessarily culminate in sex and its consequent intimate trials? Wasn't another brand of friendship possible, a deep, even sensuous, spiritual love, that could kick sex aside, or transcend it? That was probably idealistic, if not absurd.

In any case, her friendships did not have to include sex, even if she felt desire. She prided herself on her ability to ignore desire, bottle it up, then pour it forth at the moment it was handy to do so. It wasn't handy right now. Lustful sensations crept into her pelvis with their hot, swollen demands, like starving wolves sneaking into the circumference of a campfire at night. They were inappropriate, it seemed; everyone thought so, though she was not sure she thought so herself. She wasn't worried that Julio Bravo would return to drugs and rob her; perhaps he would commit crimes again, but in the long run that was his problem. She couldn't imagine the police busting down her door to find him (melodramatic TV fantasies), or loving him so ardently she would be destroyed if he returned to jail. She had never been not free to say good-bye. She was not put off, but intrigued by his dark, island skin, his husky rhythmic voice from the veritable Third World. She should hate his blatant machismo; theoretically, she did hate it, but she didn't hate him for it.

Later that day she remembered the final image of her island dream, an image that had passed straight out of her awareness, then reentered it with important clarity. The shrunken shadow of Julio Bravo drinking water from that poisoned stream frightened her more than Joanna's dire predictions, or Janice's vague admonition that he was "for real." Someone or something, an exalted consciousness that had reins on her own, was warning her about this man, and she was afraid.

CHAPTER
10

*J*ULIO Bravo came to visit her several times a week. He knocked on her door at odd hours, unexpected; sometimes the phone rang at eight in the morning and, oblivious to the fact he'd awakened her, he would say, "Dolores, it's Julio. I'm on my way down there, all right?" In the background she could hear the enraged scream of a small child, one of his sister's, or the roar of a passing subway. He always asked to borrow her extra portable typewriter, an old Remington from college days. He set it up on the kitchen table, made himself a cup of instant coffee, and effortlessly banged out poems, poem after poem, while Dolores labored in her studio, shaping the rough draft of one of hers by hand, dragging each meticulous line out of her quintessential knowledge with such overcare that the words themselves began to seem almost tangible, like three-dimensional sculpted forms.

As she wrote she was always conscious he was there, and consequently too conscious she was writing. She wondered if that changed her ability to write, or what she wrote; she wasn't sure. He invariably interrupted her. Pulling a chair from the kitchen into her study, and tilting it back against the wall, he would light a Camel and let it burn down to his fingertips as he read his latest masterpiece aloud, or "rapped."

Their communication continued to be more of a monologue than a dialogue, and once Dolores got used to this, it proved a relief. She was glad to give her blaring voice a rest, to leave the grandstand to someone else for a change. Like many noisy, angry people she secretly thought of herself as "quiet," even "shy," and yearned to be serene. Julio let her achieve this ambition. Listening to him was not unlike attending an inspiring dramatic play. His nonstop stories, like any first-rate pieces of theater, seemed to have been created with her in mind. Passively she allowed herself to be moved, to laugh, to nod, to agree. Though his tales about the "nightlife," his family, jail, romance, his present adjustment to the "street," came from a different universe than the one she occupied, they confirmed her ideas—they spoke to a basic part of herself, as Shakespeare and the Greeks did. When she needed to get away from Julio, she simply tuned him out and resided in her own thoughts, alone; the pleasant, consistent rhythms of his voice were like an unobtrusive Muzak. When she talked herself it was usually to help him with his poetry, encourage or advise. She had to admit that she liked having him around. Without making a point of it, he never touched her. He seemed to know she was afraid. Perversely, Dolores, who didn't want him to touch her, found her own hands drawn to him, twitching toward the stretched opacity of his brown skin, propelled by invisible, sporadic engines.

He made himself discreetly at home in her apartment. He took off his shoes, boiled his own coffee water, wiped the table, and unstuck windows. Walking into her kitchen he said at once, "What is that *smell*, my man?" Dolores hadn't noticed any smell, but sniffed hard, and surmised it was a dead mouse. Mice came in periodically through the holes under the sink, and she poisoned them. Julio checked the garbage, then opened the refrigerator door. "It's in here," he said. He prowled through the plastic bags of vegetables, forgotten jars of leftovers, and finally unearthed the offending rotted cantaloupe, withered to a soggy ball in the bottom depths; she never managed to eat the melons she bought. Julio dumped it, without disgust, into the garbage can. Despite this proprietary ease, he tacitly acknowledged he was in her territory; he asked before he used the phone, and waited until she offered before he ate anything. He didn't turn on the television or the radio, once she'd told him she hated disruptive electronic sounds.

He said he was good at fixing things and set to work one morning on her bathroom door, which never closed without a jaw-rattling slam and shrill grinding of wood. Though Julio never bothered to close the door at all when he went to the bathroom, and Dolores had barely registered the emphatic racket of her slam, he attacked this domestic problem with zeal. "This fucker don't close right because the wood has warped and swole up," he informed her, unscrewing the door from its hinges and chiseling away at the offending warp. Hack, hack, slam, grind—the noise of the door-fixing project kept her from working for more than an hour, which should have been vastly annoying but was not. She sat peacefully in her kitchen observing Julio, minus shirt, sweating and chiseling with smooth muscles. She watched his arms, his tight, high ass, almost relishing her unwanted desire for him, safely suspended. It now seemed independent, divorced from its object, if that object was, in fact, Julio Bravo. It would soon float up and attach itself to someone else, she thought. Meanwhile she could live with it. Yearning, she mused, might be more interesting than satisfaction. Over the racket Julio suddenly asked her a question. "Was you ever married, Dolores?"

Odd, she thought, that he didn't know; she assumed he had absorbed the basic facts of her personal history, by osmosis, if no other way. Then he added, "I *know* there have been men in your life because you are a good-looking woman." He waited for her reply.

The complete story of her love life, Dolores realized, would not present her in the most commanding light. The reason she had never succumbed to psychotherapy at the most devastating points in her chequered romantic career was the look of horror she imagined on the therapist's face as she marched her unkempt, raving crowd of lovers before him in a single file. Taken one by one they were fascinating, certainly unique, but all together they were too much alike to represent only brief departures of her sanity. There was the Czechoslovakian maniac, the bisexual black dancer, the Japanese karate champ who couldn't speak a word of English, the father of two, normal enough at first glance, but ultimately possessed of a predilection for alcoholism and the ménage à trois; plus innumerable weak-kneed imposters—the handsome college chum who had rejected her the minute she arrived in Los Angeles to live with him, all baggage in hand, the miserable Eric, who finally confessed he stared into space and couldn't make love because he was mourning the seduction of his wife by his best friend (it was news to Dolores that he had a wife), and several less memorable characters, who had all gone as far as they could, faltered, and limped off to someone very little like Dolores in the end. Despite the fact that this parade included a bunch of jerks she had dumped herself for their dreary, irritating qualities (like Don Mansion), she thought of them as having abandoned her, like the others. She didn't want Julio to know about her countless unfortunate choices; they would make her seem foolish and promiscuous, a loser, too available to anyone, to him—inaccurate these mature, celibate days. She had definitely become more discriminating, probably the reason she was alone. She decided to mention only Harold, the kind, devoted architect who had asked her to marry him. "No, I was never married," she said. "I don't believe in marriage. I came close to marrying this one guy I was with for a few years. He wanted to get married, but I didn't. He was an architect."

"Oh yeah . . . !" said Julio, attentive. He stopped chiseling and wiped his wet face with a rag. "There was this cat up in Corsica who was an architect. They busted him for having an ounce of marijuana on him. One ounce, my man. For one fucking ounce he was doing a three to life bid!"

"It wasn't Harold," Dolores said. "He only drank beer. Drank beer and watched TV. He used to beat me," she added melodramatically. She hadn't intended to tell Julio that, it just slipped out, maybe, she thought later, because she had an unconscious wish to let him know there was something similar in their disparate worlds—violence. These so-called beatings had occurred on only two occasions. Once Harold had slammed her into the bathroom

145

wall, practically breaking her finger, which hit the soap dish, after she'd announced during a fight that she was going straight out to a bar to pick up someone more interesting than he was. Another time, in the third year of their relationship, he had banged her head repeatedly against the wall of a hotel room in Greece, when she'd informed him she was seriously considering entering a nunnery in Patnos. That time she had been scared and so had he; he could have killed her.

Julio looked at her, uncomfortably tender. "How could any man lay a hand on you, *nene*?" he asked. "I could never hit no woman." He had obviously forgotten slapping the dyke, or else did not consider her a woman. "But, *vaya*," he continued, "when I have wanted to hit a woman I know that I and that woman do not belong together. A woman should not be able to make a man feel that way, that vi-olence; when she is making him feel that way she is hurting herself, my man, even if he does not raise his hand to her." Dolores nodded as usual; Julio never ceased to astonish her with his folksy wisdoms.

"I guess I'm not cut out for marriage," she said. "No one wants to marry me. I think Harold was my last chance to blow it." She trembled to hear herself admit that marriage had rejected her, when she usually claimed she had rejected marriage; she must be feeling sorry for herself. "If I marry I would have to marry for love," she added quickly, "not because I feel desperate for a man, or some kind of companionship. I know I can be alone now," she said sadly, "for better or worse."

Julio's eyes, often veiled, expressionless, whatever the emotional content of his words, now glowed with warm understanding. "Dolores," he said, "right off I could see you was one of them free, modern fe-males. You got this big space around you, dig? It ain't no cold, empty space, man; it is a nice, warm space like the sky on a nice day. Nobody should ever take that away from you. I could never take it away from you, my man. There is no *way* that I would try; that space be where your poetry is coming from. If I was your man I would know that space is belonging to you, that you need it. A dude could beat you to death and he would still not get no part of that space for hisself."

As usual Julio left at sunset; he had to clean up the office of his friend, the lawyer, and lock the door, he said. He claimed to be working part-time for this lawyer, though the terms of his employment, which allowed him to spend more than half the week in Dolores's apartment, writing poetry and yakking away, were unclear. When Dolores questioned him he was evasive. He spoke enthusiastically about "Charlie" and everything he had done for him ("Charlie is all right, my man") but he didn't exactly reveal what he did for Charlie—probably some basic janitorial work he was embarrassed to describe. On the days he did not appear at Dolores's he said he'd reported to the parole, or was following up on leads for jobs. There were a lot of good possibilities. It looked like his parole officer was going to grant him permission to get a driver's license after all, an unusual privilege for a repeat offender. "Do you know," he told her, "that if a dude on parole tries to kill hisself that they can lock him up again for that?" He might also go to printing school, he said, and get paid to study under some federal program, or learn to fix boilers, but they only paid you the minimum wage. Dolores liked the idea of printing school. "That relates to your writing," she said. His writing was improving. She suggested he propose an article about the prison riot, a kind of personal retrospective, to the *SoHo*

News. She would help him. He still wanted to work with kids. He had contacted Sharif, his old Corsica buddy, and Sharif was checking into it, man.

When Julio was gone Dolores's life continued in its usual outlines. She ate three healthy meals, as many vegetables as she could get down, went to her yoga class, and sat at her desk, laboring over her poetry. Yet something had changed. Julio's absence left a wake, like the wave that sucks noisily at the pebbles on the beach, then cuts back into the soundless sea. Her apartment seemed unusually quiet and dark, as if the 100-watt bulbs were about to die in their sockets. She spent most evenings alone. Several of her friends were away or had absconded with new lovers. She and Joanna had not recovered from their argument; they seldom saw each other or talked on the phone, and when they did they discussed the usual inanities, but in reserved, formal tones. Dolores didn't mention Julio's visits, the only novelty worth mentioning; Joanna wouldn't believe what was happening between them, basically nothing.

She did everything in a daze. She slumped on the couch pretending to read, unable to recall later what she'd read or thought about instead of reading. Household tasks took hours; she stared into space between each dish she managed to wash, watered one plant per half hour. She sat down and gazed into her hand mirror when she was determined to scrub the kitchen floor. The perimeters of time blurred; she looked up and saw it was three o'clock when she was sure it was still morning. A vague anxiety, indicating she teetered on an invisible brink, slowed her actions. Her hands floated about her; her feet moved with the uncertain momentum of a hospital patient's emerging from anesthesia.

In this mesmerized state she made important decisions. One morning the phone rang, a reverie-splitting peal. It was her literary agent, for the first time in weeks, announcing a promising free-lance opportunity—a job writing a series of twentieth-century poets' biographies for a major publishing company. The writer would be contracted to write two of the short biographies a year for an advance of six thousand dollars apiece with royalties.

"Naturally I thought of you, darling," her agent said, "because you *are* a poet. It takes one to know one."

The possibility of raking in twelve grand a year writing respectable books, books she could mention, head high, without embarrassment, not fruits or mattresses or *Family Circle*, work that would leave her ample time to write her own poetry, if she could, other articles if she had to, travel, struck Dolores as too good to be true—a boon from the gods, almost terrifying in its positive, karmic implications. What could be easier than writing a poet's biography? A little research, a lucid style, a touch of analysis; no, it had to be harder than that; nothing was easy. "Do you think I'm qualified?" she asked nervously, pressing back the Julio-inspired fog.

"Darling, *please!*" said her agent. "Is the Pope Catholic?" Dolores heard her draw heavily on her cigarette, almost heard the smoke travel down her windpipe. "I never have had a single doubt you were qualified . . . and I mean that in the deepest sense, dear. I'm not talking about silly biographies either. The first time I read those stunning short lyrics, and I mean they were *stunning*, I knew you were a poet, a *good* poet." Her voice was fierce in its praise. Dolores marveled; she didn't identify herself with this young genius her agent extolled.

Her agent sighed. "Unfortunately, poets, even brilliant poets, simply do not make money, dear. Unfortunately, if Sir Walter Raleigh were alive today he'd be painting apartments for three-fifty an hour." Her agent often told her how lucky she was to be able to write horrendous bullshit (which she termed "commercial prose"), and said how few writers of her talent could. Lucky for her agent, too, Dolores thought, who would never make a dime off her stunning poetry. Without her "commercial prose" she probably wouldn't have this agent, who occasionally sent her manuscript of poems to a publisher, pessimistically predicting the rejection that soon arrived.

"We all need money," her agent continued, "and as we get older we need more money. Even *you* will need money, darling, although I know you can live like a clam." She seemed to think she had to talk Dolores into the biography job.

"My funds are running a little low," Dolores said. That was putting it mildly. In fact, she was at the tail end of her Fruits payment and would soon have to resort to her small bank account, money saved while living in a cheap slum apartment on the Lower East Side, her Rock Bottom Down and Out Emergency Escape and Cure Fund, which she'd planned to use only to fly to Australia in the event of nuclear war, or to pay the hospital bill if she was run down by a truck, assuming she would want to live on afterward. Through her vagueness, in which nothing seemed pressing, she had already contemplated beginning the painful hustle for free-lance work, forcing herself to pick up the phone and make the stammering beggar's calls to magazines, fumbling for words when she should be pushy and self-confident, forgetting the real gist of the proposals she'd called to sell. She couldn't bother her agent with these small potatoes. Now, what she needed had arrived on divine wings. Her agent told her to put some sample articles in the mail, but not to worry, she and the editor of the series, Jean, were old friends, from their junior assistant days at Doubleday; Jean trusted her, absolutely. If she told Jean she had a good writer, Jean would know that writer was good. Jean was on vacation at the moment, however, and didn't quite have her figures worked out. Dolores must meet Jean; they would adore each other. It would probably take a few weeks, maybe a month, to negotiate the final contract. It might be a little more than twelve thousand, dear, or a little less.

Though she superstitiously believed that mentioning promising possibilities was guaranteed to make them disappear, Dolores could not prevent herself from telling Julio about the biographies. She had a painful stiff neck, wrenched in yoga class, an injury that freed self-restraint while making all physical movement awkward and uncomfortable. It almost embarrassed her to tell him about her fabulous middle-class opportunity, when he had none, had never had any. Yet she felt it was only fair to continue to emphasize the distance between them, to keep its mileage clearly established in both their minds.

"Twelve thousand bucks a year for writing a couple of silly little books!" she said gleefully. "If I can write ten pages a day I'll be finished with a draft in about fifteen days. Add another two months for research and revision and the entire project will take only two and a half months! That's only five months a year to write two books and rake in twelve grand!" Once she'd begun she couldn't stop crowing. It was safe to crow because she didn't believe this lightning bolt of good luck would actually strike.

Julio was only mildly impressed. "One hundred and two yards ain't real money, girl," he said. "Shit, you can not even put a down payment on a house in Queens wit' that! I was pulling down twelve hundred dollars a day when I was only sixteen years old! If I had not blown all that money on narcotics, my man, if I had put it into some kind of stocks, or real estate, I would be a fucking millionaire by now. That is the way so-ciety keeps the little people down, Dolores. The man be telling us if we work hard, real hard, if we be honest, if we have *suerte*, maybe one day, just maybe, we will have enough to get something of our own, when it is the man himself who be owning everything, the military-industrial com-plex and the oil companies. Fuck, that com-plex owns the whole world, my man. Even when that com-plex lets you in on a little piece of the action, next thing you know it be asking you to give it back in taxes so it can buff on over to Indo-China or somewhere so it can kill a few gooks and take what belongs to them."

He sprawled on the couch like a general-potentate himself, dripping cigarette ashes on the rug, minus his shirt and shoes, as usual; the instant any draft that could be termed "warm" wafted, Julio shed as many garments as possible. One muscular, tattooed arm was thrown over his head, emphasizing the ridge that ran along the underside of his triceps, the curve from chest to groin, and the cleft between his pectorals. "Look at my father, man. He has been working his ass off for the phone company for twenty years now, maybe twenty-five, and what has he got to show for it—*nada*! Less than nothing, Dolores.

But he don't give a fuck." Julio smiled indulgently. "My father is one straight dude, Dolores. He spent a night in the Tombs in '52 for some parking ticket bullshit, and his hair turned white in twenty-four hours, snow white, my man."

"Your father works for the telephone company?" Dolores repeated incredulously, turning her sore neck painfully in Julio's direction. She had always assumed that Julio's father had deserted the family, leaving his wife and children to starve on welfare in an unheated basement.

"My father," Julio mused. "I love my father, man. He do not dig me, he do not dig me at all, but I love him. When I got out of the joint I went to my father and I said to him, 'Now I know that I have fucked up in the past, *Papí;* I have fucked up *bad.* But now I have another chance and I am going to need your help. I am determined to change, my man.' My father, he did not ask me no questions. He said, 'Julito, *hijo,* you are a son of a bitch but I will give you what I can.' Then he was telling me about straightening myself out, and how if he be seeing me on the corner wit' them no-good bad-ass no-doing junkies he is going to put his foot so far up my ass I will be tasting shoe polish, and like that. He was always that way, my father, kicking my ass when it needed to be kicked, but no matter what they had me down for, he would be there soon as he heard about it, trying to bail me out, talking to the police. Dolores, when I get my bar and some bread, man, the first thing I am going to buy is a house in Puerto Rico, near Cabo Rojo, for my father. That is where he was born. He is always talking how he has got to go back to P.R. to die. That is his dream, man. I want to give him that. *Me entiende, niña?"* He had recently discovered Dolores's high school Spanish, and now salted his monologues with additional incomprehensible expressions.

This was the first Dolores had heard about a bar. Julio went on to explain. "Yeah . . ." he said, gazing toward a mystical horizon. "That is what I really want. My own place, a place like my partner, Blue, was having, a nice place, my man, wit' live music, Latin music. I could really get into that, having my own bar, running it myself. Some dudes hire another dude to run their place for them, but I would want to be right there, rapping with the chicks and the hustlers, a bottle of champagne on my table all the time, knowing it was my place, running it."

"That's a nice fantasy," Dolores said, "for the far future." It was obviously just a fantasy.

"I think I will call it 'The Cell,' my man," Julio laughed. "Ain't that a boss name for a bar run by an ex-offender? *Chevere!* Right now the parole will not even let me work in no bar, Dolores, because I would be in a scene where I might meet bad asso-ciations. In five years, when I am done wit' the parole, and I have the bread, man, that will be the time. I do not want to work for nobody else, Dolores."

Neither did Dolores. She had literally almost suffocated in the offices that employed her in her postcollege graduation days in New York. Trapped between grim, straight walls without windows, she had felt like she was asleep the whole time she was working, a few feeble brain cells flickering among the living dead. "Sometimes you have to do that for a while," she said. "I had to." The voice of pious logic trying to pass off things she didn't believe as irrefutable truth. "Anyway, it costs thousands and thousands of dollars to open a bar, maybe hundreds of thousands. You have to be rich to open a bar, or borrow money, or get a rich partner. You couldn't possibly save that much in five years, no matter what kind of job you got." She felt justified in extinguishing fantasies that had to do with owning things, even her own; capitalistic fantasies, she should point out to him.

"I could get me a rich partner," he said. "I could get me a rich partner right now," he added mysteriously. "But then it would not be mine. I want my bar to be mine, Dolores."

Totally unrealistic, she thought. Men getting out of jail must be prone to all sorts of unrealistic fantasies they cooked up in those dreary years behind bars. She had noticed that Julio changed his aspirations constantly, like a child talking about what he will do when he grows up. He would adjust to reality soon enough, she supposed. Too bad, in a way, to have to abandon childlike dreams for boring adult reality and some rotten nine-to-five job. "Maybe you could become a writer," she said, "or go to college. You're certainly smart enough." She reminded him constantly to check up on job openings, let him use her phone. She had heard that the Fortune Society, an organization for ex-offenders, gave a course in applying for jobs, and had tried to turn him on to that.

Julio volunteered to massage her sore neck. She needed a massage so badly she conveniently forgot the consequences of letting him touch her again. She had been considering the chiropractor on Houston Street, which would have run her at least forty bucks. She lay on her stomach on the bedroom rug, already tense, annoyed with herself for permitting a situation she'd sworn she'd avoid. Julio straddled her back and applied his fingertips to her aching neck, hot, strong fingers, which dug into the muscles like blunt, exorcising pitchforks. The instant his warm fingers touched her skin the intimacy between them sprung from its abstract realm into a trembling, palpable shape, impossible to ignore. She felt the hot presence of his groin over her buttocks, though no part of his body but his fingers touched hers. She could smell his slightly sweaty, fried, vaguely perfumed odor, some kind of cheap, pungent aftershave. The hairy nakedness of his chest set the molecules over her back into frantic collisions. Without warning, every cell of her body, interior, exterior, vibrated and expanded, started flowing up to him. She felt frightened, stuck on a careening roller coaster; it was too late to change her mind, jump up, make some excuse, to say "forget it." She prayed the phone would ring, or a knock would sound at the door—not likely. His warm, tobacco breath grazed the back of her neck. She forced herself to lie rigidly still, afraid if she moved a fraction of an inch she would turn over and grab him.

"Relax, Dolores!" Julio commanded. "I can not do you no good if you don't relax." His voice shook perceptibly. He felt it too. He began to talk fast. "My mother used to beg me to give her a massage when she was alive. She would ask me, 'Julito, put your hands on me.' "

"I'm not the sort of person who likes to be massaged," Dolores said. "They say highly verbal people who drink a lot of coffee can't stand a massage." She was obviously babbling.

He worked diligently on her back; his palms pressed the muscles down evenly, ironing them upward toward her neck. Then he attacked her neck again, releasing, almost against her will, its tight, resistant pain. Her entire body was softening into an agonizing, high-pressure, barely contained comfort, almost unbearable, yet pleasurable, like the intense heat of a locked sauna. She couldn't talk anymore. She could scarcely breathe; her own exhalations rasped in her throat. At last she gasped, "Thanks. Okay, Julio. That's good enough. Really! I feel much better." She rose slowly, first to her knees, then to her feet.

Julio stood awkwardly, his hands placed a few inches from his sides, like a dazed gorilla. "How does it feel now, *nene*?" he asked. His eyes were direct.

"Much better," she said, trying, without success, to force the usual brisk, ward-off tone into her sensually deranged voice. Their eyes met; she looked promptly away. "You give a mighty professional massage," she said. "You could probably make money at it."

"I could have made it more sexy," he said suddenly. "I could have used it to seduce you if I had wanted to. But you would not have trusted me after that."

Dolores faced him at last. There was no way to brush off his sincerity with a coy or professorial comment. "No!" she said. "You can't seduce me. It wouldn't be right. It wouldn't be right for us to start fucking. We have to talk about that."

"We could make love and talk about it after," Julio said.

"No," Dolores said. "We can't. We really can't! There are too many things to think about. It wouldn't be just a fuck. We've known each other too long already. We have a friendship at stake. I'm your teacher. You just got out of jail. You don't have a job yet. You aren't settled. For all I know you might go back to jail. You always have in the past. I hope you won't. I don't believe you will, but I have to think about that. What if I was to fall for you and then you landed back in jail? What if the cops came looking for you? Or the parole?" She was surprised to hear Joanna's speech pouring spontaneously out of her

157

own mouth, a flood of the very ideas she'd rejected. She went on. "Don't forget there's an enormous social barrier between us. There isn't anything we can do about that. I'm a middle-class white woman from a New Jersey suburb, Julio. I don't always like it, but that's the way it is. You would start to feel that if we really got involved. So would I. I don't see how we can fuck and not get involved. Besides, you're a macho. I don't mean that as criticism, I like machos, but you are. You wouldn't feel that comfortable with me. I'm a modern woman, you said so yourself. I'm no virgin. I've had a lot of lovers. . . . We'd have so many problems. You can't imagine them now."

"Dolores," said Julio. "I did not say it would be just a fuck. I said we would make love, my man. Dolores, I don't know if I know what love is, dig? But I know I feel something as close to love as I can feel for you. *Yo estoy enchulao contigo, nene.* I liked you right away, the first time I seen you, when you came into the penitentiary."

"Well, I liked you too," Dolores said. That was not exactly the truth.

"You are worrying about all these *problemas*, my man," Julio continued. "I can understand that, *niña*. I know I have let a lot of people down. But Dolores, believe me, I ain't going back to jail. I will die before I go back to jail. When I was in the nightlife, I never let my woman get involved. 'Don't look for me up here,' I be saying to my partner. 'When you are looking for me, you look for me in the street.' Dolores, I intend to get a job. You know that there are jobs waiting for me. *Sí, esto es importante.* I know that I am a macho. If I do not have some money in my pocket, I do not feel right with a woman. Dolores, I know you ain't no virgin. That makes me no difference. I am a macho, but I am not a macho in that kind of way.

158

I can learn, man. I know you are my teacher. I dig that! You have to keep teaching me, Dolores. I want you to keep teaching me. We are two different people; that is a fact. You are white, I am a Borrinqueño, but that do not make no difference to me. I do not feel that in *mi corazón. Mira,* I am not going back to jail. No way!"

"Julio, I just can't," Dolores said loudly, and felt the vibrations in her body subside, the heavy pelvic weight deflate, once and for all. Telling him in her own voice she could not banish vestiges of desire like a cold bath. She felt empty and clear.

"Nene, I understand you," Julio said. "It is all right. I can be friends wit' you until I prove to you that everything I am saying is correct."

"Well, there's no hurry," Dolores said, enormously relieved.

CHAPTER
11

---

*T*HE next day Dolores fucked Julio Bravo. Yes, in retrospect she was sure she had made the definitive, point-of-no-return sexual gesture herself. That night, after he'd gone back to the South Bronx, as usual, she sat alone at her desk, trying to order her scattered sensibilities by establishing her motives in her journal:

> I must be insane! Only one short day after I'd informed him I never would and listed innumerable good reasons why—I succumbed to Julio Bravo. What mad quirk permits me to commit such wildly inconsistent actions? When I examine my motives honestly, however, what seems inconsistent is my previous decision not to love this man, whatever love means.

What vestige of middle-class cowardice and racism
created the irrational fears that commanded no? Obviously I am, or was, thoroughly gripped by the ideas
of the class that spawned me, and absorbed its hysterical prohibitions against ex-offenders, Puerto Ri-
cans, anyone with darker skin, different background,
through my pores, though my intellect rebelled. Iron-
ically, if Julio was a war hero, a corrupt politician
who had killed, ripped off, or bombed in the name of
patriotic duty, no one alive would deny his suitability
for a woman like me, provided he also had a college
education. But because he committed a few adolescent felonies I myself judged him "inappropriate,"
even in dreams. I was forced to judge him that by my
world. Now is the time to flush these poisons out of
my mind and trust my own perceptions—that he is a
man with the rare, almost antiquated quality of true
manliness, a quality women themselves have been
misguided enough to try to strip away from men, a
man who in some profoundly spiritual recess is innocent and whole. His confusions (obviously great)
come from the same source as mine—society! I would
never say such things to justify a sensation as cheap,
as easily obtained, as soon over, as orgasm, would I?
Could any intimacy divert me so radically from the
truth if that truth was clearly negative—dangerous or
self-destructive? No, I must believe the hands that
reached for Julio were the extensions of my uncor-
rupted self; they knew the truth better than my
brainwashed mind. Well, on to the poignant details,
to wit:

Julio showed up with a red ten-speed bike he'd
borrowed from his lawyer friend's son (he said). In a
second I had stowed my unfinished poem in its folder

and we rode out together into the spring wind, the young heat. This is the only part of it that really disturbs me—my willingness to dump my life work for any promise of adventure. Julio is a madman on a bicycle. He dodged in and out of the congested traffic, ran red lights, oblivious to shouts, honking horns, near collisions, grabbed onto the backs of buses, made abrupt U-turns in the middle of the street, weaved and dipped, and rode back against the flow of speeding cars to find me, trailing behind on my dilapidated Raleigh. I followed as fast as I could. Usually Miss Cautious Old Maid on my bike, I renounced fear, entrusted my life to the fates, and felt my obsessive self-preservation abandon me, like a decaged bird. My heart was flipping against my rib cage. I ran red lights when he did, rode too fast, scared to death, yet exhilarated. Suddenly a car door leaped open in front of me; I had a split second to decide whether I would slam into the door and break every bone in my body or dart back into the careening traffic lane, directly in front of an oncoming bus. Some reflex chose the bus. It missed me! I felt an iron trap in my skull crack open. I soared! I was high, stoned on near accident. My blood swam upward, expanded my head.

I took Julio over to the Lower East Side to see the building where I had lived in poorer, more daring days. Perhaps I wanted to prove to him again that we shared some common experience—life in a slum. But Tenth Street now resembles Berlin after the war. Everything has deteriorated there. The once shabby tenements have become gutted, burned-out shells; fragments of their innards—nails, twisted metal fixtures, random boards—litter the potholed streets. No tenants inhabit their blank windows. A few ominous types drifted about, staring at us with purposefully nonseeing eyes. "This is one of the worst blocks in New York," I announced to Julio. "I'm *hip!*" he said, impressed. The *Times* said that about Tenth Street years ago, and now, it is beyond the worst, ready to be torn down. A ghost of terror shadowed me into the sunny afternoon. I remembered the first mugging in the vestibule, saw the dark, featureless face, the knife again. After that I ran from the corner, key extended in hand, ready to plunge it into the lock, shut the black forms following me out of the hall, which contained who knew what other menaces. I remembered the murder of the girl in the apartment below, the crosses burned, the Spanish wailing dirge outside the door. I remembered seeing moonlit figures on the fire escape outside my window, waiting for me to leave. This past was not nostalgic. I felt hot and scared. I couldn't get out of there fast enough.

We rode to the park along the East River. Glass lined the paths. The wind was up and that soiled, moist, rotting, perverted sea smell that is only New York, only the East River, seemed obliquely sensual, like the photograph of a favorite place, invoking memories just beyond the grasp. A solitary heavy garbage scow plowed by. Kids shouted in the field, playing baseball. Although summer is about to begin I already sensed the sad chill of fall and the gray of dismal winter in the air. New York is seasonless in its artificial immensity.

We rode by Katz's on Houston Street and Julio ran inside and came out with four hot dogs, two each, a few gooey candy bars and sweet sodas. Though I never eat that kind of crap, I wolfed down the entire sugary, preservative-ridden feast and felt wonderfully satisfied. We ate in a little park that seemed part of an old folks' apartment complex. Afterward we straddled a concrete ledge, facing each other. Julio's smooth skin was suddenly a breath away. How did we get to this mesmerized proximity from the speed of riding, eating, and talking? We sat there, cautiously immobilized. It was one of those rare moments that hangs outside the measures of time, an acute, compressed moment, in which the old constrictions of the self evaporate. I was staring into his eyes, light, brown, almost gay eyes, until they ceased to register as "eyes" and merely stretched on forever, like an expanse of horizon. Other surroundings faded. Then, without thinking twice, I started kissing him, or we were just kissing. No, the move I made toward his full, carved lips was imperceptible, but I made it; I take the responsibility, come what may. I did not *succumb,* I conquered! We kissed greedily, like sex-starved teen-agers who have not yet become jaded to the novelty of a kiss. Kissing was all, not an introduction to serious, adult pleasures. Old people were walking by; I could hear their insecure steps, feel their stares. But nothing, not the disapproving eye of God, holocaust or tidal wave, not my thoughts, still obstinately muttering their brainwashed reservations, could have torn me from Julio's mouth. We were both amazed. He said in a weakened voice, "Man, you sure do kiss good!" He said the word *good* as if it was spelled with fourteen o's— *gooooooooooooood!*—as if the word *good* was something you could eat. Abruptly he pulled me down on the grass on top of him, and we lay there like that without moving. All the lines and planes of his body attached themselves to mine, despite the difference in our height, stretched themselves over my skin like a fabric. I could still hear the tentative, shocked footsteps of the senior citizens. The grass smelled dirty, a faint miasma of dog piss and fertilizer, the bottoms of shoes. It didn't matter. Finally, we staggered to our feet. I was shaking. Julio had a frank hard-on; the outlines of his cock, its ridges and veins, showed through his tight jeans. (I probably imagined those details). He made some funny crack about it I wish I remembered but can't. How quickly we forget our lives!

We rode the bikes back to my place. I couldn't see where I was going, only Julio's body on the bike in front of me. It was a wonder I wasn't killed! By the time we got home my bladder was ready to burst. I ran for the bathroom. "I knew it," Julio laughed. "I *knew* it!" Why should I remember that? I was in an outer limbo, where only the eccentric inessential registered. I came out of the bathroom, strutted past him in a quivering walk, and threw myself down on the bedroom rug in a gesture of absolute surrender. We rejoined and started kissing again, but this time it was the usual, urgent kiss, headed rapidly elsewhere. Then, of course, we fucked—like "bunnies," as Joanna would say.

Afterward I dissolved into a state of liquid comfort. My solid body liquefied into a salty, limpid sea. I surfaced enough to ask him, "It was good, wasn't it? Didn't you think it was good?" The anxious formulas we are compelled to utter after sex are, I guess, an essential part of the ritual. "Yeah . . ." Julio said. "It was *gooooood.*" (The same, edible *good.*) "*Niña*, I

wanted you from the first time I seen you at Briarstone. You was beautiful, my man, when you came
walking into that ugly room." He shook his head.
"The one thing I did not imagine was the moaning."

Did I moan? I wasn't aware of it. It was such a peculiar idea, to imagine myself *moaning*, or making a
sound that could later be defined as *the moaning*, as if
it were some wild beast's howl, separate from me. I
tried to moan again, but couldn't do it. I always
thought I was rather quiet during sex. What else did
he say? How fast the significant details disappear. Oh
yes, he said, "I knew you was a freak even up at
Briarstone, when you used to be wearing them
boots." I guess he meant my red boots, and that I
was a "freak" for sex. I never thought of myself as a
"freak"! How weird to be called one! A salivating,
moaning, hot freak! I like that. It redefines my
prudish self. All those references to his fantasies
about me in jail! Was he plotting my seduction of
him, or his of me, from the moment we met, the moment I saw him on his file cabinet in the prison? Was
every word he addressed to me since part of an elab-
orate, well-constructed con? Well, it doesn't matter.

Later, he padded gently through my sexual parts,
separating their multi-folding leaves with his fingers.
"You have a fat pussy, *mi fresquita*," he said. "This is a
fat pussy!" This was apparently a compliment,
though what a "fat" pussy signifies, and how it dif-
fers from a thin one, I have no idea. What's a *fresquita*?
I didn't ask. I wanted him to think that I knew.
"When you are off your period," he said, "I am going
to suck this fat pussy." Then we did it again. Maybe
we did it a third time. I can't remember; numbers re-
cede.

166

"I thought you was going to make me wait," Julio said at some point.

"I was," I answered.

Posterity will no doubt want to know what it is like to make love to a Puerto Rican repeat offender. The answer may disappoint. The answer is "Normal." Cock size: Normal; quality of foreplay: tenderly firm and Normal; length of time from beginning of sex act to end: Normal; climax: Normal. Yes, it was all quite normal, your basic erotic routine. It was just plain sex, nothing more, or less. I was not transported beyond this earthly plane, nor did flames leap from my womb, as from the womb of Lady Chatterley. I still thought about what I needed from the Grand Union. I was still conscious of the rhythmic squeak the floorboards made beneath our plunging bodies, the lingering ache in my neck, the embarrassing snap in my stiff knee joints when I wrapped my legs around his back. It was just sex, not better, not worse, or even especially different than it has ever been with any other normal man I've known. Yet *normal* is exactly the way sex should be. Normal is superb! Normal is stupefying! I had almost forgotten about Normal.

Afterward I watched while Julio smoked his fifty-seventh Camel that day, watched the smooth muscles move under his skin, his sinewy flexed hands and wrists, his assured male gestures. I watched him pick his frizzy hairdo with a rakelike comb, still subdued by the moist passivity every woman feels after she's been decently fucked by a good, uptight, normal man. And with my lapse into this near-ecstatic, slightly disturbing, all feminine, liquid state came, as always for me, a wave of smothering fears, dragging behind a basically idiotic, unanswerable question, a huge, demanding question that jumps up and declares itself despite my earnest attempt to ignore it, despite my wish that sex should remain only a simple, physiological process, like digestion, that it alone should not be able to wrench debilitating anxieties out of their hiding place, a question that inevitably takes the form of a nervous, agitated cry, namely: *What will happen now?*

Before I forget, there is something "different" about Julio Bravo. He has three bullet holes on the inside of his right thigh, just above the knee, three round, slightly concave scars. I touched them, and he said they were souvenirs (*recuerdos*) of the Corsica riot. It is unusual, for me, at any rate, to fuck a man whose legs are riddled with bullet holes.

CHAPTER
12

---

*T*HE first thing that happened, or maybe it wasn't the first thing, but the first significant thing, or even the last significant thing, was that Julio Bravo disappeared. He disappeared as he must have always disappeared, Dolores thought, vanished from the lives of those he had sucked into his inner typhoon until no part of them remained unfragmented but their love for him; no, the right word for this precarious, crazed feeling was not *love*.

After the first seduction Julio appeared again in the morning. The minute she opened the door to his brown, unsmiling face she knew everything had changed. The fucking changed everything. Her mind was not clear enough to analyze the reasons for the swift transformation of their former relationship, but the old rituals of coffee, typewriter, poetry, and "rap" lay discarded by the curb of an environment that had suddenly become secret and intense. The configuration of meaning she had attached to him exploded. She was not fucking "Julio," but an abstract human form, a flesh-contained combustive energy that was not a familiar body at all. Or was this all in her imagination? She didn't know. Her life had become unrecognizable; barely formulated thoughts flapped about the disorganized heap of her physical surroundings, incapable of composing themselves into definitive cognitive shapes and opinions. She no longer knew anything at all. She couldn't remember exactly what happened or when. Their conversations ranged haphazardly over an ungoverned period of time, not clearly distinguishable as the present or past.

It seemed to Dolores that their copulations took place in slow motion, like a film made under water. The plants, furnishings, and ornaments in her apartment floated by the indefinite, soft-lined motions of this sex like fish and algae adrift in a sea. Her insides, too, seemed changed to water. "Do you know when I come?" Julio asked her. His voice wavered up through a thick liquid. During sex he dropped the "Dig its," "my mans," Hispanic endearments, and staccato rhythms from his sentences, stripped them down to telegraphic communiqués, which made his voice the voice of someone else. She could answer simply by rolling her eyeballs, or grunting. "Wrap your legs around my back," he said with a constricted urgency having nothing to do with her legs or his back. He followed her into every corner with sex. He ate her out in the damp bathtub and came into her from behind, placing one of her legs on the seat of her bicycle as she crouched over the sink, gripping the cold, enamel edge with her hands. She refused to let him fuck her in the ass, silently, by slipping that aperture out of his hard path. He told her that his second sister, Dalila, had stabbed her husband in the groin after he'd tried to "hit her in the sitter" one time too often. His sister had hemorrhoids and she could not get into that. "Maybe I could," Dolores said; would physical pain make much of a difference, one way or another? But he didn't seem to care. He didn't really try it.

They often fucked on the linty little rug on her studio floor beneath her typewriter glaring over the desk top, its dutiful black keys baring their white letters like the teeth of a faintly mincing smile. They knocked over plants. She got tired of it. It wore her out; this "it" enervated her in an imprecise way, leaving her energy only for "it." Sex wasn't the right name for "it," this carniverous appetite that left her mouth dry and stale, like the aftermath of too much booze and cigarettes, to be banished only by more of the same narcotized hunger. Everywhere they fucked they left wet stains, Camel ashes, matted-down, wrinkled, moist sections of whatever fabric they'd pressed themselves upon.

In the hiatus desert moments between the fuckings and blowings and eatings their former teacher-student relationship reemerged like an ironic joke; minus contained desire her advice was listless, embarrassed by the abandoned sex. They lay beside each other on the rug. Dolores briefly wondered if the old Italian ladies in the apartment across the airshaft could see their naked bodies. It didn't matter, really. "I be pacing the floor when I go for a job," Julio said. "That puts them uptight, like they do not know what I am going to do." He said they asked him on the application forms what was his color. "*Coño*, I wrote down *chartreuse*, my man."

171

Dolores frowned. The unswept floor was getting dusty, filthy. He had a finger up her. When he wasn't actually fucking Julio seemed nervous. He pulled aimlessly at his hands, at his foreskin, scratched his head vigorously, as if to unearth some recalcitrant parasite burrowing into the follicles of his scalp. He yawned huge, roaring yawns and cracked his knuckles at the same time. He smoked a joint and his eyes drifted into trapped corners. Day by day his anxiety expanded. Fucking seemed to discharge it, then increase it. It spread to Dolores, attached itself to her like an itching skin. She smoked his Camels; she couldn't believe she was smoking again. When he told his stories now, they no longer seemed the blithe adventures of an errant knight, but demanding visions that had broken away from their past moorings and floated into the present. When he talked he no longer addressed her, she thought, but some compelling version of himself. Sometimes she tuned out to protect herself from hearing exactly what he said, but significant, isolated words floated in through the viscous shield.

"I was sitting on the steps of this building and I seen this dude, Ramon," he said. They were lying on the living room couch. His legs were around her neck and the back of her head was resting in his groin. She felt the soft bags of his genitals sink into the nape of her neck. " '*Oye*, my man, can you give me a chip?' I asked him. '*Vete a cojer por el culo, pendejo*. I don't have none,' he said. Then I seen this girl on the steps. Her hands was full of jewelry, gold rings and necklaces and shit. I told her what had gone down and she says to me, 'Why that son of a bitch just tole me he copped. I seen it, a whole sack of coke.' " Julio asked her if she was sure, because if she was, Ramon was bullshitting behind the statement he had just made to him. "I saw it, Duke," she said. "I am telling you, man, I saw it."

"So I got my partner and we go up the steps. I knocked on the door—rap, rap, rap. 'Who is it?' he yelled. 'It's me, Julito. You know what I want.' 'Listen, my man, I haven't got it,' he said.

" 'Yours is coming soon, *hombre*,' I told him, and me and my partner busted through the door. We took it right off its frame. He screamed like a fe-male when he heard us coming through, '*Mamí! Mamí!*' I knew that dude's mother, man; she was ninety-one years old." Dolores felt Julio's fingers stroke her throat softly; the tips were calloused and warm. " 'Don't you worry, señora,' I said to his mother; 'just tell your *mamito* to give us what we came here for.' He was back in the corner, Ramon. 'I am telling you, *hombre*. I don't got *nothin.*'

" 'You lying punk son of a bitch,' I says. 'Someone tole me different.' We started to look around and we tore that fucking place apart. We could not find nothing though. I put him on the bed and I said, 'Take down your pants, motherfucker.' 'C'mon now, my man,' he said. He was crying. 'I tole you I don't *got* no shit.' '*Quizás pero*,' I said, 'but take down your pants all the same.' He took them down and I stuck my .45 up his ass, and I said, 'Now if you want to be here tomorrow morning tell me where you put the stuff.' He said, 'It's in the cupboard, *cabrón*. It's right there in the fucking cupboard, man. Get it for him, *Mamí*.' The shit be right there in the cupboard, like he said, a whole fucking sack of it. I took about thirty-five bags and went up to the roof with my partner. I said, 'C'mon, my man, we are going to get high now.' I played around wit' my gimmicks but I did not get off. My partner got off and said, 'This is beautiful shit, my man,' and I said, '*Chevere!* I just wanted to make sure it was all right.' He got pissed off. 'What! You mean to tell me you was using me as a guinea pig?' 'That is the way it be, brotherman,' I said. After that I'd come knocking at the door at all hours of the night. '*Quién es?*' Ramon would say. 'It is Julito. You know what I want.' And he would shoot the dope out the door."

Julio reversed his position on the couch and fell on top of Dolores, artlessly smothering her with his short, heavy bulk; she felt the hairs of his chest stuffing up her mouth and nostrils. Before she'd never liked hairy men. His hands on her back were ice cold, feverish at the fingertips. Maybe it was her back that was hot or cold. That story had made her feel almost physically sick.

"Would you really have killed him?" she asked, her voice stifled by Julio's chest. "What if you had killed him?"

"Then it would have been his time to die," he replied. He tried to enter her. At first his dick was too soft, but as he felt her persistent desire reach out for him, independently of her will, it got hard again and he pushed it in. It was starting to hurt; she was getting sore, but it didn't stop her from wanting it. She was pissing more than she should. It must be irritating her bladder. She closed the walls of her cunt around it; she could grab it tight, and then push at it with her muscles inside; this sensation pleased him. "How do you *do* that, girl?" he'd asked.

"Would you say that if some strung-out junkie shot you?" she asked. "That your time had come?" He barely moved in her. That drove her wild, made her thrash out for it.

"*Sí*," he answered. "I would say the same thing. It makes me no difference. Once I die I am dead. Can you feel that, *mujer de Dios*?"

174

"Woman of God?" Dolores translated weakly. She came. Sometimes she came in a feeble rush, without really feeling the buildup of convulsive spasms, almost in spite of herself. "Of course I can feel it," she said afterward.

He laughed, a phantom of his wicked, earthy laugh, now abstracted to an echo he no longer seemed to register himself. "I just want to hear you say that you do," he answered. "It don't mean woman of god. It sounds like that, but that ain't what it means."

"What does it mean?"

"I don't know in English," Julio said, and then he pulled out and lay perfectly still, rigid, obviously worrying. He didn't come, she thought.

"Julio, let's go outside!" she demanded suddenly. The room was too stuffy, filled with smoke and the acid odor of sex. She couldn't stand it anymore. She stood up to put on her clothes, than sank weakly back down to the rug. The street would be the same, dense and claustrophobic. She couldn't get away from it. She liked lolling around naked. Sensitive currents in the air flitted across her skin. Her body felt like an open field, inviting seeds and insect life to inhabit it. Julio was still lying on the couch, pensive and absorbed. His breath was raspy. He smoked too much. He was clearly thinking some unsettled, nerve-racking thought. "What I am doing now wit' you, Dolores, was the only thing I was thinking about in jail," he finally said. It was a peculiar sentence, spoken without the implied emotion. Did he mean the fulfillment of his fantasies about her had disappointed him, or enraptured him, or had nothing at all to do with what he thought now?

"Did I ever tell you I was raped once?" Dolores often practiced this sentence silently, but never said it aloud.

She supposed she didn't want him to know, or didn't want to know he hadn't guessed. No, it wasn't important if he knew or not, wasn't important anymore.

"When I was working wit' Blue," Julio went on, "we got into them drug gangs in The Bronx. We went after their action, man. I be playing the cop. I had a phony shield and a .38 and I would bust into the dealer's place and tell them they was all under arrest. I was not tall enough to be no cop, so I got me a pair of them elevator shoes. 'You are under arrest,' I would tell them. 'Put up your hands and don't move. Believe me, I would enjoy putting you motherfuckers in the ground.' " His voice was low and tough. "I sounded just like a fucking pig, my man. Then I would take them out to the car, put them in the backseat, and Blue would take care of the rest. In case the real po-lice be coming along while we was making an arrest we had rigged up a crash car that would slam into the squad car while we buffed. We would make those punks tell us where they be keeping their stash and their bread and then we would be on the telephone, asking their people for ransom. Later I found out Blue was having the relatives taken off, whether they came up with the dough or not. I did not dig that, my man. I had me a black silk suit, custom-made; that was one beautiful suit, my man. We busted into these joints in Brooklyn, guns smoking. I went with him to back him up whenever he went to make a drop. He'd say, 'C'mon, Duke,' and I would put on my suit and go with him wherever he was going. I left the jacket of that suit at a party one time. Blue wanted me to quit shooting. 'You can't do that and work wit' me,' he'd say. 'Duke, I want you be my main man, but not with that shit in your veins.' I was out of town when they got him. They busted into his old lady's apartment. They shot him and then they kept shooting;

they shot his dead body, man, twenty, thirty times with a Thompson submachine gun. They killed his woman and their two-year-old kid. I went over to Brooklyn to get away from the heat in The Bronx. When they be asking me, 'Ain't your name Duke?' I would tell them, 'Naw, man, I don't know no Duke. My name is Julio.'

"Someone paid me to fuck up the snitch. I went back to The Bronx. The snitch ast me, 'What do you want?' I said, 'I am here to fuck you up, my man.' 'Who sent you?' he said. 'That ain't wit' you,' I said. He asked me if it was Ramon's people. 'How much are they paying you?' he wanted to know. 'Ten yards,' I tole him. It was only five. He said, 'I will give you fifteen yards to fuck him up for me, *hombre*.' 'In cash and now,' I said. He went into the back room and got the money. Then I went back to the dude who had paid me to fuck him up. 'I am here to fuck you up,' I said. It went on like that, back and forth." Dolores smiled and caught a glimpse of herself in the mirror; her smile was grotesque, like the grinning teeth of a nude skull.

"Dolores," Julio asked irrelevantly. "If you was working in a bank and some cat wearing a Halloween mask was to come up to the window and say, 'Give me the money in your drawer or I am going to blow you away,' would you press the alarm?"

She was running her hand back and forth over the same spot on his inner thigh; the skin was smooth and cool, like wax. The smoothness seemed part of her own fingers. "I haven't the slightest idea what I'd do," she said. "Maybe I wouldn't care if I died at that particular moment. It would depend on how I felt, how you looked at me, how I felt about my job, my love life. I don't know." She spoke rapidly, in an irritated voice. "I can't imagine myself working in a bank." Julio put her hand on his dick. She snatched it back. "Listen to me!" she exclaimed. "Forget it! If they get you for another felony you'll be stuck in jail for the rest of your life. They'll throw away the key. I wouldn't blame them!" She stopped abruptly. She was determined to quit lecturing. It made her feel like his social worker, a role that didn't go with being his lover. She couldn't tell him anything he didn't know himself. He knew what jail was like.

"Dolores," Julio said, with a loud, gasping sigh. "I want to get me a gun. I am trying to put it out of my mind, believe me, *nene,* but it keeps coming back to me, like one of them nightmares. I see the gun in my sleep. I can touch it. I can feel it. I don't want to rob no bank."

Dolores made a disgusted sound. It was far beyond her comprehension, to want a gun, to rob a bank. She couldn't think of any new argument, one that would really register with him. Whenever she tried to convince him he said, *"Sí"* or "Yeah" as if he understood, but he wasn't hearing her. Nothing she could say would mean anything to him.

"I need a gun now," he continued. "Some nigger in Rhoda's be givin' this young Spanish dude I know a hard time last night. 'Listen, my man,' I said to him, 'why don't you fuck wit' someone your own size?' I hit him. I hit him hard, Dolores. I can not stand to see no full-grown son of a bitch take advantage of no kid. He went out holding his face, bleeding at the nose. 'There will be another time, Julito,' he said to me. I know that dude would not be one to get it on with his hands. Now I can not go back to the South Bronx no more unless I am strapped down."

"So stay away from the South Bronx!" she said. "Why don't you sleep here at night instead of going back

there?" She said that without considering the consequences.

"I can't stay here, *nene*," Julio said. "The parole be
thinking that I am living wit' my sister. They check out
that shit. Besides, you need your freedom, your place."
After he left at night Dolores always ate something she
could buy in the small grocery downstairs, cream cheese,
crackers, bread, salami, nothing healthy at all, and fell
asleep, waiting for the next day, when he would come
again. She was too tired, or too freaked out, to go to her
yoga class, to write.

"Guns are evil," Dolores said emphatically. His left
hand was squeezing her breast, gently, absentmindedly.
"Don't touch me!" she said. "Listen to what I'm telling
you for once. What's happening to you? What happened
to all your resolutions? Next you'll be back into heroin."

"There is one thing that I know and that is I will die
first," Julio said.

"When you pick up a gun you assume you have the
right to put an end to someone else's life."

"That is cor-*rect*," he said.

"And you think you have that right?" Dolores continued. Whenever she talked to him about these things she
felt like she had her back against a brick wall. It was all
so desperate in a way she couldn't grasp. She had never
imagined herself pontificating about guns or killing, especially in bed. "It's evil," she said lamely. "It's truly
evil. No one has the right to take away life." She knew
she believed that. "Life is not your prerogative."

"When I was a little kid," Julio said, "my mother took
me to a *bruja* up in The Bronx. That is a witch, Dolores,
like an exorcist. She was thinking this *bruja* lady could
take the bad juju out of me. Dig it, we went into this

179

broken-down place on Willis Avenue. I remember that *bruja,* my man; she was ancient, old, wit' eyes sunk deep into her skull, Dracula eyes. They was burning, like fire. Her skin looked like one hundred years old, dead and dried up, like old newspaper. The air there was bad, sweet and sick-like. At first I be scared. I be wondering how come it is so hot in that room wit' them dusty curtains and red candles. I be wondering why the *bruja* do not open no windows. It was winter, man, but it must have been ninety-five degrees in there. Then I realized it was me that was hot; my skin was heating up, getting hotter and burning like a fire. Everything began to jump up and down—the *bruja'*s face, the other people there. All of a sudden she screams at my mother, 'Take him out of here, because he is going to kill someone!' "

He was hard again. He pushed her head down and Dolores began sucking him, feeling sick inside. Too much sex. She wished Julio would go away. He put his palm on her head. "Play wit' my balls," he ordered softly. He moaned unhappily, as if in pain. *"Vaya,* you know how to suck dick, *mi fresquita.* Who be teaching you to suck dick like that?"

Afterward she lay on her stomach in the yoga resting position, her cheek turned away from him. He was driving her crazy. It was out of her hands, what he did, didn't do. It was important to remember that.

"I would never go back to the house when I was a kid," he said. "I was telling my mother it was because I seen a monster outside the door. I used to stay at other kids' houses and tell their mothers I was an orphan. Then my mother would come looking for me. 'Does Julito belong to you?' they would ask her. They did not believe her when she said yes. Where we was living then there was rats."

Dolores began to cry. She didn't know why, exactly, but the tears felt cool, relieving, like rain in a hot place. She rarely cried, but now she made the most of it. She snuffed and wiped her tears. She relished the gritty, tired feeling they created in her eyes. *"Tú estás llorando, nene linda,"* Julio commented, though his attention was focused elsewhere. He cracked his knuckles again and ran his fingers repeatedly over his chest.

"Do you still think about Graciela?" she asked through the dregs of her tears, trying to direct her anxiety toward the most logical focus—other women. She was always jealous.

"Who?" Julio questioned. "Gracie? Sure I be thinking about her."

"Well, what do you think?"

Julio was cautious, evasive. "I don't be thinking nothing, Dolores. Nothing you don't already know."

"Julio, I just don't know what to do. Nothing I say makes any difference. You don't even hear me."

He grabbed her face in his hands. "You keep talking to me, *nene*. Talk! You are saying what I be needing to hear. *Oye,* I need to hear the things you be saying. I am trying to understand." His voice cracked with urgency. "Most of the time I am just rapping. It do not mean nothing. I am going to get me a job. Soon, now. Sharif is working on it, man. My sister called him because I be talking about guns to her. He came over. We smoked a joint, then he said, 'All right, Julito, now what is this *bull*shit?' He tole me when I feel like that to come sit in his office all day. He can keep me busy, he said. When I talk about guns and crazy shit you say to me, 'Julito, *tú estás loco*. You are one crazy motherfucker and you will spend your life in jail.' I be listening, believe me. I be listening good." He got up and put on his tight jeans and his white polyester knit shirt with the little collar with red and blue trim. He dressed like a typical Puerto Rican, Dolores thought. It was evening. She had no idea if he still went to the lawyer's office or not. How long had they actually been fucking? Later she looked in her journal and discovered it was only a week, no, a little more, nine days, counting the day when he'd had to report to the parole. "You can save me, Dolores," he said. *"Mujer de Dios."*

"That's not my job," she returned. That was the right thing to say. It was certainly the truth.

At the door Julio was agitated. "You are helping me," he said. "Believe me, *nene.*"

"But I'm not doing enough," she replied, drained, exhausted, fucked through every pore. She felt she had lost her power to help him, possibly her desire to help him; with sex he had gotten the power over her. They were silent. He didn't look into her eyes. "Why don't you stay for dinner tomorrow at least," she said. "I'll fix a duck. Didn't you tell me you wanted to try it? Duck à l'orange." She imagined herself cutting the orange peel into julienne strips. It seemed a ludicrous and impossible task.

"Chevere," Julio said, briefly smiling his real smile. "Duck, man. Julito eats duck!" He laughed and kissed her. But the next day he never arrived.

CHAPTER

13

*A*S the morning passed and Julio Bravo's abrupt knock did not reach her door, Dolores plunged, almost gratefully, into the ordeal of "waiting." Waiting was a necessary ingredient in the love affair as she knew it—the point at which passion and fear coalesced into a sharp, easily defined pain, the consummation of the dark side of love, the side she could definitely feel and believe. She began to "wait" almost before Julio was late, certainly before she knew he wasn't coming, knew beyond a doubt that he had abandoned her. By ten o'clock in the morning she was waiting, maybe not for him, but for the blank, petrified space of waiting itself, the space that doubled its oblivious emotional breadth every hour. She sat glued to her great, suffering anxiety, unable to move, read, or think normally. The suspended agony of waiting for a lover, she thought, was like finding herself transplanted to the arid desert of a foreign land, where she'd known from the moment she landed she would not survive.

She tried, as always in these situations, to reconstruct what she might have done or said to make the man disappear. She had told him that to "save him" was not her job; that might be true, but it had been a cold, cynical response to his need for her help. She hadn't shown enough real sympathy for his problems. She had wanted to escape the intensity of it all, because she was afraid of intimacy, no doubt, and he had understood that and run away. Oh, it was no use examining the reasons *ad nauseam;* he was gone; she'd never know exactly why, and she didn't suppose she could have acted differently. No, in the end, she'd had no choice but to be her terrible self.

She watched her futile body wander from room to room, passing its hands aimlessly over objects. She felt a constricting pressure swell behind her eyelids, frustrated, unshed tears, that soon spread their watery uncertainty into her guts and legs. Every second harbored the possible ring of the telephone, the sound of his rough voice, his knock at the door; every second dragged by, conspicuously empty. There was nothing she could do to make him appear; that was the worst part, she was helpless. Finally, at 11:30 A.M. she gave in to the only constructive possibility; she picked up the phone and dialed the number he had given her long ago, his sister's number. She hated to call men, especially to resolve her anxieties about them, or to find them when they'd disappeared; such attitudes were relics from unliberated days, she reminded herself. After two shortened rings, a hollow, mechanical voice answered and stated in portentous tones, "I'm sor-ry, but the number you have dialed has been temp-or-ar-ily disconnected." He hadn't told her his phone was out; why should he though? She'd never called him or said she wanted to. He had mentioned that his sister was not responsible, did not use her welfare checks to pay her bills.

By noon her mood had changed and she was angry. He had no right to do this to her. Nobody had the right. He was wasting her valuable time. She would explain to him a woman couldn't do anything else while she waited for a man, that the man controlled her time with his absence; he certainly could have called. Inconsiderate. There was no reason on earth he couldn't have called. Dolores waits for no man, she said defiantly to herself, and went outside. The bright sunlight pierced her eyes, and she blinked like a winter creature emerging from its cave. The beautiful day was a reproach. There wasn't anything she wanted to do out here. She couldn't remember what she'd ever done. Walk? Go to the park? Why? She walked slowly, heading nowhere. Her anxiety was out of proportion to the cause, she told herself. He'd probably show up tonight at dinnertime. She had invited him for dinner, after all, not breakfast or lunch. There was no rule that said he had to come in the morning, just because he mostly had before. Last night she had dragged herself to the Grand Union, cashed a check, and pushed a full cart down its fluorescent aisles. The congealed duck was now unfreezing its icy flesh in her kitchen. She was submerged in her private, neurotic trauma, basically egocentric. This ferocious anxiety was strictly her problem, inspired by her unhappy, romantic past, or her warped psyche, not Julio Bravo. Why did she assume because he was late he wasn't coming at all? Perhaps he didn't have the subway fare, or had an important family problem to

185

attend to. He might be in some kind of trouble. He'd been in a bad state yesterday. He'd talked about trouble—the man in the bar, the gun. He might be dead or in jail again and she was worrying that he had abandoned her; selfish worry! And with these mitigating thoughts she knew she was trying to excuse him, so she could greet him without pent-up anger when he arrived and quickly resume fucking him again. She had seen him less than twenty-four hours ago. Some intuition told her he was all right, and she knew the same intuition was telling her it was over, as it had been before it began, when she'd waited for him at the subway.

She went to her favorite café and ordered a cappuccino. This was the part of her routine she had missed when solely occupied with him—her solitary moments in this café, where she could think her own thoughts anonymously in public. She caught a glimpse of herself in the antique mirror over the baroque silver espresso machine and saw that her face had become gray, old; deep, black circles puffed the skin under her eyes. At this very moment, she thought, he might be knocking at my door, wondering where I am, worrying. This idea afflicted her with a morose panic. If she missed him she would never know, and she would go on waiting. Without asking for the check, she threw a crumpled dollar on the table and rushed home.

She fumbled with the key, unreasonably expecting to find Julio behind the door, and was again confronted by the undisturbed, bleak disorder of her apartment, the sun shining ruefully through the rain- and dust-marked windows. All that remained of Julio was the metal ashtray, overflowing with butts. Immediately the walls pressed in, confining her to the dim, spaceless cave of her own mind, empty, except for its miserable burden of expectation, its concentration on passing time, on meaningless sounds. She tried to numb her perceptions, cast her thoughts away, banish her psychic existence and merge with the couch like an inanimate substance, devoid of pain. No, she could not dismiss the pain—blunt, unreasonable, stupid suffering—her perverse celebration of her greatest metaphysical fear, loss of love, fear of abandonment. This fear, she told herself, had nothing to do with Julio at all, nothing to do with vanishing lovers, nothing, even, to do with the brave, independent person she thought of as herself. This fear, totally illogical, issued from some atavistic, reptilian female organ, stimulated into action by copulation. She never felt it when she didn't have a lover, only when she had one who wasn't there.

The telephone rang, shrill and alarming in the silence. It's not him, she told herself, don't think it's him, and approached the receiver, expectation forcefully contained. It wasn't Julio, but her friend Sophie, whose resonant French-accented voice popped a real world, the one she'd occupied before Julio Bravo, back into focus. It had been weeks, Dolores realized, since they'd talked or gone out for their traditional Thursday-night drink. She hadn't called Sophie or anyone else. She had only thought of Julio, whether he was present or not.

"What happened to you?" Sophie exclaimed. "I have been so worried. You do not call. You are never at home!"

That wasn't true; she had been at home, but couldn't answer the phone when they were fucking, or about to fuck, or had just finished fucking, which had been almost all the time. Had the phone rung at night? She couldn't remember; possibly she had sunk into some abstract hole, where no awareness penetrated, when he had gone back to The Bronx. "I'm sorry," Dolores said, "I've . . ."

187

"You have a lover! Marvelous!" *Marvelous* was one of Sophie's favorite English words; she gave it the full weight of her slightly hysterical warmth, opposing it vocally to its antonyms, ever present in her mind.

"I did," Dolores said, "but it's all over now, I guess." This pronouncement was so floridly pessimistic it sounded untrue and reassured her. It couldn't "all be over" so quickly, without warning. He had merely stood her up, a crime, yes, but not equivalent to abandonment. He would probably show up sometime today, or tomorrow.

Sophie gasped, as she always did, when presented with any news she could interpret as *"désastre."* Her anxious spirit reached out for disaster; other people's only seemed to forewarn her own, always lurking on the outskirts of her elegant life, her vibrant serenity. With the slightest warning, at the most minute hint of anything amiss, she would become terror-stricken and devoid of hope. In this way, she was exactly like Dolores. "Do you want me to come to you?" she asked, as if volunteering her services at a deathbed.

"Oh yes," Dolores sighed, admitting in a rush her vast need for consolation. There was no face she wanted to see more than the warm, living, female face of Sophie.

Dolores immediately noticed that Sophie's pregnancy had greatly advanced. Her stomach, which had grown large and round beneath the shrinking fabric of her ragged velvet skirts, now seemed to float independently before her small body, like a trembling planet, attached only by slender strings of gravity. From the moment she had missed her period, Sophie, who had wanted a child for years and considered herself sterile, had worried it was a tubular pregnancy, because someone she knew had died from one. When this proved false, she feared the child would be born a monster, because she was over thirty-five, or that its father, a much younger man who adored her, and now squeezed fresh orange juice to sate her acid thirst three times a day, would abandon her, or that the child would be premature and die, or sicken and die, or would eventually catch its bedclothes on the gas stove and die, or that she would die while it was being born. Even after amniocentesis revealed the fetus to be a healthy boy (already named after Sophie's favorite medieval hero: Gawain), she still suspected that the test had failed, that not all the chromosomes had been accounted for, and the child would emerge an idiot, or afflicted with one of the few diseases the exam could not detect. She had actually considered taking the test again, but her doctor had told her that would be dangerous. As her pregnancy progressed without *désastre*, however, some unpredictable radiance had possessed her in spite of herself. Though she still attempted to nourish disastrous thoughts so she would not be taken by surprise if they turned out to be true, her physiological state itself all but vanquished them, brought with it the undeniable assurance of a mysterious grace. Sophie was utterly and fervently happy.

Dolores immediately sensed this organic joy, noted it with amazed mistrust, like the configurations of a lunar landscape. She offered Sophie the spindly kitchen chair, first covering its hard seat with a pillow from the bedroom, and uneasily watched her lower her suspended bulk down upon it. Though Dolores had hoped to be nursed and consoled herself, she now found herself in the presence of a condition more subtly demanding than her own. She made banana daiquiris, omitting the rum from Sophie's, who no longer drank booze or coffee or ate chocolate or could bear the smell of meat. She spiked her own heavily, uneasy in the presence of this ecstatic friend, replete with a delight that must be fragile, might not withstand the sick desperation she exuded. Perhaps she shouldn't spill the whole story of Julio Bravo; it might influence the fetus, or Sophie might think it would. Nevertheless, the opportunity to confide at last to a kindred, feminine soul who would surely empathize was irresistible. Why hadn't she told Sophie right away? She was guaranteed to understand. In her own bohemian past, her peripatetic voyages from one European country to another, there had been figures no less bizarre than Julio Bravo: a decadent Englishman who had spent every day lounging in his bath, drinking tea and chatting with a giant blue parrot; a suicidal Russian emigré painter; an Italian prince who had proved to be homosexual, despite his ardent gifts of expensive jewels. Her current lover, the fetus's father, was a Jew who had been raised in a South American jungle, where his parents had eluded Hitler; a wild young man, who wore his black hair long and tousled, he shouted about art and politics in his personal version of English, still marred by remnants of guttural forest sounds. No, normal men were not for Sophie any more than for her. Even the child, Dolores was sure, would never be a "normal" man.

She launched the story of Julio Bravo, making it good, embellishing details. She told about his vow to kill her rapist in jail, his first visit to her apartment, her reluctance to get involved. She described his earthy warmth, sensitivity, his role in the Corsica riot, his desire to battle the forces of repression and injustice, a desire she felt akin to her own real truths. She built up to the first time they made passionate love in an old folks' park, and then, to Julio's desperate struggle to stay out of trouble, his desire for guns, their heavy conversation yesterday, and then, to his apparent disappearance, though she wasn't one hundred percent sure he'd disappeared. It was a great story, she knew, and Sophie loved a story; but she felt uncomfortable telling it. She was inflating Julio into an unreal hero, like a movie star, or the protagonist of a novel, someone larger than life who could be regarded from afar with innocuous excitement. Even when she emphasized her own fears, her current dilemma, she knew she was leaving something important out—some essential information that would express how it felt to know this man was inextricably attached to her intimate self.

In the middle of the story, Sophie, who had been punctuating Dolores's monologue with small French exclamations—"Oof!" and "Yes?" and "Ooo lala!"—shifted uncomfortably, and her hand traveled to her large, planet container. Dolores stopped talking.

"It is nothing," Sophie said, eyes shining. "It is just that he moves so much now."

Dolores continued, unsure if Sophie really listened, or if she only pretended to listen, while focused on the busy creature inside and its waves of organic joy. She did not interrupt with the many questions she'd asked when Dolores had delivered such traumatized tales before, only, "Is he handsome?"

"Very," Dolores said. "At least I think so." She described Julio's elegant conquistador face, his goatee, his gold earring, his sinister tattoos, his bullet holes, his muscular body. She was transforming him into a painting, she thought, a portrait of a man impossible not to love. Why? So Sophie would fall for him too and exonerate her own foolhardy passion?

"Phoooo!" Sophie exhaled her enraptured admiration

syllable, yet Dolores sensed she was only trying to give this dramatic account of romantic adventure the same quality of attention she would have given it before she was pregnant. But the compelling thing inside now drew her away; the biggest adventure, her faraway eyes, her hands, pressed to her stomach, seemed to imply, was this physiological event that she could not describe, had barely, Dolores thought resentfully, even tried to describe. Apparently pregnancy was private, exclusive material, evading the powers of communication, like the actual sensation of sex. "Désastre" for Sophie, Dolores realized, would have no more to do with the jaded exasperations of a failing romance, not her own, or anyone else's; "désastre" was limited to other realms. "Désastre" would soon be the fleshy, new smelling, speechless stranger refusing to take the breast, crying at dawn, and at last, toddling to stick a fork in an electric plug. Sophie listened haphazardly. She looked at Dolores but saw instead an intangible vision. She exhaled in extravagant French, not for Dolores, not for any man, but for the breath of life itself.

Dolores began to feel even more miserable. Though she doubted what she said interested Sophie she convulsively ran down the positive possibilities, trying to convince herself. "It's Father's Day, isn't it?" she asked. "I forgot it was Father's Day. He has children. Maybe he's visiting them. Maybe he forgot about Father's Day when he said he'd come. He might be visiting his own father. He loves his father, he said. He wants to buy him a house in Puerto Rico. But he could have called, don't you think? No matter what, he could have called. I don't know, maybe it's not part of his macho culture to call a woman when he's going to be late. I'll have to talk to him about that." She should shut up. She should can this pointless verbal energy and attempt to come to grips with the fact that her angst about Julio Bravo had little to do with Julio himself; it had to do with her own state of mind, eternally anxious.

Sophie jumped.

"What's the matter?" Dolores asked.

"He is swimming from side to side like a fish," she answered.

"Gee whiz!" Dolores exclaimed, then realized that sounded just slightly sarcastic. She wanted to remedy it with a sympathetic remark, but couldn't think of one. She knew the expression on her face could in no way reveal the slightest understanding of what it was like to have a child swimming around inside you. "Do you want another daiquiri?" she asked. She suddenly resented Sophie for not drinking alcohol. One little drink wouldn't obliterate the kid's brain cells.

"No, I don't think so," she said. She had to be getting home for her afternoon nap. As she gathered up her bag and gauzy shawl she told Dolores she was sure Julio would be back. "I really want to meet this one," she added with a warm, possibly phony smile. Dolores had not introduced Julio to any of her friends. There hadn't been time.

"Well, *I'm* not pregnant," she said irrelevantly, and resisted adding, "Thank God!"

Sophie glanced at her, a little sadly, she thought. Perhaps she was thinking what a shame it was that Dolores was condemned to this ridiculous, lonely life full of trivial agonies, that all her joys and sorrows focused on the comings and goings of hopelessly inappropriate men who couldn't love her, and she would never know the true satisfaction of creating life. That made Dolores angry. What was right for one person was not necessarily right for another. She created poetry, after all, immortal life. She clamped her lips. At all costs she must avoid a long speech about why she didn't want a child. She should be glad that Sophie cared enough to come over and console her in a hard moment, when she would obviously have preferred to be alone with the ecstasy in her womb. She had an unexpected influx of affectionate thoughts for Joanna, who, despite her middle-class desires for things and success, did not want babies either, who always opened her mouth, stuck out her tongue, and said "Eccchhhhh!" when anyone asked when she and Tom were planning to have one.

When Sophie left, her eyes still shining with private bliss, she put a concerned hand on Dolores's arm. "Be careful, Dolores," she said.

Dolores inexplicably felt on the verge of tears. "You too," she quavered, then wondered why she had said that. It was an awkward non sequitur, like saying "Thanks for calling" to someone you had called yourself.

Alone again, she allowed herself the full, almost self-indulgent agony of feeling wretchedly alone. The crisis was over somehow. She was no longer waiting. She could, she thought, survive a solitary existence, minus someone to love her, minus babies, minus all the things every woman was supposed to have. She could even survive the stolid, isolated certainty of her abandoned state, but she could not survive the tortuous process of being abandoned. Though it was only five o'clock she knew Julio wasn't going to come—maybe never again—and even if he did, even if he came tomorrow, loving, full of apologies, she would always feel that he had abandoned her and she was alone. She pulled herself together and began to clean her apartment.

It was filthy. She emptied ashtrays filled with Camel

butts and roach ends. She changed the come-stained sheets. She washed endless glasses and cups with juice and coffee stains hardened in the bottoms. She threw out crusts of bread and wiped crumbs off the tabletop. She stuffed the chilly duck in the refrigerator, where it would probably decompose. She sprayed the cockroach hideouts and took the stinking, half-liquefied garbage downstairs. She watered the plants. She wiped the layer of thin, gritty dust off her desk top. Then she vacuumed her entire apartment. She would eventually have to wash the windows.

As she cleared off the couch she found a small piece of paper stuck between its cushions. One word, "DiFiglia's," and a number, "132," was written on it. DiFiglia's was the name of a neighborhood bar, an old Italian joint that had recently sold out and renovated its inside to attract chic, uptown tourists. Deserted by the local artists, it was now filled with the most obnoxious, bourgeois, pretentious people who came there hoping to meet artists and paid a small fortune for drinks. The swank interior had even served as the set for a scene in a Woody Allen film. The handwriting looked like Julio's. Why would he write "DiFiglia's" on a piece of paper? Maybe he had a job possibility there? No, he wasn't allowed to work in a bar, he'd said. Probably someone else dropped the paper, eons ago. She threw it away.

After the massive cleanup operation she felt clean herself, free and uncluttered inside. She had faced the bottom once again, she thought, and had surfaced alive, alone, but unvanquished. The bottom really had nothing to do with Julio Bravo, or men who had dumped her before; it was simply there, itself, inviolable, waiting, the true void where we are all alone.

She fixed a salad and realized how hungry she'd been

for something green. She had lost weight, though all she'd been eating was starch and cheese and sweets. She lay on her fresh sheets and felt simply content that her apartment was clean. She was spiritually and physically organized. Tomorrow she would call her agent and find out what was happening with the poets' biographies. She would go to the library and do some preliminary research. She would iron every blouse in her closet. Soon she would try to write again. She picked up an old copy of a woman's magazine and read a short story with surprising concentration and peace of mind—a banal, badly written short story. How can they publish such garbage, she wondered. She felt sorry for short-story writers. At least poets knew they'd never make any money, so they could afford to stay pure. She realized, then, that her mind was already safely on other subjects. She was not really thinking about Julio Bravo. It was almost embarrassing to admit that after an entire day wasted agonizing over the whys and wherefores of his disappearance, she was almost relieved he was gone.

CHAPTER
14

*H*ER agent advised her that the contract for the poets' biographies would be coming through in a couple of weeks. To celebrate Dolores rampaged the thrift shops in the East Eighties. Grubbing through musty, tangled piles of clothes, smelling vaguely of dry-cleaning fluids, deodorants, and unknown perfumed bodies, she unearthed a magnificent yellow '40s blouse with a witty pocket that resembled lips, one dollar, and a pair of elbow-length kid gloves, lined with silk, but not the alligator purse she'd been searching for. She thrust Julio Bravo out the back door of her mind like yesterday's newspaper and felt strong; she could do it; evacuate a male that had obsessed her from her thoughts and fill the quivering space he'd occupied with other ideas.

She called friends. Nothing much had transpired in their lives. She told off the jerk who came to read the Con Ed meter at 7:30 A.M.; why in hell did he have to bang on the door and shout "Gas man!" loud enough to wake the dead; she was asleep, but she wasn't deaf! She welcomed back the ranting, astringent self that had retreated before the onslaught of Julio Bravo. Something vital in her wilted under the heat of "love." She had never yelled at Julio, never even spoken harshly to him, not really, and now never would. He had vanished. That was clear. She hadn't heard a word from him. He had obviously found their affair too threatening. Predictable, since she was, after all, a college-educated, middle-class writer and he was a Puerto Rican jailbird from the South Bronx. She filled her psychic reservoir with noble, forgiving feelings. It was all right. She couldn't hate him for being what he was, or pretend he had disillusioned her. It never would have lasted much longer. She would soon have come to her senses and gotten rid of him. She could now analyze their brief relationship like a remote, literary text. By fucking him she had surrendered her positive influence over him, and thus deprived him of the part of herself he wanted most, and thought he would secure by fucking her. She began to write him a letter, explaining this ironic fact, and telling him they could still be friends, that he needed her; then, feeling those sentiments were too self-righteous and condescending, she ripped it up.

Beneath the batterings of her mind, his image grew distorted. His face, in her memory, was now deformed, its cheeks bulging, nose wide and infected with cauliflower lumps, frizzy hair ballooning grotesquely. His powerful body had become a shrunken, muscle-bound dwarf's. He was ugly and inappropriate, and she was better off without him. She recalled the weird things he had told her; he was clearly off his rocker, possibly dangerous, if not to her, to himself and other people. She was lucky this unwise dalliance had not resulted in disaster. In her third yoga class her body finally cooperated with her mind, gave up, at long last, the final vestige of its sexual preoccupation; yes, something in her tense solar plexus relaxed with an uneasy crack and sigh.

On the way home from the thrift shop she ran into Gregory again on the street, walking with *The New York Times* clutched protectively to his chest. He stopped and visibly gathered himself, honing the formal approach he'd used with her since she'd rejected him. Her friend Eve had dumped him for a twenty-one-year-old student in a policeman's college, and he had burst into Dolores's apartment, drunk, his fair-skinned face inflamed, and announced he was choosing her as a replacement. Dolores had been incredulous. It was impossible for her to identify herself with the "want" this bereft lover of a friend expressed for her. He told her he had invited Eve and her young lover to join him for champagne, then thrown the bottle out the window at them when they'd departed together; it had crashed on the street, splattering glass and Brut. His desire for Dolores seemed to have concocted itself in an empty vial.

"How's your criminal?" Gregory asked now. He evidently still remembered her unfortunate revelation the day she had rushed back and forth from the subway looking for Julio. He posed the question in a facetious tone that enabled it to be taken seriously or ignored. "Did you ever find him? Or shouldn't I ask?"

"Yes," she answered, imitating his chic, superficial tone, with possible honest underpinnings, "unfortunately." She felt able to comment on her adventure with

199

Julio now, with the detached exuberance of a television talk-show guest.

Gregory invited her to have dinner with him, as if he couldn't quite stop himself. She dressed carefully. The yellow blouse went perfectly with her navy rayon crepe skirt. This was exactly what she needed, an expenses-paid date with an appropriate man in an excellent restaurant. This was the treatment an attractive female poet, living the single life in New York, deserved and should take for granted. Almost a year had passed since his deranged proposal. Perhaps now she should, in fairness to herself, give him serious consideration. It was about time she chose a lover with her wits about her, a reasonable companion, who would help her live a nice, secure life. There was nothing wrong with a "nice" life. Gregory was handsome, if you liked the effete type; he was basically monogamous; he was rich, especially compared to her; and he liked intelligent women, unlike most men. In time she might develop passionate feelings for him the way normal women did for men, in response to deep affection and mutual respect. Irrational passion never lasted long anyway. She'd just had proof of that.

She met him at La Charcuterie. "What are you working on now, pray tell?" he asked. She leaned forward into the candlelight. It was the same question, she thought, that all rational, middle-class human beings asked each other over dinner in expensive, New York restaurants. Every decent person, who wished to reveal his own basic worth then express his sincere interest in others' lives, answered this question solemnly then asked it in return. The expression *working on*, by itself, manifested a dignified importance. God forbid you weren't working on anything, like poor Julio Bravo. She told Gregory about the poets' biographies, making them sound far more interesting than she now thought them to be, skipping the amount of money involved (Gregory would think it paltry), but implying it was vast. She then moved on to her artistic vocation and discussed her poetry, which for the last three days had been going, she could really say it, almost well. She had slipped a recent sample, a violent, scary piece, tight and controlled, into her bag in case the opportunity arose to show it off. She had the feeling he was impressed with her, and she liked that.

"I'm trying to re-create the formal surface of rhymed, metered verse without resorting to traditional forms of rhyme and meter," she said, watching her hands wave expressively and thinking how these flapping appendages belied her serious, canonizing voice, "because most of those forms are just too old-fashioned for our modern thoughts and diction." She felt bored with herself. Why should it be dull to describe one's significant ideas, those related to supreme artistic effort, or important ambitions and goals? Real communication must involve, more than this self-centered exchange of projects in progress, a dynamic connection that moved beneath the surface of words. She extracted a pink mussel from its corroded shell and dipped it into the rich brandy sauce. This fattening meal would probably make her sick.

Gregory then told her what he was working on—a punk rock star's loft. "It's a fantastic space," he said, "lined with windows, southern exposure. But my outrageous friend, Johnny Cruel, wants the ceilings, walls, including the windows, draped with silver vinyl, like the inside of a dirigible, as he so eloquently puts it. Daylight burns his eyes, or so he attests." He raised a morsel of pâté on bread. "Try the pâté. It's superior."

"He hates light?" she asked. Gregory slipped the pâté into her mouth with his own fingers.

"He most emphatically hates light," he said. "What's more, he commanded that one end of the loft be painted a vivid, metallic red. I'm doing my best to dissuade him from that!"

"Why? It sounds different, at least."

He told her that he was considering buying a building in Hoboken. "I've rejected owning things before," he said, "but now I'm at a place where I think it feels comfortable."

Of course it feels comfortable when you're loaded, Dolores thought, slightly irritated. Everyone she knew talked about homeownership in tones of righteous self-improvement, as if it were a necessary spiritual exercise. "I don't ever want to own anything," she proclaimed, and was about to launch a ferocious invective stating why when Gregory interrupted her.

He leaned forward and removed his wire-rimmed glasses. His pale blue eyes seemed overexposed without them. "Let's can the trivia," he said. "You should have taken me when I offered myself to you."

"Oh . . ." Dolores said, surprised off guard, and promptly dribbled a pool of mussel sauce on her new yellow blouse. She plunged the edge of her napkin in her glass of ice water and dabbed compulsively at the stain. She felt Gregory's eyes staring at her fixedly. She looked up. He smiled, enjoying the lack of composure he'd produced. "I should have?" she asked, distractedly. "But you were in a state of unrequited love," she said, recovering, making the term "unrequited love" sound superficial, like a frivolous vacation in the Caribbean. He continued to stare at her, smiling, almost mockingly. "Besides, you told me yourself you were going out with every woman you could lay your hands on after Eve left." ("I do it very well," he'd said, "or at least that's

what they tell me.") Eve had told her that she and Gregory hadn't made love for an entire year. She said it was
something to do with the conjunction of the planet Saturn
with her moon sign and his sun sign, which Dolores
tended to doubt, particularly after Eve raved dramatically,
"I let him strip me of the essence of my womanhood, my
connections to the earth and water!"

"Well, you would have suffered for three months while
I bedded every wench in lower Manhattan for revenge,
and then you would have had me," Gregory said evenly.
She thought she detected a strained note of sincerity beneath his calculated attitude.

"Oh," she said again, that inarticulate, dumbfounded
oh. "But you must be involved with someone else by
now, aren't you?"

"Ah *oui,*" he said. "I guess she's the best friend I have
at the moment . . . but I don't quite know where it's all
going. Sometimes I bother myself about it, and sometimes I don't, but . . ." He let the *but* trail off purposefully.

"But what?" Dolores asked.

"Just a simple *but* . . ." He looked at her meaningfully.

"Do love affairs have to have passports?" Dolores
asked, aware that she was avoiding his eyes, along with
the issue he'd proposed.

He didn't answer. "I think I saw you with her on the
street once," she continued nervously. She could feel
herself circumventing him, edging away, despite her determination to be receptive and available. "A pretty
blonde? A little shorter than Eve?"

"Short and blonde and half female coyote," he stated.

"How is Eve? Do you ever see her anymore?" Dolores
asked. She herself had lost contact with Eve, who had
camped with one friend, then another, then completely

203

disappeared. She never wanted to live with a man again, she'd told Dolores.

"Eve and I were bored with each other," Gregory said. "I didn't see it that way at the time. My ego got the best of me. Now I can look at the situation objectively. . . . You, of course, have more lovers than you can count."

The love affair, Dolores thought, was the topic of conversation that automatically followed "work," as if it were printed on an invisible agenda. "Not a one," she said. "None at all." She observed Gregory's incredulous expression. She liked playing the role of an attractive, could-be femme fatale, who, for reasons unknown, preferred the sanctified grounds of celibacy to the company of men; it gave her mystery. She often told people she had no lovers, even when there were occasional lovers around, then surprised a sudden fear that revelation created in herself. There was no way she could connect other people's certitude that she was admired by men with her own certitude that she was not.

She ate a staggeringly rich chestnut mousse, unnecessarily topped with whipped cream, and felt her stomach press uncomfortably against the walls of her straight skirt. The bill arrived, and Gregory picked it up with the possessive nonchalance of a king bestowing casual favors on a pauper. He took his American Express card out of his wallet. "Shall we have a nightcap?" he asked coolly. He was inviting her up to his place. She agreed. There was something here to settle, and once in his posh, twelve-hundred-dollar-a-month studio, she could settle it, or back out. He took her arm formally, and they strolled, as if they had been cast in a drama that took place on the deck of a ship. In heels she was a bit taller than he was. She looked down at his smooth, shiny red hair. It was impossible to discern the exact shape of his body, always concealed, no matter how snug his trousers or slim-lined his shirts. Once, when she had gone to visit Eve, he had opened the door wearing khaki shorts that revealed legs as round and muscleless as a child's, sprouting curly red adult hairs.

As they walked toward his place they passed DiFiglia's. Dolores deliberately noted the number over the door, "132." "I can't stand that snooty place," she said spitefully.

"Really?" said Gregory. "They have the best Sunday brunch in Manhattan. Caviar omelets, spicy Bloody Marys, warm croissants with gooseberry jam. Definitely three-star. We'll have to go sometime."

"It's an asinine place," she insisted. (How could he think of food after their gluttonous meal?) Then she modulated her voice to an evil hiss. "It represents everything I hate about this pretentious neighborhood."

"Someone who feels like you do robbed them last week," he said. "A real stickup."

"When?" Dolores was jolted.

"The Sunday before last, I think. Wearing a Halloween mask. He threw the bartender on the floor, held a gun on him, and made him take off his trousers. Clever. Vinnie DiFiglia wasn't about to run out into the street after him without any pants. He didn't get much. Apparently he thought the register would be full, but they take their money to a bank drop every few hours, even on the weekend."

"Are you sure it was the Sunday before last?" Dolores asked. That was the day she had waited for Julio Bravo and found the piece of paper with "DiFiglia's, 132" written on it in the space between the couch cushions.

"Quite sure. Why? Do you know a robber who strikes only on the Sabbath?"

"I may," she answered shortly, feeling frightened inside. "Anyway, I'm sorry whoever it was didn't clean out their whole wad and blow the stupid place up!"

Gregory chuckled, but looked at her strangely. "I'm not," he said.

The walls, ceilings, even the floors of Gregory's studio were painted hospital white. He asked her to remove her shoes. Eve had taken her grove of jungle plants with her, and austere, high-tech white tables had replaced them, each lined with pencils, pens, and drawing implements, arranged in meticulously straight formations. A bare, old-fashioned sink, which seemed meant as a decoration, graced the far wall, its curved pipe exposed. Eve had told her it was impossible to wash dishes in this low-slung, useless sculpture, but Gregory had refused to install a less aesthetic, modern version.

He took a bottle of expensive pear brandy, a complete pear preserved within, from the white enamel cabinet. "Poire?" he asked. It tasted like smooth, fine-scented fire, and burned away part of the heavy French meal, which in combination with the news of the DiFiglia robbery, had given Dolores the gastric bloats. They sat facing each other. She felt uneasy. For lack of anything significant to say she whipped her poem out of her bag and read it to Gregory. He listened attentively, obviously concentrating.

Afterward he said, "When I invited you to dinner I intended it as a friendly gesture; but now that I've seen you again, talked to you, and listened to your extraordinary poem, I'm simply overwhelmed by my former passion." His voice was still protectively bemused, allowing her to take his statement seriously, or dismiss it as facetious flattery.

"Well, thank you," Dolores said, in an equally bemused

tone. "I'm always delighted to be the object of profound admiration," and felt an unidentified phobia assault her, as if the moment to take a decisive step that would carry her across a tumultuous, flooded river, thousands of feet below, to presumably safer ground had arrived and she couldn't possibly move to take it; she couldn't even think about her future, or Gregory, because her mind refused to abandon the subject of the robbery, miring her in Julio Bravo. It couldn't have been Julio who held up DiFiglia's, she thought, knowing it could have been, and if it was, she was partially to blame. There were too many coincidences—the Halloween mask, the gun up the ass, the brazen style. Yet coincidences were often deceptive, certainly not proof. She wished she'd asked Gregory if there'd been a description of the robber; now it was too late. He would find her curiosity suspicious; she had already shown too much interest. He knew she knew a criminal after all.

"Unfortunately you have someone else now," she said. Why was she copping out? She forced herself to gaze straight into his eyes, as his face loomed closer until it was hard to distinguish the outlines of his smooth features. His freckled forearm emerged from the sleeve of his shirt and his hand closed over hers, pinning it to the table. He was about to kiss her. She braced herself. His lips were dry and thin, and as they pressed forcefully into hers, she could feel the flakes on their dry surfaces, unnerving excrescences, like bits of shell in a soft-boiled egg. His tongue probed the inside of her mouth purposefully, as if a silent general were commanding, "Flicker! Run it over the inside of her lips!" He had no taste of his own, only the stale remaining essence of mussel sauce and *poire*. He kept on kissing determinedly, even after she had abandoned the whole project and simply posed her mouth inertly, waiting for it to be over. It was, she thought, a sexless, desiccated kiss, impure for its lack of passion. Worse, she could judge it from afar even while she participated. He put his hand abruptly on her breast. Dolores slipped her chest from under his grasp, wishing she could vanish from the scene like a phantom, and distraught, found her first sensual kiss with Julio Bravo had burst back into her awareness with the impact of an explosion; it was almost tangibly on her mouth, its texture, the taste of his saliva. She couldn't shut the sensation off. She stared zombie-like at Gregory's profile. The chrome desk lamp illuminated only the glint of his glasses, which he'd replaced on his face.

"The intellectuals kiss!" he stated. At least he, too, realized their union lacked some necessary ingredient. To escape comfortably, without reproaches, or guilt, she didn't mind being chalked off as a wooden, sexless intellectual herself. Then he held out his hand as if to lead her again to the deck of the ocean liner. "Shall we?"

"Shall we what?"

"Retire to the boudoir?"

She couldn't believe it. "I don't think it's going to work," she said.

He let his hand drop theatrically. "I can tell you think that." He didn't look at her, or really look away; his poise was perfectly established, his emotions controlled. No more agonies for him; he had known, to begin with, that he risked nothing. "You can stay," he said, "or leave. Whatever you prefer."

She jumped up and put on her sweater. She was drunk, she realized, when the room wavered. "I do have to go," she said. "It's late." She looked around frenetically. For what? An alarm clock? He sat calmly at the table, watching her unhinged flutterings with his deliberate smile.

"I have to get up early and get to work," she said. The diligent writer. He nodded curtly. Why was she so befuddled, semiparalyzed with guilt and confusion? Why did she feel like a degenerate, adolescent cockteaser? Nothing earthshaking had transpired. They had made out for a minute; so what? You could kiss a man who had taken you to dinner in an expensive restaurant and not go to bed with him. It wasn't illegal. "It was a great dinner," she said. He stared at her without expression, sitting, spine erect, in the straight-backed chair. "No, really, I enjoyed it," she protested, as if he'd contradicted her, then practically bolted out the door. She'd forgotten her shoes. Humiliated, she came back and put them on. "I'm sorry, Gregory," she muttered, then left, without looking back.

Outside the night was still warm, and people strolled in the streets, despite the late hour, nearly two, said the clock inside a locked store. She turned toward home and bed, where she could sleep, shut it all into oblivion. A nauseating hopelessness settled in the pit of her stomach along with the dregs of the rich meal. Acceptable life partners were clearly denied her by some punitive, mystical spirit that had placed the impetus for rejection in her own body, her own mind, so she could blame not the powers of fate for her unending isolation, but herself.

She walked west for a block, then stopped, turned and walked east. Where was she going? Pacing the streets like a madwoman. What an ego to tell her she should have grabbed him when she had the chance. Such arrogance! She could have had him! Had what? Poor Eve! She tried to focus on Gregory, to condemn him, so she could dismiss her own fatal error; but Julio Bravo, his true image restored, his tough, handsome pirate's face, his smooth muscles and bullet-ridden body, complete with strong thighs, rough hands, penis, even feet, was vividly reestablished on the screen of her mind, larger than life. She was thirty-two and growing older; she would die alone. Everyone died alone, but she would die having been alone her entire life. She was resigned, but she could no longer pretend she didn't care. She looked in the window of DiFiglia's, scrutinized its hot, smoky, untempting crowd, realized she was drawn to this place she theoretically despised, because she wanted to be at the scene of Julio's crime, if, in fact, he had committed it, in order to feel his presence more acutely; sick! She tore herself away and walked inexorably toward the subway, but it was only as she crossed the gray, bleak platform of the Fourteenth Street station to change for the graffiti-scrawled express that she fully realized where she was going—to the South Bronx. She had once asked Julio which subway he took to get to her place. It was this one. His sister's address, the address she'd written on the envelope of the letter she hadn't sent, printing it with painstaking care, as if it were to travel to an obscure foreign country, was inscribed in her memory. She sat numbly on the blue plastic seat, so tired, so out of it, she felt she was dreaming.

210

CHAPTER
15

---

*L*AST night I went to the South Bronx to find Julio
Bravo. There were no logical reasons: An unimpassioned kiss from a man I might love, but can't,
evoking a vision of true passion, provided the suicidal, sex-sick inspiration. I took the subway, rattled
metallically through an endless tunnel, and emerged
on an elevated track into the open night, starless,
depthless as an onyx window, bleeding with red and
green watery flashes of neon lights. I was half asleep,
drunk on wine and brandy, and some deranged fear
of my own inclinations. When I saw the subway stations bore the names of anonymous streets instead of
the usual numbers, I realized I had no idea where I
was going—to Julio Bravo's sister's address, but

---

where was that?—and, in fact, I wasn't sure if I was
in the South Bronx, or some other part of The Bronx,
or in the proverbial Bronx at all. I had only one fellow
passenger, an ageless black woman, whose deathly
tired face in a fluorescent-lighted stream made her
seem a shrunken traveler to the underworld. It was
impossible to invade her ossified reverie to ask directions; I would have had to scream to make my voice
audible over the scraping grind of the subway
wheels, an impossible thought, to confront my own
voice on this nightmare voyage. Finally the old lady
shuffled off the car and I decided to follow, down an
unmoving escalator to the street below. Julio's address repeated itself in my mind—one real fact to
cling to—but I did not feel real enough in this place
to ask where it was.

There was no one to ask. The street was a grave-
yard of desertion. The old woman seemed to vanish
into an invisible Sibyl's cave. It must have been three
in the morning. I walked uncertainly to the corner,
found a street sign there, but so bent and mangled it
was impossible to tell which of the two streets it
named. I didn't know what to do, where to go. The
street was lined with dilapidated burned-out buildings, their lightless windows blinded with boards, or
silver sheets of tin, like the abandoned tenements on
Tenth Street, only hundreds of times more removed
from habitation. Streetlights with smashed globes,
also banged and twisted, hovered over the sidewalk
like crippled metal flamingos. Only one issued a thin
trickle of light, instantly blotted up by the multilay-
ered, porous darkness. Garbage alone populated the
street, a spooky, personified garbage—papers and
cardboard in ghostly shapes, twirling in an unfeelable

hot breeze, mummies of furniture, hulking chairs, hob-
bled, legless chairs, metal bedsprings, soaked mattresses with the stuffing bursting out of wounds in
their coverings, glaring, deactivated stoves, supernat-
urally white in the unilluminated alley, and injured
toilets and tubs, foundering on their sides. I fantas-
ized, or actually saw, living creatures darting from
the corners of my eyes, rainbow-wrapped, like glau-
comic visions; the outlines of a cat scattered, tail up,
into an alley. Beneath my feet a floor of shattered
glass fragments crunched.

I had no idea which way was north, east, south, or
west. I only knew the subway had traveled north. Insane to be in this place. If an iota of my common
sense remained I would have run back to the train
and beat it the hell out of there. But I had already
taken the dangerous mission, no, the lunatic fantasy,
too far. Odd, I could not summon up the compelling
desire for Julio that brought me there, or remember
why I'd wanted to find him. In my mind there was
only a photograph of a tall woman in a fancy blue
skirt picking her way through a garbage-strewn
street, a faceless woman in a dream I could be having
about myself. But I walked on, high-heeling my precarious way through potholes and rotted vegetable
matter, pitted concrete, passing infinite charred, vacant buildings, empty lots, where fires flickered like
cooking fires in jungle villages, and shadowy human
figures crouched. I didn't know where I was going, or
why, only that I moved inexorably toward a deeper
circle, simultaneously photographed by my own
brain. At any moment someone could have robbed,
stabbed, raped, even murdered me, but I was not
really *there* enough or enough myself to be afraid.

213

Then I saw the small boy, seven or twelve, who knows; his startled dark eyes stared at my strange apparition. We both halted in the middle of the devastated street and confronted each other wordlessly. I saw that he held a short, rather innocuous-looking knife, like a penknife; but still I was numbly unafraid. As I stared nervelessly at the knife he let it fall to his side and, black eyes glued to my face, put it in his pocket. Perhaps he planned to mug me, then was so amazed to see such an unlikely figure before him, he changed his mind. He wore the half-wild, unclaimed, ragged presence of a child raised by savage wolves. Whose child was he? Perhaps in some metaphysical sense he was mine. I told him the address I was looking for. He said nothing, and didn't acknowledge my voice. "Can you help me find it?" I asked. "I'll give you some money."

Without a word he turned, jerked his head over his shoulder to signify I should follow, and set off at a half run. I went after him as fast as I could in my teetering shoes, losing sight of him, then catching up again. He loped awkwardly, like a pursued animal, crouching to avoid the eagle's predatory eye, through this garbageland fire jungle. We soon came to a major artery. The ghostlike figures now moved everywhere, registering my presence coolly, noting it reductively, gauging it with deliberately nonreactive eyes. Despite the late hour, small bars, or social clubs, were open; neon signs marked their Spanish names in indelible fuchsia and blue. Bursts of salsa music escaped open doors, then clicked off in the gelid, all-quenching atmosphere of this night, clearly holding the possibility of imminent death-insured action in its tense molecules. Each sound registered in the opaque near-silence. I heard a loud argument. A woman's voice shrieked incomprehensible words. Someone else hoarsely shouted a name, or an imprecation, over and over, an abrupt, broken syllable. A pane of glass shattered its particles to the ground like brittle rain, followed by an unending, monotonous scream exhaled by a siren; the voices stopped.

Down another semideserted street, past more desolate burned-out shells, spaces alight with acrid, shuddering flames, cringing dogs, and at last we stood beside a tomblike modern building. I never expected to find Julio in a project, but hiding out in a collapsing tenement, or the back room of a bodega. The boy stuck to the straggling bushes on the defoliated lawn. I walked to the front entrance where an unwelcoming yellow light burned above the street number of Julio's address. It then occurred to me that it was almost four o'clock in the morning, at least—scarcely the time to pay a visit to anyone. But I had to do it. I turned to the little boy, still observing me with careful, unmoving eyes. "Wait for me here," I whispered. He didn't answer or indicate he understood. So far he hadn't said a word. I entered the vestibule of the building and examined the names on the mailboxes. "Bravo" was written below the name "Martinez" on 6H. "Martinez" must be his sister's married name, I thought. Should I press the buzzer? I noticed then that the main door of the building was unlocked and half ajar. The dingy, beige-tiled hall smelled of piss, like a men's latrine, as did the elevator to the sixth floor, glaring with icy fluorescent lights and unreadable bloody graffiti.

The door of the Bravo residence was marred by kicks and dents, as if some desperate marauder had battered it, or pried at it with sharp tools. I knocked softly. Total silence within. I dismissed all sense of propriety and rang the doorbell, listening, embarrassed, to its loud, disturbing buzz, unable to remember a thing about Julio Bravo, or why I had come there to find him. A question was called in a drowsy, female voice—indistinguishable words. I couldn't find my own voice to answer. I rang again. At last footsteps tramped toward the door and the peephole slid open. An eye appeared behind it. I put my face in its range of vision. "Dolores," I said, and as I uttered my own name I felt the full shame and insane absurdity of standing in that place at that moment. It was too late to run, impossible to disappear. The door jerked open. A thin, dark-skinned woman, drugged with sleep, deep circles under her frankly hostile eyes, swayed toward me, clutching a filthy, torn terry cloth robe to her body. She looked more black than Puerto Rican. A child in the back began to wail. "Shut the fuck up!" she yelled, her voice mean and uncontrolled. A wisp of limp, oily hair fell away from one of its pins. She turned back to me, her face gradually awakening and hardening to the confusion my white, middle-class presence inspired. Her eyes veiled over with suspicion; her mouth set in a malevolent smile. Beyond her rigid body blocking the door I saw a dark hallway, painted an institutional green, its dull, bare wooden floor creased with scratches. A baby stroller, missing a wheel, listed to one side, a dirty stuffed animal beside it.

"I'm sorry to bother you," I said.

She nodded, her face growing progressively antagonized.

"Are you Rosa?" I asked. I was mortified, more so

with each word. Her face spoke curses, such as "Who told you my name, white bitch?" but she just nodded coldly. "I'm a friend of Julio's," I said.

"Julito ain't here," she said quickly.

"My name is Dolores," I went on. "I used to be his teacher at Briarstone." How bizarre—what would a teacher from a prison be doing in the South Bronx looking for a former student at four in the morning? How dishonest, to hide behind my official white status, as if I could have no other, when that was not what brought me there. Why did I do that? Something to think about when I can think again. "I'm sort of worried about him."

She stood there, saying nothing, waiting. Her grim, unsmiling face, I realized, was young, quite beautiful beneath its exhausted expression of fury. There was no sign of recognition, or if my name was familiar to her or not, if she believed me or not, or if she just waited, as she had always waited, for misfortune in the form of white institutions to pass. Various bits of information Julio had told me about his sister came back. She was interested in poetry. ("I want to show you the poetry my sister be writing.") She had said, "Julito, I'm lonely. I need a man." None of this meshed with the angry wall of a face and body at the door.

"He ain't here," she said again. She was obviously not about to reveal any other information. She started to close the door.

"Do you know where he is, or where I could find him?" I asked quickly. I knew she wouldn't answer, knew I'd always known I wouldn't find him here. If I thought I'd find him I wouldn't have come. "I'm afraid he's in trouble," I said.

Her face suddenly unleashed the rage behind its frozen mask. "Lady," she said, "if I knew where that motherfucker was at I'd call the *parole!*" She looked at me a moment with a dim spark of outrage igniting her flat eyes, then shut the door firmly, without slamming it. I heard the lock hinge into place and her bare feet pad back down the hall. It dawned on me then that she might not really be his sister. At that hour, in that unreal place, I had no feelings about that; even now I'm not sure what gear my mind should be in to consider the possibility that she was someone else, the meaning of that deception, if it was one. There was no proof she wasn't his sister, just an intuition I had, possibly hysterical. There is no way I can connect anything I saw or experienced in The Bronx with the Julio I thought I knew.

Outside the little boy was still waiting. The sky was half a degree less black. It must be later, or earlier, than I'd thought. I was suddenly dead tired, tired enough to stretch out on the browned grass and close my eyes; perhaps I would wake up and find myself in my own bed. The boy looked at me with his still eyes. "Are you hungry?" I asked. His expression barely flickered. He was either deaf and dumb, or didn't speak English.

We walked to some kind of all-night restaurant, painted the same soiled institutional green as the corridor of Julio's apartment. Misshapen fried things sat in trays in the window. An old woman brought milk, a bowl of greasy stew, and stale cake. The boy crammed it hungrily in his dirty face. I drank a cup of bitter coffee. A group of Spanish men played dominoes in the corner, silently, except for the tapping of the black pieces on the table. I occasionally felt them

218

give me the discreet, appraising glance, riddled with subterranean hostility, that had registered my presence everywhere. They might have thought I was a social worker.

"What's your name?" I asked the boy, focusing my interest on him, to avoid thinking other thoughts, or asking myself further questions. He continued eating, using animal-like awkward motions to shovel the food into his mouth with his hands. The wrinkled old woman observed us, not unkindly. "Julito," she answered for him, and added some swift, Spanish admonitions to the little boy, who did not look up from his mangy gobbling.

"Julito?" I repeated incredulously, and felt my face produce an ironic smile. When we left the luncheonette I gave the little Julito five dollars, all I had, except the token to get home. He snatched it out of my hand with a squirrel-like rapacious hunger and scampered away. I could see the elevated subway track nearby.

I walked slowly up the long, rusted metal stairway to the platform. In the middle of my climb I suddenly felt dizzy and everything went black. The steps beneath my feet dissolved and I was sure I was falling, the floating, stomachless plunge of a disembodied soul falling down into profound nothing in a nightmare about death. The fall lasted a second, then stopped, and I found my sweating hand still clutching the banister, and my feet stolidly implanted on the metal stairs. I must have almost fainted out of weariness or some consummation of emotional anxiety; but that physiological sensation of falling, dreaming, when I was wide awake and standing upright, conjoined the scattered, abstract fears of the entire night into an immense, tangible panic. I have to confess that breath-stopping, sweating, quaking, all-consuming terror was satisfying somehow; its violent jolt purged the delusion I was not myself and made me understand I was where I wanted to be, and what I had come for. After it subsided I knew, beyond rational knowing, that my presence in this South Bronx infernal world had invoked Julio Bravo, put me in touch with him, and like it or not, for better or worse, live or die, I would soon see him again.

CHAPTER
16

JULIO Bravo returned a week later, as Dolores braced herself to witness the late-afternoon bris of Sophie's son, Gawain, born three weeks ahead of schedule, complete with all limbs, organs, sparse hair, and fingernails. She had gone to inspect the infant in his hospital bed, where he, along with other shriveled specimens, writhed under bright lights, grimacing like a tortured soul forced to reenter the earthly plane. Though Dolores knew what a bris was, she had always thought it a mythological rite, occasionally resurrected in Israeli desert outposts. That Sophie, who had begun a doctoral dissertation on the lives of Christian saints, and often quoted their writings, would initiate her son to the world via this ancient, no-madic ceremony, attested to either her true pagan nature or some fanatic, traditional streak Dolores hadn't realized existed in modern Jews. She was probably just ignorant about Judaism, she thought, absentmindedly opening the door when she heard the knock (but to slice off part of the penis of a newborn child in front of a hip, Soho crowd . . .) and saw Julio Bravo shifting from foot to foot in the hall.

Despite all the loaded images, negative, positive, over-blown and grotesque, she had heaped upon him in her mind, his reality was shocking, if only because he was nothing more or less than himself. He was just a man, wearing a short-sleeved green synthetic knit shirt with a colored decal above the breast pocket, waffled beige pants with a wide belt flap, and the usual sneakers. There was nothing of the South Bronx fires, the bottomless fall, or the lapsed life of burned-out buildings that clung to his strong, clean presence. If anything, he seemed more sub-stantial and wholesome than he had before. His hair was a little shorter and he filled out his own precise outlines with a lush spirit of opulence. He smiled at her, all sexy confidence, grabbed her and bit the sinewy joint that joined her neck and shoulder. She unwittingly inhaled his hot, intoxicating smell, which related more to her confused memory of him than he did himself.

"Where were you?" she accused.

"I missed you, *nene linda*," he said, his rhythmic ac-cents muffled by her neck. "*Coño*, girl, I was missing you a lot."

"You didn't miss me enough to call," she said, hearing at once the false note in her self-righteous fury, attempt-ing ineffectively to push him back. She was too startled by the counterindications of his real presence to emote anger correctly. She was always furious until fury was called for, and then it sputtered and died. "I thought something terrible happened to you! I thought you were back in jail! I went up to The Bronx to look for you!" He was still wrapped around her, squeezing her unyielding waist with his strong hands.

Julio unfolded his rich, mirthful laugh. "Yeahhhh. . . . My sister tole me," he said. "She did not know who you was, my man. She be thinking you was one of them lady detectives."

"It's not funny, Julio. You have no respect for me." Dreary, outraged femininity. How many times had she said or thought these prim, ineffective words in similar situations? "I told your *sister* who I was," she said, emphasizing *sister* with pointed tones she hoped were ironic or nasty.

"There is no one that I respect more than you, *nene.* You know that," he said, lowering himself catlike into her kitchen chair and looking at her directly.

"Why didn't you call me?"

"I *couldn't* call!" he said.

"I notice you don't have any broken fingers." Excellent sarcasm. She went to the mirror, not sure if she was flouncing or stomping, and began putting on her makeup, pretending to ignore him. Her hands were trembling, and the lines around her indignant mouth were set in ugly furrows, like a bitter old woman's. She would rather suffer masochistic tortures, she thought, than play this outraged female role, much less play it badly.

"*Nene,* come here to me," he said.

"Don't try to con me, Julio." Her quavering voice now sounded like a hurt child's. He got up, came behind her, pulled open her pink kimono, and softly began to caress her bare torso. In the mirror she could see his dark hands on the pale breasts she'd never liked, because they were

---

223

too flat and shapeless. His fingers walked down her stomach, then probed the elastic of her underwear.

"I am telling you that I missed you, Dolores."

"I don't accept that," she said. "That's not an explanation. You can't show up here after weeks and weeks, and expect . . ." A spasm of desire, not easily transcended, interrupted her tirade. "Anyway, I have to go to a bris. Right now."

His features, partly visible behind her in the mirror, squeezed together, as if concentrating on a difficult, abstract question. She felt his hard dick swell through his pants against her buttocks. His hands convulsed around her breasts, and his face, lying sideways against her upper arm, eyes open, but unseeing, was expressionless, impersonally steeped in a biological involvement of his own. "Julio . . ." she said, a weak warning, a diminishing no, and she gave it up as false coyness, out of whack with the essence of what was happening. She watched him finger her nipples, her crotch, heard him breathe heavily behind her, saw his hands go to his belt, unfasten it hastily, pull down her bikini underwear, then begin to fuck her intensely from behind, feeling neither desire nor lack of it, vaguely amused by the spectacle they created in her celibate mirror. She was the same wishy-washy boob she'd always been, she thought sadly, a so-called liberated woman who picked the wrong men, then let them walk all over her, do anything they wanted to her, abandon her callously, then fuck her the minute they walked in the door. It was unfortunate to be this kind of woman. She watched her wretched, masochistic self, a self without the moral strength to be either angry, or glad to see him again, get fucked standing up like a broken mare in the mirror, and crouched a little to make it easier for him. His hands roughly pulled her buttocks toward his body. She wondered if Julio himself judged her a spineless creature he had thoroughly conned then bent to his will. His face was still crumpled into some private absorption with the sex itself, or something else, who knows. No, she thought, still being fucked, he did not look at the situation from her middle-class viewpoint. He could love her and abandon her and return when he wanted; to him, no doubt, this was the role women were supposed to play, had always played. He had probably treated every woman he had ever known the same.

After he came he still held her. "I went into a slump, Dolores," he said.

"What kind of slump?" she asked quickly, still watching the two of them in the mirror.

He let go of her and sat down again, lit a cigarette, and gazed at the smoke with worried eyes. "You look good to me, *niña,*" he said listlessly, but he wasn't looking at her. "*Real* good!" That's what he'd said when he'd first gotten out of jail, she recalled; it was probably a stock line, delivered now, without enthusiasm. It was getting late; she'd miss the bris.

"Why won't you talk to me?" she asked. She didn't feel angry anymore.

"I will talk," he said, "but not now."

She put on her dress and he followed her out the door, obviously preoccupied. He turned when she did and continued up the block. It seemed he was coming with her, uninvited. "Do you know what a bris is?" she asked. "A Jewish circumcision ceremony. A friend of mine just had a baby boy."

"In Cabo Rojo," he said, "there was this dude who circumcised hisself . . . wit' a knife, my man." He made a violent, hacking gesture with his hand. "They put him in jail for that, man, because they said any dude who

225

could do that to hisself could kill somebody. I knew a dude who had to have it done like that when he was already growed. He went into the hospital. After that he did not have no feeling in his dick. He said to me, 'Julito, I don't feel nothing no more!' He was crying like a baby, that sorry motherfucker.'' He laughed, but his mood was not gay, rendering the laugh dry, almost ominous. He repeated the punch line, " 'I don't feel nothin', Julito. . . .' "

They were going to pass DiFiglia's, Dolores realized, remembering. She could see the chic bar looming closer at the end of the block. Should she ask him, straight out, if he had robbed it? Or take him by surprise and tell him she knew he had? She looked at him intently to see if his expression had changed, if he noticed the bar, or looked deliberately away. No, he was merely walking, a slightly dispirited version of his usual toe-heel salsa bounce, and did not seem to be looking at anything in particular, or struggling with a guilt-ridden conscience. "Dolores," he said, "I blew my parole."

"What does that mean?" she asked.

He didn't answer. "Is that Vincent DiFiglia?" he asked instead, looking up at the sign over the bar.

"I don't know," she said carefully. "Whoever it is is pure Mafia though."

"He is definitely Mafia," Julio said. "I was up in Corsica wit' Vince, my man. Do you know they let that cocksucker leave the joint once a month to go to the dentist? They be coming to get him in a big Continental wit' a dome on the top. That is against prison regulations, Dolores . . . to go to the dentist outside the walls. That was not no dentist he was going to. When he be coming back we was all asking him, 'How is your teeth, *maricón*?' but nobody said nothin' to the hacks. Nobody wanted to dry snitch on the family, man." They walked a few steps in silence. "Maybe he went to the dentist, that *pendejo*, but he was taking care of other shit at the same time. He took care of business from the joint, my man."

"You could drop in and say hello," she said, watching his reaction, testing him.

He laughed. "*Coño*, I want to walk to the end of this block alive," he said enigmatically.

"What are you laughing for?" she asked. "Your situation doesn't sound particularly funny to me. What do you mean you blew your parole? Are the cops after you?"

"Don't say no more about it now, Dolores." His voice was suddenly earnest in its warning, a voice that said, "Don't give me any shit, bitch!" Dolores abandoned her plan to accuse him of the robbery. He would never offer an easily deciphered reply; he was too smart for that. His very life had depended on him being smart like that. Would he be walking calmly past a place he had just held up? Wouldn't he be afraid someone would come out and spot him? No, he (or the robber) had been wearing a Halloween mask, Gregory said. On the other hand, he might deliberately walk by as cool as could be, to allay her suspicions, if he thought she had any. If she let on she knew, or said she thought he'd committed the crime, it might mean trouble for her, she thought, with a negative chill. Even if he hadn't done it, he would think she no longer believed in him, didn't trust him. . . . She gave it up. She might be thinking such thoughts because she needed an excuse to avoid accusing him, not because she was afraid of the consequences, but because she didn't want to know. He had already told her he had "blown his parole." Did that mean he was back into crime, or only that he hadn't reported to the parole board? They rode the elevator to Sophie's loft in silence.

The bris had not yet begun. Dolores entered the noisy afternoon party with Julio in tow, suddenly aware she was about to bring the secret, obsessive side of her life into direct collision with her sane, middle-class existence, and the pleasant, ordinary friends who created it. She registered, or imagined, a nearly audible halt in all conversation, a collective intake of breath that drowned out the music on the stereo. Thankfully, most of the faces were not familiar. Not everybody here knew her, or would think it highly astonishing that a woman had entered with a Latin man. You couldn't, she thought, tell he was an ex-con by looking at him.

Julio stood beside her, unselfconsciously surveying the scene, hands on his hips. She noticed again, as if for the first time, the sinister black tarantula on his wrist, the muscular power of his fluid body, the smooth tawniness of his skin and carved features. It was she, she realized, and she alone who was staring at him transfixed. He was undeniably beautiful; in this room filled with pale, bland faces, he was as exotic as a sinuous wild leopard in a cage of house cats. She was amazed that nobody had rushed over to admire him, to touch him with a fearful, tempted hand; she could barely keep from stroking him herself.

Joanna was the first to greet them. "Julio Bravo, I presume," she said in a loud, deliberately jovial voice. She did not look at Dolores.

"*Sí!*" Julio said. "Call me Julito." He smiled his wicked pirate's smile.

"This is Joanna, one of my closest friends," Dolores put in hastily.

Joanna pointedly ignored her. "Okay, Who-leeto," she said, pronouncing the *ito* somehow wrongly. "I'm real glad to meet cha." She was being her brusque, cowgirl self, though there was something contrived in her manner, as if she were determined to preserve her personality in a foreign land. "Welcome to the whacking off!"

Julio loved that. "The whacking off!" he repeated, laughing his I-caught-you-saying-something-you-weren't-supposed-to-say laugh. "Yeahhhh . . ." he said, "they are gonna take it off. My people don't do that shit, my man. We are pure Carib. Los Indios don't do none of that shit to their sons."

"He's a cutie!" Joanna said loudly to Dolores, giving Julio an openly salacious wink. Dolores noticed she was wearing a gorgeous new silk camisole, with exquisite lace at the top. Ordinarily she would have commented on it jealously, saying, as they always did to each other, "Why didn't you get one for *me*?" but she didn't want Julio to know that side of her, her avaricious, clothes-hungry self. On the other hand, she couldn't very well ask Julio if he'd held up DiFiglia's in front of Joanna, or discuss his parole problems, or play social worker, or grab him, or deal with him in any familiar way. Between her friend and her inappropriate lover she was stripped of words; the separate identities she had achieved with each of them were now completely null and void, leaving her with none. She stood awkwardly.

"You are the first fe-male to call me *cute*," Julio said. He cracked his knuckles noisily and looked around. "This is one beautiful crib," he exclaimed. "*Linda*, my man!" Sophie's elegant loft, left her as a kind of divorce settlement by a former lover, the Russian painter, who had mysteriously absconded for Morocco, never to return, was jammed with antique curios, books, Oriental carpets, and hung with the lover's youthful masterpieces.

Sophie emerged from the bedroom. She was still pale from the birth process, and her body, minus its firm, planet container, had deflated into a series of bloated folds, which hung loosely around her once trim form. It was horrible, what had happened to her body, Dolores thought, eyeing it with perverse fascination. "This must be Julio," Sophie said, in her warmest voice. "Marvelous! She was worried about you," she said, turning toward him.

"I have been worried about myself, my man," he replied.

"How's the *petit*?" Dolores asked.

Sophie's expression changed at once. "He isn't eating," she said dramatically. Her tone summarized the tragedy of world starvation. "I put him to my breast and he does not suck."

"*Vaya*, you got to put some sugar water in a bottle and give it to him," Julio advised. "First rub it on his lips so he gets the taste. That is what my first wife was giving to my son when he wouldn't take the tit."

Sophie smiled vaguely. "Oh, I do not think so," she said, "not white sugar!" Whereas once he would have interested her, now he did not; no one could. Absent-mindedly she turned to another guest who ran up, crying, "Darling, you look fantastic! Only six hours! You were so lucky!"

"I would not be eating nothing neither if somebody was going to whack off my dick," Julio said while Sophie was still in earshot. Dolores cringed.

Joanna chortled. They were getting along fine.

"I saw the little bugger," Joanna said. "There wasn't much there to whack off as far as I could tell." A friend pulled her arm and she, too, turned away; Dolores soon heard the names of galleries, grants, and other artists. Apparently there was nothing about Julio Bravo that stopped anyone but her in his tracks or halted social wheels in their relentless turnings.

"I like that chick Joanna," Julio said. "She is all right, my man."

"What do you mean you blew your parole?" Dolores asked again, knowing she wasn't supposed to ask, but what other dialogue in their history of words was adapted to this place, or to this almost normal "date" they were having?

"I can not tell you that here, niña," he said patiently. He poured himself a glass of wine, eyeing the guests carefully.

A crowd formed near the door of the bedroom where the circumcision was about to begin. Dolores recognized some of the guests from Sophie's prepregnant parties, initially subdued affairs, which inevitably erupted into passionate gorging, arguing, and dancing. These friends now milled a little awkwardly around the bedroom door, wearing cleaner clothes than usual, clearly unsure how they should behave or what they should say. They nodded, almost embarrassed, at one another. The bris, however, seemed to have brought forth mainly relatives, who shrieked and bustled like enthusiastic proprietors. Dolores had never thought of Sophie as a person with relatives. Everyone was swilling large quantities of brandy and wine, stuffing down cold cuts, Italian cookies, and nuts. Dolores heard a voice say, "Do you know it's traditionally forbidden to drink alcohol until after the ceremony." "Too late now!" another voice cried.

Dolores elbowed her way firmly to the door. A poet should see all. The small infant lay on its back on a table, its face and torso a virulent, strawberry red. It cried softly, drawing its sausagey legs up protectively around its

231

minute penis. Sophie stood, back to the wall, outside the bedroom, staring, with catatonic determination, into space. "Don't worry," Dolores said nonsensically, unequipped to provide comfort at this moment she did not understand. Sophie didn't seem to hear. "It'll be all right," she persisted, feeling foolish.

The confusion pressed and babbled around the door. "Did they do it yet?" someone asked. "Let me see."

"I want to see," the child of one of the relatives whined.

"No, sweetheart," her mother said.

"Why don't they bring him out here!" a baritone voice boomed.

One of Sophie's cousins, a gangly young man wearing a *yarmulke*, stood at the baby's head and held him down, pressing his small arms firmly into the table. The tall, pink-faced rabbi repeated mechanical prayers in Hebrew, simultaneously preparing metal instruments and giving instructions to Sophie's lover, who also hovered anxiously over the table. An old man, apparently an uncle, wearing a *yarmulke* too, swooped down on the process with a camera. "No, Moishe!" Sophie said. "No photographs! Not until later!" She spoke loudly and distinctly, as if to a child who refused to understand. Dolores looked at Sophie. "Why not?" she asked, but Sophie didn't answer, possibly didn't hear. She had risen to a plateau earthbound voices did not reach; as she made her son a Jew, she became her own medieval saint, Dolores thought, provoked.

Julio had poured himself a water glass of brandy and stood beside her now, gulping it down rapidly. "*Una fiesta!*" he said loudly, over the chant of Hebrew prayers. "A whacking-off fiesta!" There were glances. "Shhhhhhhh," someone said. Dolores was mortified, by

Julio, but more by the jerk who dared to shush him. He might be crude, but he was right.

Sophie's lover still twitched in the inner sanctum, mopping his sweating forehead with a clean Pamper. He handed things to the rabbi with shaking hands. The old man again plunged toward the door with his camera. "No, Moishe!" Sophie admonished. "No flashbulbs! Wait! Please!"

The child had begun to scream loudly and continuously, its wizened face growing unbelievably red, as if all the blood in its body was about to burst through its skin in geysers. The screaming, though feeble in actual volume, seemed to obliterate all other sounds with sheer, persistent intensity. It was completely unnerving, that relentless, ear-piercing scream. Dolores craned her neck and got a clear look at the knife; no, not a knife, exactly, but a sort of corkscrew. The rabbi picked it up and lowered it majestically toward the infant's body. When it made contact with its flesh, Dolores closed her eyes, shuddered, and involuntarily pressed her hands to her ears. *"Baruch atoh adonai elohainu,"* she heard the moyel chant. "All finished! *Mazeltov!"* Dolores opened her eyes and looked back into the room. The smiling rabbi lifted the still screaming infant high into the air. One of his hands was rigid and clenched, frozen by a spasm of shock. His scream cut off in midgasp, and he fell completely silent. He seemed to have passed out, though his tiny eyes were still open. "All done!" Sophie's aborigine lover sang. He was elated and smiling. "All fin-ished!" Sophie tore into the room and snatched the baby. There was something deranged about the way she ran to him, Dolores thought, as if she were not conscious of herself running, awkwardly tripping over the rug, as if nothing, not space, not time, not even her own body stood between her and possession of her child, which she now clutched tightly to her breast, whispering and crooning. It was as if she were no longer herself, but an infant's attachment.

"I saw it," Julio said loudly, excitedly. His eyes were bloodshot and his face noticeably paler. "I saw it, man! The whole thing!"

"We have to shut the door now," Sophie said firmly. She was afraid of germs; the child might contract a flu.

Adelaide, one of Sophie's best friends, said, sotto voce, "This is ridiculous! I cannot tell you how many bris I saw in Israel. You are supposed to cheer and pass the child around, to celebrate. Either you do it that way or you don't do it at all."

Joanna said to Julio, "Well, now that they whacked it off they can start teaching him how to use it!"

Julio was pacing and drinking, smiling and frowning convulsively. "Yeah . . ." he said. "I saw it, my man," he repeated. "I saw them cut it off!" There was a kind of flipped-out, uncontrolled terror in his voice.

"Julio . . ." Dolores asked. "Are you okay?" She touched his arm. The tight skin was hot.

The jovial moyel, now in street clothes, came to the dining room table and began passing out his business cards. There was relieved laughter and jokes. "Do you circumcize daughters?" someone asked, and everyone roared. Adelaide lit a joint and passed it to Dolores.

"You never know," a notoriously gay friend of Sophie's said, pocketing a card.

Dolores was still shaken, not by the brief operation itself, which she hadn't actually seen, but by the child's stiffened hand, its inflamed redness, its screaming, its sudden suffocated silence. It was incredible, she thought. After no alcohol, sugar, or coffee during pregnancy, after

234

amniocentesis, after Lamaze breathing exercises, after natural childbirth without anesthesia, after the perfect nursing environment—out came the knife! It was incredible that everyone here, except Julio, who had probably shot people in cold blood, accepted this brutal, primitive initiation as nothing more or less than a time-honored, sanctified celebration. All these middle-class penis cutters could drink, laugh, and joke, but not a one of them could question what they had just seen (or not seen, since nobody but Julio had looked). That was religion! As long as it was *your* religion it was beyond reproach.

"They whacked it off," Julio said. He was drawing provoked stares. "Yeah, man . . . *whacked*! Before they cut it they put a little metal thing in there, man, like a bell. When they pulled back the skin it was purple underneath, like a dog's dick." Someone laughed uncomfortably. "I did not see no blood," he continued compulsively. "Just a little dab. That wasn't no knife either. It was like a knife, but it was not no knife."

"There is something horrible about it," Dolores whispered to Joanna, who was listening to Julio with obvious amusement, "to symbolically attack a man's malehood in the name of God." Her voice grew louder in spite of herself. "Isn't it saying, 'Forget about your dick and think about religion?' I wouldn't do that to any kid of mine."

"Oh, I don't know . . ." Joanna answered. "It's supposed to be cleaner or something. I'm sure glad Tommy has all of his though. The first time I saw the little beauty I said, 'Now what the hell am I supposed to do with *this*?' Then I figured it allllll out." She made unmistakable pulling and wriggling motions with her fingers. " 'Boy oh boy,' I said to myself, 'there's a lot more here to play with!' "

"Why is it supposed to be cleaner?" Dolores asked.

"Isn't it very old-fashioned, to do it in public like this?"

"There was a dude in Puerto Rico," Dolores heard Julio's voice behind her, pronouncing *Puerto Rico* with authentic rolling *r*'s, "who circumcised hisself with a kitchen knife. Cut off his own thing, my man. They put him in jail for that, because they said any dude who could do that to hisself could kill somebody." A middle-aged woman with obviously hennaed hair was looking at Julio as if she had just seen a mastodon.

"Is everything okay?" Joanna asked significantly.

"I guess so," Dolores answered. "It's a long story. I was going to tell you, but . . ."

"I like him," Joanna said quickly, almost anxiously, and Dolores saw that she was lying, or if not exactly telling untruths, using the innocuous, all-approving word *like* when she meant something different, meant, perhaps, that she understood Julio as a source of fervent passion and liked, not him, but the idea of that. She could misrepresent her approval, even to herself, in the name of a friendship she had missed sorely, missed more than Dolores, in her ingrained, resolute isolation ever could. Dolores felt tearful, and put an awkward hand on Joanna's shoulder.

"Well, he's not circumcised either," she said, and realized that she cooperated with the lie by trivializing the passion that drew her to Julio, a passion now too warped, too ingrown and convoluted to explain, in order to apologize.

When they left she felt stares follow them. Julio had made a complete spectacle out of himself. She could almost hear the outraged gossip begin behind them. "Who was that *creep*? What is an attractive woman like her doing with *him*?" And her friends would say gravely, "She has a lot of problems." They rode down in the ele-

236

vator. Julio was smoking nervously. "Shit, man," he said. "That was heavy fucking shit. How can that baby's own *mamí* and *papí* do that to him? What is that poor sucker going to say when he is growed and looks at his johnson? He is going to say, 'Fuck it, my man. I did not have no *choice* about that.' Some bad plexes are going to come down in that little boy's head behind that."

"It's their religion," Dolores said lamely. "It may seem barbaric to you and me but they've been doing it for centuries. The Muslims do it too. It's supposed to be cleaner. Actually, they circumcise every boy baby born in an American hospital whether he's Jewish or not, unless the parents sign a special paper saying they can't."

"I can not believe that, Dolores," Julio said.

CHAPTER
17

*B*ACK at her place Julio paced the floor. He cracked his knuckles, lit cigarettes and let them burn down in the ashtrays. He sat down and got up again. He made a phone call, hitting his fist on the tabletop while he listened to repetitions of the ring. Apparently no one answered. He slammed down the receiver and went to the toilet. He seemed totally off the wall, possessed by a ferocious anxiety, unleashed by the bris, or all the booze he'd gulped down. Dolores vowed she would not ask any more questions, but she followed him from room to room, standing in the doorway, waiting, hands cold, her stomach stitching itself into a tight pocket. He turned on the radio and dialed it rapidly through transformations of music and static to the Latin station. A loud, mournful Spanish ballad, *"Túuuuuuuu . . . Eres tú . . ."* immediately created its annoying ambience. "I can't dance," he said tensely, as if someone had asked him. "No way. When I be taking a girl to the club she was asking me, 'Julito, why don't you want to get down wit' me?' 'Because I will make you look *bad, nene,*' I said to her. 'You should be dancing with someone who will make you look *good.*'" He looked at Dolores with distracted, bloodshot eyes, as if registering for the first time that she was there. He showed no sign of leaving for the South Bronx, as he always had before in the evening.

Finally he seized her and maneuvered her to the bed, lay on top of her, pressing his clothed torso ungently into hers, got up, unbelted his pants, then flopped back down on his back and lay staring at the ceiling. "NOOOOTI-CIAS!" the radio sang cheerfully, then melodically repeated, *"Noticias! Noticias! Noticias!"* The announcer's voice followed, a macho baritone, delivering its fast, rhythmic news. Julio grew more agitated. He got up, exhaled noisily, dug a joint out of his pants pocket, then lay down again. The ashes dropped to his chest. He pulled insistently on the skin of his limp penis, like a young child, unaware of what he was doing. Fearfully she put her hand on his arm, some desire to calm him, and felt a volatile electricity moving beneath his skin, a scary, twitching current in her palm.

"I blew my parole, man . . ." he said, in a different way than he had before, quietly, as if he were telling himself a sad truth he didn't quite believe. Once he'd spoken he seemed calmer. She waited for him to go on, increasing the pressure on his forearm.

"I was out in Connecticut," he continued. "I was with some people that I know. A couple of homeboys." Her

239

first feeling was illogical relief. If he'd been in Connecticut he couldn't have robbed DiFiglia's.

"I thought you were looking for a job," she said flatly, unable to locate her emphatic, social worker's scolding voice in her nervous throat, in the dynamic she felt missing between them.

"I *was* trying to get a job, Dolores. *Tú saba.* I tried!"

"What happened to the boiler school?" she asked in the same dull voice. "That federal program?"

"I went down there," he said. "One day. They was going to teach me to fix the fucking boilers, man. I had signed up to be a super-visor, to *watch* the dudes that be fixing the boilers. That *pingú* who be running that program put out a wire on that job, my man."

She honestly couldn't blame him for not wanting to fix boilers, she thought, or to be anywhere near boilers for that matter. Why should she pretend to want something for him she couldn't want for any other interesting person she cared for? Just because it was a job? Because it was straight? "So you didn't report?" she asked, thinking, yes, he still could have robbed DiFiglia's.

He waited before answering. "Naw . . ."

"What will they do to you if they catch you?"

"They ain't going to catch me, Dolores," he said. "They won't do nothin', man. They will put me back in the penitentiary on a parole violation. A three months' bid . . . maybe six months. I have not committed no crimes that they know about."

It came out in spite of her, before she could tell herself she didn't want to know. "What crimes *did* you commit?"

"I cannot tell you that, *niña*. That is not wit' you." He paused, then conciliated. "I did a little juggling, that's all. I didn't put no one in the ground."

"Maybe you could think up an excuse," she said, "tell

them you went upstate looking for a job, and you got sick." Maybe, she thought, she could ask a friend of hers who lived near Syracuse to write a letter, saying he'd been there. No, that wasn't fair, to get other people involved. It was his problem; she had to remember that.

"I thought about that," he said. "I thought about it good. But what if it don't work, my man? I do not want to go back to jail, Dolores; *vaya,* not for three months, not for one day, not even for *una hora.* I will die before I go back to jail." He sat up on the edge of the bed, his back to her. "I have already spent too much of my life in jail. Dig it, I was in a hotel room up in Connecticut, man, waiting for my partners to come down, and I be going out and buying canned food, sardines, and like that, and lining up the cans in my window, just like I was doing at Briarstone. One day I looked at them cans and I said, 'Julito, you have spent too much *time* in the jails, *hombre.* Dig it, the jail be in your head, now, even when you are not *in* the jail.' We was riding on them roads up in Connecticut. Those are beautiful roads, Dolores, *linda.* They put Borinquen into my mind. I be looking at all them nice trees, them lakes, man, them purple bushes that be smelling like per-fume. Beautiful, my man! I seen lawns and flowers and kids playing baseball and shit, and I said, 'This is one fucking beautiful country. You do not know nothing about this country, my man. *Nada!* You do not know shit. You only know about hustling, and cement, and con-crete and metal bars. You do not know nothing about *la vida,* Julito.' "

The radio was now blasting an emphatic cha-cha. She wanted to keep touching him, to put her hand on his dejected back, now that he had removed his arm, but sensed he didn't want her to, or wouldn't feel it. "So why didn't you stay out of trouble, then?" *Out of trouble;*

so Protestant and medicinal. "You could have gotten a job. You had a lot of contacts. You didn't really try! I don't think you even wanted a job, Julio." She waited for him to reply, but he remained silent. She sat up and leaned over, looking into his face. "It doesn't make any sense! You blew it, knowing what you just told me!"

"I know it do not make no sense." He dug the heel of his hand into his perspiring forehead and pressed it up toward his hairline.

"You're completely self-destructive. I don't—"

"Dolores," he said. "When I was fifteen years old and putting narcotics into my arm, I knew back then I was wanting to destroy myself. It don't come from my mind, man. I do not know why it be like that with me."

She sat very still, looking at him carefully. She felt like an audience, watching a tragic drama. She supposed she understood him at last, and that understanding itself carried her farther away from him by the minute, like an invisible train.

"I was thinking, Dolores," he said, "that I can buff out of New York. I can go out to Vegas, where I have people, and open my bar."

"They could arrest you out there, too, couldn't they?"

"I can get my man to make me a fake ID," he said. ". . . But I can not go out there stone broke with nothin' in my pocket, because those people will be saying, 'Julito came out here with nothing. He is going to look for trouble here.' "

She waited. He was definitely moving farther and farther away.

"I know about a sting I can pull where I could pick up thirty grand," he said quickly. "Pick it up easy, man. It is a big place, but I know the layout, because Rosa was working there for a while. I know what my cut would be. I be talking to these dudes, telling them this way to go in there, that way to do the thing. 'You are *loco, hombre,*' they was saying to me. 'You are one crazy motherfucker, Julito. What you are talking about is dying.' We was playing six-card stud. That is like poker, Dolores. I said, 'Listen, my man. Whether you are going for a lot or a little, the same card comes up if you got it.' "

"That's ridiculous!" she said. "Why don't you go for a couple of million. Hold up an armored truck, or something, if you're going to risk your freedom, your so-called *vida* for money. . . . Maybe you could buy your way into Paraguay. Thirty thousand bucks is peanuts!"

He took her seriously. "I ain't ready for Paraguay," he said.

"What is it, Julio?" she asked. He was lost to her, that was certain; the sad gulf widened between them. "What is it? The excitement, the money, the revolution? If you had to pin it down to one thing, what . . . ?"

"It ain't none of them things, Dolores," he said. "It is just what I do."

She registered that silently, then said, "I think you should turn yourself into the parole." Her voice grew convincing again. "You could do a few months, like you said. Then you'd be free again. You could start all over, fresh. You'd have time to cool out in there, think things over. Why not? There's no way for you to go forward now from your present situation. They're bound to arrest you sooner or later. The parole board would find out if you started working, wouldn't they?" She couldn't get rid of the job idea. That was all she could find to preach about, a dreary, menial salvation, though he had just told her, more or less, that was not an option for him, probably never had been.

243

"Three months in the joint can turn into three years," he said. "One of the Corsica brothers, he was in on a parole violation, man, for driving without no license or some shit like that. He was the first to die when the troopers came in. One of the first."

"RADIO WADO," the radio sang, "W . . . A . . . D . . . O." A rapid, jingling commercial followed. She thought for a minute, consciously judging and premeditating her next sentence, considering its final point-of-no-return consequences. She knew she had to say it. "I can't . . . be with you if you're an outlaw." As soon as the words left her reluctant mouth she knew they were the truth. They resounded with the full, righteous tone of the no-nonsense truth.

"Outlaw?" His worried face smiled. *"Outlaw!"* he repeated. He laughed his I-caught-you laugh.

"It was one thing when you got out of jail and swore to me . . ." she went on incoherently. "Now it's all different. It's desperate. Now it's a lie. I never said I would . . ." In these half-definite sentences she barely wanted to say she was giving him up, finally and forever. When she finished he would leave and be gone. She felt miserable now, not so much for herself as for him, his terrible plight, which no longer seemed to her romantic, Jesse James or Robin Hood, only pathetic and defeated. Once he was gone she would begin to recover; she would learn from this. There was nothing she could do to help him now. She was surprised by her clear, uncomplicated desire to protect herself, to get out of it. When the chips were down she was not so self-destructive after all.

"I can not go back to The Bronx right now," he said.

"Because of the parole? Isn't there anywhere you can stay besides your sister's?" He would be gone, as if she had dreamed him; she would close her eyes as he walked out the door and open them to find him absent from her life, and soon, her mind.

"It ain't only the parole I am worried about," he said ominously.

What did that mean? That someone else was after him? She looked at him. He was studying his fingernails. She began a stammering question, but didn't finish it. "Then it's dangerous for me to know you," she said, "to have you in my apartment."

"I swear to you no one will ever hurt you while I am here, Dolores."

"Julio, you can't stay here!" She heard the panic rise in her voice, high-pitched and quaking, despite her desire to sound firm, mature, in charge.

"I don't have nowhere else to go, *nene*," he said quietly, as if explaining a basic fact to an impatient child. ". . . until I split for Vegas," he added.

CHAPTER
18

*F*INALLY Dolores went to bed, leaving Julio pacing before the faded voice and blurred image of her ancient television with the dying tube. She had been watching him pace and twitch for hours, interrupting his frantic self-absorption only to make continual, frustrated calls to someone who never answered the phone. When she tried to talk to him he shot her a bleary, uncoordinated glance, or answered monosyllabically, as if unwilling to be reminded she was there. It was getting on her nerves. She gave up, lay down, and fell into an unconscious stupor that passed for sleep.

In the morning she awoke, already sweating in the humid light that pierced the blinds, then remembered the problem that engulfed her. Where was Julio? She walked into the kitchen and found him sitting at the round maple table, cleaning a black gun. He must have had it on him, or brought it in a paper bag, concealed in his clothes, or maybe he had gone out last night and acquired it. He didn't look up, merely tensed beneath the unhappy scrutiny of her eyes; he butted out a cigarette in the overflowing ashtray, and continued work.

"How nice!" she exclaimed, strident sarcasm concealing her fear. "A lovely gun!" He didn't answer. "Shall I direct you to the nearest bank? Or perhaps you'd prefer a grocery store?"

"Yeahhhh . . ." he said absentmindedly, not in affirmation. The small screwdriver from her bike-repair kit, a pencil, some Q-Tips, her spot remover, and a small can of 3 in 1 oil he must have had with him were set precisely on the table. He had gotten one of her demolished T-shirts out of the rag closet and cut it into small squares. As she watched he pushed something on the gun, and it seemed to spring apart in his hands. She had never before meditated on the significance of guns, but if she had she would not have imagined them possessing this tangible aura of imminent evil possibility.

"Where did you get it?" she asked. No reply. He took one of the cotton squares, soaked it in spot remover, wrapped it around the end of the screwdriver, and began plunging this contraption into the narrow cylinder. In spite of her repugnance she couldn't help watching with a glued fascination. His hands manipulated the gun with a basic, masterful assurance, as if they had come to the thing, the operation, to which they decidedly belonged.

"Is it loaded?" she asked tremulously.

"You cannot clean a gun when it is loaded, Dolores," he said, without looking at her.

"Did you get it from Vinnie DiFiglia?" she asked,

thinking that was the key; he had not robbed DiFiglia's, but he had used his underworld contacts there. A muscle in his face twitched, but he didn't answer. She had only seen guns gripped by cowboys and gangsters in movies or idiot TV shows, or displayed inanimately behind protective glass cases in dull museums. Even the gun in his crazy stories had seemed an appropriate dramatic prop, never real. "I never saw a gun before," she volunteered, then chattered, "I mean, not this close, not where I could touch it." What she meant, she thought, was that she had never seen a gun in the hands of anyone she knew, anyone who wanted to use it. He remained silent. The gun absorbed his entire attention; he had brought the full weight of his male focus upon it, as she'd seen other men focus on football games, beer, or a game of chess. It was an obliterating, obsessive focus she had never understood. She had always felt finessed by it. She wondered where the bullets were, if they were in his pocket, or if he didn't have any yet.

"This is ridiculous!" she said loudly, sinking down into the other chair. She watched him press a button near the base of the handle and remove a square-shaped hollow chamber.

"Is that where you put the bullets?" she asked.

"That is the clip," he replied, in a voice that notified her he didn't much like these questions; she was hassling him. He was working inside the main part of the weapon with a Q-Tip.

She thought she'd better shut up, ignore him, go into the bedroom and wait for him to leave. Eventually he would have to leave; he couldn't stay here forever. Yet something held her to him, to this gun, to the tension between them. She didn't have the slightest idea what one said on the subject of guns, she thought, realizing she was tempted to abandon her boring moral stance and find out everything about it, especially what he was thinking and what he was planning to do. He had begun polishing the blue-black metal with a cloth, tenderly, deliberately. It was like a scene from a book or movie that thrills precisely because you know it could never happen to you—a desperate convict on the run, cleaning a gun at a middle-class poet's kitchen table. She could imagine telling it, an excellent story, to her delighted friends sometime in the future when it would all be over. *And then I walked out of the bedroom and found him cleaning a gun.*

He glanced up, his eyes neither cold, nor warm, nor communicative. "You are looking at me like a child," he said.

"You are a child," she replied, "a bad little boy who thinks he's the Lone Ranger."

"No," he said, "I mean you got the eyes of a child. Sometimes you be looking at me scared, *real* scared. Other times it is like you are trying to be friendly, and then you are just spaced out."

"Well, what do you expect?" she asked. "It's not every day someone cleans a Colt .45 at my kitchen table." Miserably cute.

"It ain't a Colt," he said cautiously. "It is a Beretta." He picked up the gun, compact and reassembled in his hand, and tossed it a few inches in the air, letting its weight fall back into his palm with a solid, audible plop. "This is a beautiful piece, Dolores. This is a beautiful Eye-talian gun, my man. *Mira,* it looks like a small gun, but it is powerful. I could hit a penny across the room with this gun."

"Wonderful!" she exclaimed.

He held it up, squinted his eye, and aimed the barrel

at an invisible spot outside the window. She flinched, but he did not squeeze the trigger. Maybe that meant it was loaded now, though she guessed she would have noticed if he'd loaded it. "Every time you squeeze the trigger another bullet goes into the chamber," he explained. "That is why they be calling it an automatic." He sat down and continued polishing.

"I see someone's time has come," she commented.

"Dolores," he said. "What happens, happens."

"I used to believe that, before I met you." She waited to see if he'd respond. He polished with complete concentration. His passionate rapport with this diabolical piece of metal excluded her. She went on, "Now I think there are some people who make their own fate and blame it on everything and everyone but themselves." She sensed that he cringed, if ever so slightly, when she spoke; he was not immune to her opinion.

"Things fall apart; the center cannot hold; Mere anarchy is loosed upon the world," she quoted. "The blood-dimmed tide is loosed . . ."

He put down the gun and gripped the edge of the table. "Sometimes you keep that mouth of yours running, Dolores . . ."

"You could obviously use a little poetry right now," she commented, hearing the anger in her voice respond to the anger in his. Yes, she was angry; she ought to be. He had no right to be here, in her apartment, with this gun; he was taking advantage of her. "So what are you going to do?" she asked him. He pressed the clip back into the gun and laid it carefully on the table, without answering.

"You don't trust me anymore?" she asked.

"It is not that I don't trust you. It is that this is not wit' you."

"It is too *wit'* me," she said, imitating him. "You're in my place, you're my . . . friend." She had been going to say *lover* but that impassioned term now seemed not only inaccurate, but unwise. "You're staying here even after I asked you to leave," she said, thinking, you're going too far. His face was a stony blank.

She kept talking, almost in spite of herself; it would be better to keep quiet; he didn't want her to talk to him. "Listen to me, Julio. You don't really want to do this." She didn't, she thought, know precisely what he wanted to do. "I can't sit here politely and watch you destroy yourself. If you'd stayed in the South Bronx, or somewhere, and dug your own grave it wouldn't be my problem. But now you're here in my place; you're my responsibility. I feel responsible, anyway." It was bullshit, this responsible savior role. She didn't care what happened to him anymore; she just wanted him and his Beretta to get out of her apartment. "I don't know . . . maybe that's why you came here," she went on, "because you *expected* me to stop you. You wanted me to. How can I? I can't. I can't take that gun away from you; you're not a child with a toy. All I can say is you owe it to yourself to forget it, this stupid plan, whatever it is . . . robbing some store. . . . You're worth more than that. You say you can't stand to go back to jail, but if you do this" (that abstract, fearful *this*) "you'll get twenty-five years for sure. You know that. They're bound to catch you. You have a record, fingerprints. They've always caught you before. You'll get caught and you'll go back to jail forever." She was raving, off on a tirade, sponsored not by any sincere motive to save him, but to save herself from having to deal with him anymore. She had jumped up and was waving her arms like a berserk puppet. He watched her with wary eyes, his hands posed alertly by

251

the gun, as she ejected sporadic, half-baked sentences that only barely clung together. "I know this isn't what you really want." She felt like she was shouting, her vocal cords straining. "What about your family? Your father . . . his house in Puerto Rico? What about *us*!" She heard at once the false note in that artless romantic statement, knew he must have heard it too; he wasn't insensitive, even in this insensitive state. "It doesn't make sense; it's crazy!" She felt she was about to zoom off into space, propelled by a hysterical energy that must be inspired by sheer terror, or a need to scream down this glacial wall of stiffness between them. "Julio . . . *please* . . . turn yourself in now, before they find out about . . . while all they've got on you is this parole violation. Go back to jail for three months if you have to. What's three months? You've spent years in there and survived. Go down and talk to them. Tell them the truth . . . you were in a slump. . . . If you can't talk to them, maybe I can talk to them. I can talk to them for you. I'll call the police . . ." She heard the word *police* project itself from her disorderly mouth with dismay. The minute the syllables formed themselves and hung audibly in the air, she knew she'd made a serious mistake; she should have said *parole board*.

Julio stood up now too, carefully, as if he was balancing on a narrow ledge. The guarded expression in his eyes, the tight set of his mouth, were unfamiliar; even the way his features were arranged seemed to have undergone a peculiar, disorganizing shift.

"I wasn't really going to do it," she said quickly, trying to quiet her still loud voice. "I meant parole board, not police." To him it's the same thing, she thought, knowing now, from his new face, that distinctions between law-enforcing agencies no longer mattered to him.

"I know you are not going to do it, *niña*," he said, and the old, affectionate term, spoken in a voice that was as stern, as devoid of familiar expression as the outlines of his face, was chilling.

They stood staring at each other. He was clearly not seeing her as he had before. Her mind continued to chatter on. *I betrayed him,* she thought; *he thinks I'll betray him.* The phone rang, once, twice, three times, and its insistent peal seemed to descend, almost soundlessly, from a planet in the stratosphere.

"Dolores," Julio finally said, softly and deliberately, as if he'd come to some temporary decision. "I want you to go into the other room and sit on a chair. You sit down on your chair and stay put. I want you to sit down in your chair and write some of your po-etry. I do not want to hear your voice no more."

"I have to go out for some groceries," she whimpered idiotically, "there's nothing to eat in here." His narrowed eyes told her he meant it. "So it's a matter of life and death," she said shakily, wondering why she'd said that—a line from a mystery thriller. And then she went into her study, sat down at her desk, and rested her head on her typewriter. Her breath came in short gasps, as if she'd been jumping. She was in a situation she couldn't grasp; it was better to play it cool, now, accept the fact she'd blown it and lost control. It was altogether reasonable from his point of view—she could well betray him. When he had wanted to save himself, she was an ideal friend, an ally, a sounding board, a moral presence from another class, but now that he was determined to go to hell with himself, her white skin, middle-class apartment, and ideas had automatically placed her in the category of Enemy.

She waited, trying to interpret the slight sounds he

made in the other room; it was like being kept captive, without bonds or bars. She held out her hand and watched it shake. Was there a real reason to be so scared of him, or was she overreacting? The phone rang again, and she got up to cross the room and answer it. Julio appeared at once; he had sensed her intent, heard her movement. He blocked the doorway, his face pale and strained. "Let it ring, *niña*." The hard, anonymous *niña* again. Why wouldn't he let her answer? It didn't make sense. Yes, it did; he didn't want her near the telephone, not after she'd threatened to call the police, or he thought she had. He was afraid she'd tell anyone who called he was here, about the gun. And obviously he didn't want anyone to know he was here because he . . . the shrill sound repeated itself, four or five rings, then terminated abruptly. She wondered who was trying to reach her, if it was the same person who'd called before. No one, she thought, would think it odd if she didn't answer; no one was expecting her, or planning to see her. She could be dead here a week before anyone would suspect anything was wrong.

She sat at her desk as he'd ordered her, listening to her own uneven breath, to him, scraping back the chair, pacing to the phone, and making the same, unanswered call. At last she was unable to sit still any longer. She got up and went into the kitchen. He looked up quickly, but did not tell her to sit back down. Moving slowly and carefully, as if she were approaching a wild animal, without inciting it to rage or flight, she walked behind him and rested her hand on his shoulder, which flexed rigidly beneath her fingers. She didn't know why she should want to touch him under the circumstances, but she did, not only to win back his trust and close the precarious distance between them, but because, for some perverse reason, she still half desired him, or if not the threatening stranger he'd become, the version of him she'd always desired. His shoulder felt comfortingly familiar beneath her hand. She felt him relax slightly, then reach up and put his hand on top of hers. She wound both her arms around his neck and leaned her entire weight into his back. She wanted to know he would let her this close to him, to bring him back to her. Insanity; a normal woman would be fully conscious of the danger she was in. A normal woman would be planning to escape, to slip a sleeping pill in his coffee, or signal a neighbor to call the cops. Yet it was impossible for her to believe this man she'd fucked so many times would harm her. Her fingers moved to his belly, squeezed its folds, pressed tracks down to the hard lump of his dick. He tilted back in the chair and leaned his head against her breastbone; but there was no palpable ease or surrender in the gesture.

"Dolores," he said, almost apologetically, "I cannot let you walk out of here. Believe me, *nene*, I did not plan it to be like this. I did not want to make you responsible." She clung to him, like a shipwreck victim, as she digested the possibly ominous significance of that. Did he mean he wasn't going to let her leave her apartment for the time being, or that he would never let her leave at all, because whatever he had done or was going to do, she would know he had and report him? When he decided to make his move, would he bind and gag her, or simply kill her with the agile, thoughtless blow with which he'd killed a fly? Her outlines, already blurred to him, would evaporate in the fogged intentions of his eyes, and he would see her as nothing more than a troublesome blot to wipe away. Maybe that was how he'd committed crimes in the past, almost accidentally, directed by the will of a separate being that suddenly inhabited him. He had killed other people; he had told her that. She couldn't claim she hadn't known. No, that was paranoid; he had never killed a woman, or a friend, at least not as far as she knew. But then, he wouldn't have told her if he had. She knew she would never have turned him in—that had been a slip of the tongue, a faux pas—and he must know it too. She should tell him that, yet to say it aloud, again, would make it sound like a terrorized plea, and thus, less convincing. She decided to keep her mouth shut.

She sat down in the other chair, trying to relax. He was still fiddling compulsively with the gun, surely loaded by now, and smoking cigarettes. Think of something to say, she thought, keep him talking. He likes to talk. "If you were so into guns," she said, "you should have joined the Army. They might have made you a general."

"*Coño*," he said, in an immediately invigorated voice, his old, jovial, storytelling tone, "I *tried* to join the Marines when I was jitterbugging. I had the short hair already, a baldy. I went down to the recruitment office and I said to the dude, '*Vaya*, I want to go over to Nam and kill some gooks for you, my man!' He was wearing a blue uniform, full of them medals and shit. He said to me, 'What is your name young man and how old are you?' 'Dig it,' I tole him, 'my name is Duke and I am nineteen.' I was only fifteen then. 'Well, Duke,' he says, 'fill out this application form and we'll send you down for a physical.' 'I don't need no physical, brother,' I said. 'I am from the street and I am *strong*. Just give me my machine gun and my uniform and send me out to Nam. *Pa'lante!* I have been wanting to go over there.' He looked at me strange-like. 'Do you use narcotics, Duke?' he ast me. '*Sí, hombre*,' I told him. 'I use heroin and cocaine.' I could not see lying to the dude. His face got real tight and he ast me to fill out the application and bring it down there the next day." Julio laughed ruefully. "By the time I be getting my 4-F I was already in the Tombs. I thought, 'Shee-it! I must be fucking *bad* if they won't send me to Vietnam.' "

Dolores listened to her own nervous cackle objectively, wondering if she was laughing only because he would be suspicious if she refused. She had always laughed, always thought his crazy stories were funny, or if not humorous, entertaining. Now she realized they were not about a fucked-up mythical character he'd invented; they were about himself. It was amazing how fast he could switch personas, begin telling the old war stories in the same old way. She stared at him, consciously separating his multisignificance into components, like a jigsaw puzzle she couldn't make fit—the charming convict she'd thought she could help, her student, the man she'd fucked in every corner of every room, and now, the dangerous criminal he himself had endlessly described, holding her in some ambiguous captivity in her own apartment. The gun lay between them on the table, surrounded by its self-generating cloud of poisoned stillness, like a sleeping snake. She swallowed another impulsive, terror-stricken question, *What are you going to do with me when you leave?* The phone rang and this time she pretended she didn't hear it.

She went into the bathroom to get away from his oppressive presence, the fearful questions it imposed. "I'm going to the bathroom . . ." she announced hesitantly, realizing she was asking his permission. She sat on the toilet and tried to think, to marshal her mind toward the topic, How to Get Out of This Dangerous Situation. She was really too scared to think. Yet despite her increasing

257

panic, the "dangerous situation" seemed remote, unrelated to her, like the concept of a third world war. Perhaps her brain was taking the easy way out and dismissing the problem, because there was no solution. She was trapped, at the mercy of his unpredictable whims. Even through the door she felt him sitting at the table, waiting, visualized his hands, still on the gun. Was he planning some definite fate for her, or would he trust his instincts to dispose of her in the right way when the time came? He didn't know a lot about her. It would be easy for him to forget what she'd meant to him, if anything. She hadn't told him much about herself; she hadn't acted like she usually did. She had been nothing more or less than her fascination with him, a rapt, silent audience, and now there was a good possibility he'd kill her for that; her knowledge of him would stand in his way.

That had been her sorry idea of excitement, she thought sadly, to turn herself into a receptacle for an "interesting" man, to divest her own true being in order to receive him more completely. She had substituted her passive obsession with a bizarre figure for real action, and had called this supine state "adventure," instead of undertaking real adventures that would have made her an interesting person herself. And now that this pseudo "adventure" had reached its inevitable conclusion, a so-called dangerous situation, she was too immured in passivity to think of a way out, or come to grips with the fact it was happening.

From inside the bathroom she heard him walk to the telephone and dial, then heard his staccato accents, angry tones. "Where was you, my man?" It seemed he had finally reached his party. She pressed her ear to the door, eavesdropping. "Sí . . . yeah . . ." he was saying. "Dig it, I got the piece." Then he spoke in rapid Spanish. Now, whatever was going to happen would begin. She felt her insides drop, as if she had dived off a cliff. Without a conscious plan in mind, she turned on the bathtub faucet full force, and under cover of the watery roar, opened the bathroom door. He couldn't see her from where he was without turning completely around. She shrunk along the wall toward the kitchen table. Any minute his call might be over. He was still talking. It sounded like he was making arrangements; even in intent Spanish she made out addresses and names. Her purse was on the chair. She lifted it up and, almost as an afterthought, slipped the gun into it. Then, so quietly she couldn't believe she was capable of such silent motion, she inched her way through the kitchen to her apartment door. The lock made a loud, hollow click, but the door opened almost noiselessly on its hinges. She left it ajar, then tore down the steps, running as fast as she could, clumsily, like she ran in dreams, when her legs moved with a possessed energy, but didn't take her anywhere.

Outside her building she froze for a moment, imagining she heard him behind her, then ran to Houston Street and, thank God, flagged a taxi right away. She was gasping for breath, though she hadn't run very far. Her heart made stabbing thrusts against her chest, like the dull point of a knife. The cabbie turned and looked at her inquiringly. She couldn't think where to go, or speak; she made a vague forward gesture with her hand. She didn't look back to see if Julio had followed her.

CHAPTER
19

*D*OLORES got out of the cab at the Port Authority bus terminal. Her knees felt like they had dissolved, but she still ran through the crowded station, dodging hurrying figures, ramming her hipbones into other people's luggage, out of breath; she was sure Julio was not far behind her, pursuing on demonic wings. She considered dumping the gun, a throbbing weight in her purse, into a large trash bin in the middle of the terminal, but she couldn't halt her panicked, forward momentum. Besides, there were too many people who might see, might recapture it; Julio himself, inevitably behind her, might pick it up and kill her on the spot. It was a mistake to have taken it; it was more dangerous to have it on her than to have left it there.

As the cab whizzed up Eighth Avenue she had decided to visit her mother in New Jersey. The familiar terminal, the fumy gateway to holidays, summer weekends, occasions that called her to the now disturbing vacuity of her childhood home, had loomed up with the comforting promise of refuge. Her father, she vaguely recalled, was away on business, and her mother inhabited their large suburban house alone. She could easily pretend she had wanted to surprise her, to keep her company in her solitude. In fact, she knew as she hurried to the platform, it was she who needed her mother, needed her as she had when she was sick in bed as a child, and her mother had wrestled with her fevers, soothing her forehead with cold washcloths, bringing her special meals on a tray adorned with flowers from the garden.

The bus roared through the tunnel and down the highway, past the polluted, fiery fields of chemical industry, and at last crossed the intersection Dolores thought of as her personal childhood landmark, the strip of highway where she had waited for the school bus for eight grade-school years. An odd, gray fortress of a building, almost medieval in design, marked the spot; her mother called it the "bird factory" because it had been used to raise birds. Once, on a snowy night, the whitening lawn of their nearby house had filled with the bright green, amethyst and yellow wings of parakeets and canaries, released from their cement prison because they were diseased. Tears had come to her mother's eyes; the birds, she said, would die in their only flight for freedom. Later, Dolores's parents had moved from that house to another in the next town, and the "bird factory" had been transformed into a hosiery mill, now abandoned, surrounded by rampant weeds splintering its asphalt drive. *And then I ran out the door and went to visit my mother with the gun in my purse,* Dolores thought, mentally rehearsing the story she would tell later, though the audience of amazed faces had lost its identifying features in her mind. In the suffusing image of vivid, dying birds, Julio Bravo, not her childhood, seemed an insubstantial dream.

She called her mother from the Lakeland depot. It was late, already dusk. She told her she had been walking past the Port Authority on the way home from the library and suddenly decided to surprise her with a visit. "It was a whim," she said, knowing her tones must reek of falsehood. It was a suspicious statement; all her visits to New Jersey were thoroughly planned in advance, via endless long-distance telephone calls. "I thought you might be lonely here all by yourself," she said, also suspicious. It was not like her to offer up solicitude to her mother.

Her mother's voice was not exactly ecstatic. She had almost banished the unexpected from the twilight of her life, and preferred all events to repeat themselves in predictable patterns. "I've been calling you and calling you," she said, vigorously reproachful, "but you're never at home. . . . I've already eaten," she warned. "You know I don't fuss much when Dad isn't here." (Subtly accusing her of visiting New Jersey for a free meal.)

There was a lengthy, perhaps punitive, delay. Dolores stood, shifting feet, in front of the depot, trying to be grateful to breathe sweet, country air, shivering in the evening chill. Too late she had realized she was wearing only filthy khaki shorts, a T-shirt, none too clean either, and Kung Fu shoes with no socks—scarcely appropriate attire for her mother's bastion of suburban formality. She hadn't brought a thing with her, not a hairbrush, toothbrush, or comforting book, only the gun. Taking it had seemed the natural, the cor-rect thing to do at the time. Now it had become a complicated issue, with unforeseen repercussions waiting in the wings. It would have been smarter to leave it on the table and concentrate on getting out herself.

Eventually her mother drove up in the green Buick. She never left home without a hat, perched on, or crunched into, her large head, or without red lipstick, and her special glasses with the pointed rhinestone frames. The three dogs she had recently acquired from the pound, hoping to replace her beloved Pepper, who had died the winter before, after gagging for months on some unknown and much discussed obstruction in his throat, leaped frantically from the backseat, to the front, to the back again, barking and yapping, leashes entangled. They jumped en masse on Dolores, were slapped back, admonished. "Get down, Sandy," her mother said to the pale-haired terrier, some highly unusual breed, yet the least loved of the three. "You get down now. Don't pet her!" she warned Dolores. "She'll pee the minute you touch her when she's excited like that." She shoved Sandy and the smallest of the dogs, a tiny, straight-haired miniature, into the backseat; the third dog, a fairly tranquil poodly mutt, lounged on Dolores's lap.

Her mother shot her a penetrating glance. "My God!" she exclaimed. "Is that all you're wearing to come home?" She eyed Dolores's naked legs suspiciously, seeing, Dolores thought, the round, plump legs of the cooing infant she'd brought into the world, superimposed over the long, improperly nude limbs of a half-dressed, whorish slob of an adult daughter, wondering how one creature had ever emerged from the other. It must be painful to be her mother, no doubt about that.

263

"I didn't have time to change, Mom. I said it was a whim!" She heard the defensive near-whine in her voice; a voice that emerged from an atavistic, child's vocal box.

"No bra either!"

Dolores remembered she had omitted the one garment essential to home visits. "I forgot it," she said lamely.

"You'll wish you had a better memory when you end up with sagging breasts," her mother said in injured tones, then declared repetitively, "Young women who don't wear brassieres develop sagging breasts!" She was forever sending Dolores clippings from newspaper columns and women's magazines that supported this morbid opinion; the last one had been something about "joggers' nipples," though Dolores didn't jog. The tiny miniature began to bark shrilly from the backseat, for no apparent reason. "She's a tiger, that Bitsy," her mother said. "Listen to that ferocious voice!" She chuckled indulgently, inappropriate attire forgotten.

Dolores remembered the gun again and switched the purse from the space between them to the side near the car door. She feared her mother's X-ray vision would spot the fuming metal straight through the leather, as her apparent psychic sixth sense had pierced less substantial barricades to intuit peculiarities in her life. She constantly skirted the borders, nearly striking the truth of events she couldn't know happened. She had brought up the subject of rape, for example, almost every time Dolores visited for an entire year after her rape occurred, always in the abstract, like a topic from the news. Once she had called, "Just to see if something's wrong," as Dolores embarked on a one-night stand in her apartment. It was a bad idea to come here, she thought. If her mother were to acknowledge her strange appearance, drawn face, probably haggard eyes by asking, "Is something wrong?"

she would never be able to tell her, would have to answer, "No, nothing. Nothing at all," and if she didn't ask it might mean she was on the verge of guessing all. She prayed her mother wouldn't mention guns, or gun control, or the death penalty, in which she firmly believed. She might then give herself away, crack under the strain of obligatory silence and needed consolation. Unfair; she might expect her mother to dish out material sympathy if she'd come home sick, or broke, but not because she'd harbored an armed robber in her apartment and escaped with his gun.

Her mother's mind, however, was safely on other matters. She pointed out the new houses on the once country road, settling, half built, into bleeding tracts of raw earth, thoroughly dismantled of green. The paths Dolores had explored, even a few years back, had all been replaced by such muddy potential backyards. "Look at that God-awful house!" her mother said, shouting to overcome the sound of Bitsy's shrill yapping. "I suppose you call that a 'Colonial.' I will never understand why they have to cut down all the trees like that!"

"Because every citizen of Capitalist America has got to own his own little house and yard," Dolores said vindictively, knowing she included an attack on her parents' house and yard in this condemnation, on the very private property, in fact, that had spawned her. She waited, almost eagerly, for her mother's reply, hopefully the beginning of a bitter argument. Fierce battles, which had started with screaming, and ended with her mother crying, beating her with a hairbrush, and Dolores running away from home, had for years been the essence of their mother-daughter style. Now, these fights had diminished to inflammatory debates on theoretical subjects, politics or social mores, which rapidly transcended polite tones and rose to the old, high-pitched personal hysteria. To inspire them Dolores pretended to be a Communist, anarchist, or right-wing Republican—anything to get her mother started. Perversely, it was only when their screaming reached the passionate crescendo of her childhood that she felt they were truly mother and daughter again, that something like love caught fire between them.

She expected her mother to shoot back, "Would you like to live in Russia? Go ahead? Go!" (just as she used to say, "Go! Run away! I'll help you pack your bags!") but now she was more interested in talking about the dogs. "I don't know whether we're going to keep Sandy," she said. "She's still *shitting,* as you would say, whenever I leave her alone for more than an hour. I put her bed down in the basement to make her feel more secure, but it doesn't help much. I told your father I'm not going to keep cleaning up that mess. But Sandy is your father's favorite dog. You should see the way she greets him when he comes home at night! She peed all over his green sports jacket last week. I said, 'My God!' "

"Why don't you tie her up outside when you go out?" Dolores asked. "You still have the doghouse there."

Her mother's lips set angrily. "I don't want an outdoor dog," she said.

"But you have the other two, and besides, you'd only put her out there when you weren't at home, so what's the difference?"

"I just don't want that kind of dog," her mother said. Her voice faltered a bit, as if she were going to scream or weep. "I wouldn't have taken a dog I knew I was going to have to keep outside."

"But you wouldn't *be* here when she was outside," Dolores repeated, feeling the fury rise in her own voice, hating herself for the malicious pleasure she took in driving her poor old mother to the brink, and for getting herself worked up over this trivial issue to keep her mind off the gun, and Julio in her apartment.

"I told your father we'll give her six more months, and if she doesn't improve she goes back to the pound," she said firmly.

Dolores hastily stowed her purse in the closet of her old room, still painted the sickly violet she had chosen years ago. The trophy she'd won for Outstanding Journalist in high school, along with her Thespian medals, remained on the bookshelf, and her high school graduation picture was still framed on the wall. She felt drawn to this photograph of herself, bright eyes, hair curled and set precisely in what they used to call an "Italian," grinning with a buoyant innocence that stretched her round, boneless cheeks into full, fruitlike globes. (Her teeth seemed larger, slightly protruding in those days.) She had also been fatter and her breasts bigger; bra-ed up vigorously, they were visible even through the folds of her academic gown. A virgin, then, she couldn't remember wanting to be otherwise, or thinking the impure thoughts that would one day lead her to return home with a criminal lover's gun. Her own seventeen-year-old face, she thought, seemed the face of a stranger, a sane, mature young woman, years older than she herself felt now. "Do you want cold chicken or a hamburger?" she heard her mother call from the kitchen.

She sat at the Formica table while her mother prepared chicken, salad, and cake for her with embattled efficiency, talking on, telling stories about the dogs, her beloved garden, and the neighbors, many the same she had told the last time Dolores visited, more than two months ago. Nothing much happened in her mother's life anymore, but she scarcely seemed aware of that; a few novel events, punctuating the weeks of routine chores, sufficed as focal points.

She didn't ask Dolores about herself, little about her work, nothing about her friends, or *beaux,* as she'd called them when she thought there might still be hope. It was hard to fathom exactly what she imagined about her existence, or if, in fact, she avoided imagining it at all. She knew Dolores wasn't married, had produced no offspring, didn't have a prestigious nine-to-five job, in short, had reached some amorphous adulthood without posting any of the usual signs, and that was enough. She would rather not know, her distrustful lips said clearly, or perhaps it was that she did know, had divined the essence, and found it unmentionable, like a terminal disease, not to be discussed with the person who had it.

"The stupid Lardners finally invited us over for a drink," her mother was saying, referring to the neighbors she especially disliked. "Spur of the moment, of course, at nine thirty at night. I told your father, 'I don't want to go over there! I've been out in the garden all day and I'm dead tired. I'm going to bed.' He told them I didn't feel well, though I didn't see why he had to lie. If they can be rude, I can be rude too. Then Karen Lardner had the gall to call back and ask if Dad might want to come over by himself."

Dolores nodded, dropping off into what she thought of as her suburban zombie euphoria, an unmistakable sinking of the limbs and brain, which rendered her inaudible, incompetent, and unwilling. This deadly lethargic state, something like a minor stroke, attacked at exactly the moment a good daughter would jump up, cheerfully clear the table, wash the dishes, perform any helpful or constructive task. Instead, she felt so overcome by the groggy stupor she could barely open her mouth to speak or turn the pages of the latest *National Geographic*. Tonight, however, she greeted this discomforting zombiehood with relief; it annihilated her current anxieties with an obliterating fog. Here in the instant morphine of safe, domestic, uneventful New Jersey, chirping peacefully with crickets and outdoor night sounds, Julio Bravo seemed a myth, and the gun, light years away in her closet. "You told me about the Lardners," she said to her mother. She felt compelled to advise her when she repeated a story, to call her back from encroaching senility. She should just give it up; it would be easier to tune out, smile, and think about something else.

Her mother's attention returned, as usual, to dogs. "I miss Pepper," she said. "I still cry when I think of him, how he had to get sick in that damned kennel, and the jerk that ran it didn't even bother to tell me to come get him that night. I never would have waited until morning if I knew he was gone. He was about gone when we got him home, poor boy. But you know, when we put him in the basket near the fireplace, because we thought it would be warmer for him in there, he dragged himself into the bedroom because he wanted to be with us."

Dolores had heard the story of Pepper's demise many dozens of times, though, significantly, her mother hadn't called to tell her about his death until a week after it occurred, a basic vote of no-confidence, a recriminating acknowledgment that Dolores didn't deserve to know, because she had been unforgivably disgusted by the old dog's gagging, warts, half-blind eyes, and bad breath. Now, her mother repeated the story aloud as she must have repeated it in her own mind, trying to ferret out the flaw in eternal justice that, once explained, would bring the fourteen-year-old animal back from its untimely death. Pepper, she seemed to believe, had been meant to live forever, at least longer than her. Now, he lay in the vegetable garden, giving life to the asparagus, constantly reminding her mother of his compact, curly body, just beyond the veil, as she trod on the spongy earth of his grave.

"Well," Dolores said, as she always did, "he lived a good, long life." It was growing harder to press some semblance of emotion into this tired statement, which inevitably enraged her mother, possibly because it indicated that Dolores, too, was among the traitors who believed Pepper had really died.

"If that damned jerk at that kennel had taken him to the vet instead of letting him lie there in the cold . . ." she said, then mercifully turned her attention to the living. "Watch Bitsy's tricks! Up in the corner!" she ordered. "Okay! Up. Up! Good girl. Gooooood girl!" She rewarded the coyly posing dog with a yummy of some kind. "That itsy Bitsy is a smart little girl," she said in a crooning voice.

Dolores sat, still narcotized, at the table, guiltily watching her mother finish up the busy domestic functions a good, visiting daughter should perform. Her anxiety was returning, in spite of, or because of, her stupefied boredom. He might wait for her to come back, she thought, and when he found out she didn't have the gun, he would . . . Still, it would be best to get rid of it; that would eliminate the possibility of him using it; then she could decide how to explain if she actually had to face him. Her hand strayed to the head of the pale dog. Tomorrow would be here soon enough; now she should forget about it and try to relax; she would have to be calm and rested to deal with this problem effectively.

"Don't pet her," her mother sirened. "You know what will happen! She peed all over Gertrude last week!"

Her mother was getting old, Dolores thought. Her face wore its familiar defining lines and expressions hesitantly, like a disintegrating marble statue. She walked more slowly than before, and complained of arthritis. It was frightening, and for some reason, also annoying. It was especially annoying to think she ought to treat her mother differently, more kindly, indulgently, because she was old.

And then, she said mentally to the time it would all be over, *I sat at the kitchen table in New Jersey with his gun in my purse, and listened to my mother talk about her dogs.*

Dolores and her mother spent the rest of the evening in front of the large color television in her father's den. This television, too, added to her sense of drugged incubation. Larger than any television should logically be, it replaced all possible thoughts with its vast spread of vivid Technicolor. She gratefully watched whatever nonsense it proffered up, mesmerized by its hallucinogenic rays. She tried to take each moment with equanimity, not to think, to consider television a kind of meditation, eliminating her own inner, chattering dialogue. It was possible he would wreck her place for revenge. Her mother, yawning, let the dogs out. "Tomorrow I'll show you the garden," she told Dolores, adding reproachfully, "Of course, there's not much left. You missed the daffodils and the iris. All I have now is a few of the lilies." Her mother always insisted she tour the garden, and this Dolores didn't mind—walking slowly, examining the large, fragile blossoms, and hearing their poetic Latin names.

271

She went to her room and locked the door. Soon she heard heavy breathing and a light snore from her parents' bedroom down the hall; the walls of these jerry-built suburban houses were made of something only slightly heavier than cardboard. She unzipped her purse and took out the gun. It was heavy and smooth in her hand, heavier than its small, compact mass would indicate. She still didn't know if it was loaded. She touched it gingerly. Even minus bullets she expected it to suddenly expand, spill a sheet of orange flame, then explode with a deafening noise. She put it carefully down on the bed. Its inanimate silence was sinister, challenging. Lying on the pink bedspread with white tufts, the same spread she'd had as a little girl, the black gun was a foreign invader, a thing that didn't belong, and its solemn, impersonal strangeness made it seem here, even more than in the hands of Julio, real. *Then I waited until my mother was sleeping, took the gun out of my purse, and laid it on my bed.*

She picked it up again, deliberately avoiding the trigger. She had to admit she liked the way it felt; the smooth, cold touch of it was almost sensual. Written on the side of the barrel in tiny, clearly etched letters was "Pietro Beretta," and beneath that, "Gardone, V.T. Cal. .380." A mysterious round symbol with three arrows inside of three circles was also imprinted in the metal—a kind of gun mandala, perhaps. She turned it over, still handling it uneasily. A small, triangular mechanism, like a lever, was situated beneath the inscription, "P.B. Mod 70s—Made in Italy," and written next to it was the word *Taggio*. *Taggio* must be Italian for "push," she thought, or something like that. This was probably the lever that opened the gun so you could clean it. She considered pushing it, but was afraid she might not be able to put it back together again, or that it was loaded and might blow up in her hand. She had to get rid of it before she went back to New York, that was for sure, before anyone, including her, was killed or hurt by it. She shouldn't fool around with it. She would throw it in the lake and that would be the end of it.

She put the gun back in her purse and quietly let herself out the door. As she tiptoed toward the front hall one of the dogs barked. "It's nothing," she called, in case her mother had heard. "It's me. I'm in the bathroom." She would go down to the dock; nobody would be there now. She descended through the woods, the only remaining woods, part of her parents' acre of land. A crescent of slightly clouded moon barely revealed the path.

The lake, once surrounded by thick oak forest, now twinkled with the lights from the many houses that occupied its banks. The old weather-warped dock of corroded wood had been replaced by an aluminum structure, where sailfish and canoes were tethered; everyone in the new development had a fancy boat. Neat steps led down to it now, instead of the treacherous, slippery mud path. Except for the dark water of the lake itself, it scarcely resembled the place she'd swum as a kid, taken her junior lifesaving lessons, and finally come with a high school boy, tall, blond Andy someone, who had told her, here on this dock, that she had beautiful lips. She could still remember her gratified surprise, her "Me!"; it was the first time any male had ever described any part of her as beautiful. In high school she'd been considered a bony creep, though she wasn't as bony then as she was now. That night she had written her first decent poem, beginning, "Spring first sheds . . ." Now, with this gun in her purse, she could not remember what spring had shed, only the feeling the poem had given her, a transcendent excitement that mitigated the fact this boy wouldn't kiss her so-called beautiful lips, because he was really in love with some short, cute cheerleader. A feeling hard to define, but which worded itself, "This is *it!*"

Do it and get it over with, she told herself. Her mother might realize she was missing via her psychic powers, and that could lead to questions she would not be able to answer with the necessary deceptive innocence in her current state. She took the gun out of her purse, holding it by its waffled plastic handle, the way you would hold it if you were really going to shoot. She had intended to throw it hard, hurl it into the lake, where it would sink into the mud forevermore; as she had walked toward the dock she had pictured this action, almost felt her muscles perform it. She pulled back her arm, tensed her body, then felt the energy escape the intended motion. She did not complete it or let the gun go. The gun itself seemed to paralyze her hand and arm; its smooth, steel heaviness welded it to the shape of her palm. In a strange way it seemed to complete the hand that held it. She supposed guns were designed to do this, to make them more accurate, easier to fire. Her fingers did not want to let it go. It was a unique sensation, to hold this gun, viscerally unsettling. She could imagine how it had given Julio, a deprived ghetto kid, some mystical sense of power. When he was a gang member, he'd told her, he'd walked the streets of The Bronx drawing down on strangers, because it made him feel good. Crazy; she should have known he was off the wall the minute he'd told her that.

She found her finger impelled toward the trigger, unable to resist putting it there; it was obviously the place her finger was meant to go. Almost in spite of herself, she squeezed it, feeling the metal give with a delicious, smooth, pressing action. She jumped, expecting a great, hollow boom to reverberate over the water. Nothing happened at all. The lake remained silent, its depths obscured by the cloudy sky, the retreating milky moon. She still held the gun by the handle, pointing it; it wasn't impossible to imagine killing someone, but who? If you wanted to kill, to fire, it probably wouldn't matter. It was glued to her hand, to the potential of its flash, its catastrophic explosion.

It made her face hot to hold it, aim it, gave her a feeling of pure and novel excitement, as if her body had released a huge quantity of an unknown hormone, adrenaline perhaps. Quickly she squeezed the trigger again, steadying herself for the blast with a rising thrill of expectation. Again, nothing; silence. It definitely wasn't loaded; she didn't have to worry about that.

Again she envisioned herself raising her arm, throwing, letting go, felt the impetus of the motion, then realized she was standing as she had before, still, like a stone column, with the gun pointed over the lake. She liked this image of herself, a tall, thin, hollow-cheeked adult woman, pointing a silky, cold steel Beretta, a cruel Mafia gun, over the water of the overbuilt, corrupted place she'd been raised. It defied everything. *And then I stood by the shores of my childhood and fired his black gun*, she said to the time it would be over, to Posterity.

She heard a car stop at the dock and young voices. Kids still came down here to drink beer and make out. Headlights beamed through the trees. A door slammed. She put the gun quickly back in her purse, and hurried up the steps, past the car, and climbed the wooded hill to her parents' house.

CHAPTER
20

*I*N the morning Dolores took the bus back to New York, making some cockeyed excuse to her mother about work to do, calls to make, people to see—all obvious lies. She was returning of her own free will to the same "dangerous situation" she had only yesterday gone to such pains to escape; insane! It would have made more sense to hide out in New Jersey as long as humanly possible, but it wasn't possible; she was incapable of playing the demanding role of innocent daughter with the gun fuming in her purse, with her nerves stripped raw. In any case, waiting would not resolve the situation or make it go away; she would have to face Julio eventually, unless she absconded to a different city, in which case she would still have to go back to her place to pack up her things.

Unreasonably, she felt compelled to return and get it over with, to see the drama to the bitter end.

There were two possibilities: either Julio was still in her apartment or he was not. If he was, he could be waiting for her, pacing the dirty kitchen floor like a wolf, whatever positive emotion he had left for her converted to savage rage. It was impossible to imagine his reaction when he'd hung up the phone and found her and his Beretta gone. It was lucky, at least, she hadn't thrown it into the lake. Now she could simply give it back to him. She could say she had taken it in a last ditch attempt to save him from himself, from the thing he was planning to do that would destroy him, even though she knew he would be angry at first, and not see it that way. That would be consistent with everything she'd said before. Then she could tell him she'd decided he was not her responsibility after all; she couldn't change his life for him. Here's the gun; take it; do what you have to do! By now he might be cooled out enough to find this excuse plausible. In fact, she didn't know why she'd snatched the gun—she hadn't planned to, it wasn't a good idea—but she had not consciously intended to redeem him by doing so. Perhaps she could get herself to believe this honorable motive had controlled her mind. At least she knew it wasn't loaded; he couldn't take it and immediately blow her away.

Then there was the second possibility: He would not be there. She would not have a chance to explain. He would think she had taken the gun and turned him in. He would have made a run for it. In that case she'd never see him again, or he would be planning his revenge, and when the moment came for him to take it, he would not allow her to say a word. In this case the gun would be irrelevant; he could get another, or kill her some other way. It would be easy enough for him to kill her if he wanted, to lie in wait for her somewhere, to climb in the open window of her apartment on a distant summer night when she'd forgotten about it all. *Kill* was such a melodramatic word! She could not seriously imagine him plotting to "kill" her, or visualize the moment when she would die by his hand. He hadn't threatened to kill her. He had only said, "I cannot let you walk out of here," and then he had done just that. He hadn't tied her up or tried to stop her; he had let her escape. She *was* afraid of him, but not because she really thought he would "kill" her. Perhaps that finite, violent word served to concretize her amorphous fears.

She barely experienced the bus ride. She was exhausted from nerves, from lack of sleep. A spasmodic tic had started twitching beneath her right eye. She had lain awake all night, thinking these same thoughts, or versions of them, over and over. She called her apartment from the Port Authority, knowing even if he was there he wouldn't answer, thinking the call was for her. She hung up, then called back, letting the phone ring ten, fifteen, twenty times. That would notify him it was her; no ordinary caller would let it ring so long. Then, exasperated, she hung up. She hadn't proved a thing. He might still be there, or not. She considered calling Joanna and asking her to meet her at her apartment; but if she did, she would have to tell her the entire story, and she would advise her to do the sensible thing, call the police, and if she did that, she would betray him, which she didn't want to do. If she betrayed him she would have good reason to fear him. Her own real power over him, she thought, lay not in outside forces of any kind, but somewhere in herself, if she could find it, express it. To come back alone with the gun was in itself proof that she hadn't betrayed him. Instinctively he would see it that way. She wasn't up to this major confrontation; she needed sleep, peace.

She forced her heavy legs up the steps of her building, and approached the door of her apartment quietly. She listened. No sound disturbed the contained silence within. He might be sleeping, or sitting, not moving. There was no reason to assume he wasn't there. She knocked, first a timid, almost soundless knock, then louder. She was still in the hall, protected by the presence of neighbors, old Italian crones, who went constantly up and down the stairs with groceries and dogs. No answer. Fortunately her keys had been in her purse, not on the desk, as usual. As she applied them to the double lock, she realized the door was open. He must be gone. He had left, leaving the door ajar. It was impossible to lock it without a key. He might have forgotten to lock the door from the inside, or left it open for her. She pushed it lightly and peered in. If he was in the kitchen she would see him.

As soon as she stood on her own floor she knew for certain he wasn't there. The air held no choked energies. Things were exactly as she had left them—dirty dishes on the counter, piled in the sink, an ashtray full of butts, the gun-cleaning equipment, an unmade, rumpled bed— a stale, sunless atmosphere. All that remained of Julio were a few anonymous waste products, a crumpled cig- arette pack, a damp towel over the kitchen chair. He must have taken a bath. The water she had left running was off. She searched the table, then her desk for a message; there was none. She checked the pad by the telephone, discovered some heavy, concentric doodle, not hers, but no telltale words. Weird; she herself would have left a note, saying what she thought, if not good-bye. The blank lack of anything was more unsettling than his angry, confronting presence would have been. It meant the situation was, more than ever, unresolved. It meant she would never see him again, or she could expect to see him at any given moment. He would come back, as furious as when he'd left, or never return at all, meaning she had passed out of his awareness. She should be grateful, if that was the case.

She lay facedown on the bed, inhaling the last traces of his smell, the smoky male odor, the sweetish stuff he used on his hair. She was almost too tired to feel afraid; she only wished the entire business would resolve itself, in her mind, if not in reality. She had expected it to resolve itself when she walked in the door. She reached for her purse and took the gun out again. She put it down and tried to look at it objectively. She did not know if the immediate anxiety this dangerous metal thing provoked was for itself, or for the problem of Julio. He had just cut out, *buffed,* as he would say, and in all likelihood she would never know where he had gone or what had happened to him. In the long run he would evaporate from her life, leaving only the gun, an appropriate memento of his existence. She should simply get rid of it and forget it, and him, forever more. But any minute he might return, might want it back, and in that event it would be hazardous not to have it. He might have stepped out for a pack of cigarettes, and right now be climbing back up the stairs. The undiminishing reality of this gun was proof that Julio's absence had not made him disappear.

The telephone rang. That had to be him, she thought, and lurched toward the receiver. It was her literary agent. "My God, sweetie," she said. "I've been calling you for two solid days! As soon as the first check comes through—and knowing publishers as I do I can guarantee that will not be *instantly*—you must promise me you'll buy an answering machine."

"I was in New Jersey," Dolores said weakly, gradually adjusting to the fact it was not Julio's voice she was hearing. Her first impulse was to hang up as rapidly as possible in case he was trying to call. She tried to locate her business personality in her overwrought mind, still sputtering futile "what ifs" and false conclusions.

"I have the contracts, darling," her agent announced triumphantly. "I would have put them in the mail, but that might have been equivalent to tossing them into the Wide Sargasso Sea. In case you haven't noticed, the New York mail is like the Pony Express! My father in Coney Island got a letter my sister mailed from Connecticut three days before I did. The same letter, mailed the same day! The Upper West Side is Timbuktu as far as the Post Office is concerned."

Dolores listened to her agent disparage the U.S. postal system in an intense voice; it was like hearing a foreign language she didn't know very well. She wanted to hang up, to scream, "Well, what do you want?"; then she remembered it was something about the contracts. Her agent began reviewing the "terms," as she called them, telling Dolores how she had defended her benighted writer's interests against the vindictive forces of commercial publishing. Each word registered with its appropriate meaning, yet divorced from those that preceded and followed it. It was unfair; she shouldn't have to deal with her career, or anything else, now. She considered saying she had been about to take a bath, that she would return the call, but she knew if she hung up she might never return it, at least not soon, and one didn't dismiss one's agent when she'd called to say she'd consummated a deal—not if the house were on fire. She listened, still not completely comprehending, to the mesmerizing professional voice. Her agent said the first contract was for a biography of Walt Whitman, a name that registered through Dolores's logic-obscuring fog with decided negativity.

Dolores loathed Walt Whitman, the great old gruesome graybeard. She had once written an ignominious paper on him in college, an assignment, which the professor marked virulently with red ink and termed "Nearly incompetent." "O Captain My Captain"—sanctified grade-school garbage! She had never dreamed this series of projects would begin with Walt Whitman. She'd thought it was on modern poets; Walt Whitman wasn't modern! She had imagined Allen Ginsberg, Marianne Moore, possibly Wallace Stevens, even . . . the names of other American poets escaped her. Roethke? Was he American? Her memory, her intellectual identifying powers, had fled like startled ants. She could only envision pushing the coffee cups aside, crouching at her dusty desk in her still smoky study, and tediously beginning to compose an entire book on boring, boring Walt Whitman about whom she gave less of a shit. Even though she couldn't think clearly, this was unthinkable. She'd rather write about Pineapples!

Her agent rattled on. She hadn't absorbed a word she'd said for the last five minutes. She was trying to listen, but basically waiting for Julio Bravo's knock at the door, for the all-future empty hole in which it would occur or not occur. She would never in a million years be able to write an intelligent word about Walt Whitman; that and only that was a comprehensible fact. She still held the gun in her hand; it fit there with an embarrassingly comfortable sensation. Idly, she squeezed the trigger, tensing for the blast she knew it was not loaded to fire. She tried to make herself tune in. The first biography was due in the fall. It was now almost July. She would have to start work today, surely tomorrow; impossible. It was totally impossible.

"Listen," she interrupted, suddenly unable to remember her agent's name. Then, mercifully, it came to her—*Jean*. "Jean, I don't know . . ." she said.

Silence; an alerted, ready-to-snarl silence.

"All of a sudden I'm not sure I want to do it."

More silence. It was unbearable. Her agent would think she was crazy. "Until now it . . . it sounded fantastic," she stammered. "All the money . . . everything. But all of a sudden the thought of . . . I really don't want to write biographies." She was too tired and freaked out to deal with this correctly. "I'm not sure I even *can* write a biography—I never have."

"This is a fine time to tell me," her agent said, her voice even and angry.

"I realize that. Believe me. Honestly. It's a terrible thing to do to you . . . to back out like this, but I just . . ."

"Darling, it's a terrible thing to do to yourself; *I* am irrelevant," her agent said, in tones that indicated she was not irrelevant at all. "Why don't you calm down, think it over, and call me back in an hour. I think you've just experienced what is known as classic writer's panic. I *know* those panics, sweetheart. I have seen them! Believe me, only the most talented writers suffer from them, especially poets, with those delicate sensitivities. *Sylvia* had them. Even *I* have had them, and I am not a writer."

"I know I won't feel different in an hour," Dolores said desperately. In an hour she would be asleep or dead. "I'll just feel more guilty than I already feel." Something had creaked, a footstep in the apartment next door, but she'd thought it was Julio. She hadn't locked the front door again; she should lock it or face the reasons why she'd left it open, so when he walked in on her, she couldn't pretend it was an accident. She wanted him to come back so she could get whatever would happen over with now, so it would not follow her into the forevermore.

"Darling, this is a godsend," her agent said. "What are you going to do for money, if I may ask?"

The last thing Dolores could think about was money. "It's too academic," she said. "It will interfere with my own work. I feel it."

"Dolores," her agent said kindly, as if she were addressing a body in an iron lung, "you don't have to give me any more reasons. I think I understand. Probably Beatrice Wilcox will do it, or . . . well, never mind. It's embarrassing, of course, but that's not your problem. I'll think of some way to explain it to Jean; she knows poets too," at which point Dolores remembered her agent's name was not Jean. The editor's name was Jean. Her agent's name was Marian, Marian Rothstein. If the gun was loaded, she thought, I'd kill myself. She must have made a half-strangled sound.

"Dolores," her agent said in a pointed, woman-to-woman voice. "This is not like you. Tell me what's wrong."

"Nothing, Marian. . . . I'm not feeling too well."

"Are you sick?"

"No, not sick exactly."

"Don't you want to call me back about this, darling? I can let it wait until morning, I promise you. There's no panic. The contracts are already made out. Everyone will be so disappointed. You can sign them anytime this week."

"No, Marian," she persisted, unable to believe she was persisting. "I don't want to do it." That last sentence emerged with a firmness that alarmed even her own ears. She wanted to hang up and collapse. There was no way she could imagine tomorrow when she would have to collect her deranged thoughts and direct them toward Walt Whitman.

"Are you absolutely sure?" Dolores tried to concentrate and picture her agent's face, a kind, sly, elegant face, which she had only seen twice, once in her office, when she had given her her writing samples, and once at a crowded literary cocktail party, when she had rushed by in a black dress, gushing, "Darling, how are you? We must talk!" on her way to a far more major celebrity. Their limited business had been transacted on the phone.

"I'll survive," Dolores said. "Don't worry about me, I . . ."

"Is it a man?" her agent asked fiercely. Dolores remembered the sign she had seen hanging over her desk. "A Woman Without a Man Is Like a Fish Without a Bicycle." At that time this witty renunciation had impressed her favorably; Marian would be a soul sister, a companion in stalwart sacrifice.

"There is a man," she said. "Yes and no. Sort of. Marian, that's not it. If you want to know the truth I just don't want to write a single word about Walt Whitman. I hate Walt Whitman. I've always hated him." She was insane, she thought, she was making a con-scious error. "When I agreed to do it, no one said anything about Walt Whitman," she finished. "You said modern poets." Then she added hesitantly, "Maybe Jean would let me do another poet first. . . ." That, she realized, after she'd said it, was what any competent, professional, mature person would have said to begin with.

Her agent didn't seem to hear her last comment. "It's all right, dear," she said, obviously debating which of her clients she would call with this emergency bonanza when she'd gotten rid of the fucked-up poetess cretin on the other end of the line. Dolores could tell she had both dismissed and forgiven her—a confused, unliberated female, who had let some man wreak havoc with her priorities. There were numerous titles she would now wear—justly—in her agent's mind. She had passed out of the ranks of money-making writers, out of the realm of potential anything worth mentioning. She would remain a poverty-stricken, unpublished minor poet, starving, as she diddled away at her puny, lyric lines. Her agent would never call her again; she would blackball her among other agents, among publishers. Simply, quickly, and completely, she had blown her career in New York.

After hanging up Dolores laid the gun gently in her underwear drawer. Later she would find a better place to hide it. And still alert for Julio's knock, or the telephone's nonexistent ring, she passed out on the bed.

CHAPTER
21

Epilogue

*L*AST night Julio Bravo knocked at my door at two
in the morning, five months after holding me
"hostage" in my apartment, five months after leaving
here without a word for some unknown destination
in the underworld, five months after I stole his gun
then strapped it with masking tape to the pipes below the kitchen sink. (Not the best of hiding places,
in retrospect—what if the pipes had burst when I
wasn't at home?—but the one that seemed best at
that dismal moment.)

I had staggered home in the freezing rain in those
murderous gold shoes, after making a complete ass of
myself at Vasco's decadent dinner party, to collapse at
long last in bed, when the knock sounded—an in-

stantly familiar, furtive, urgent knock. I unearthed myself from seminightmares, made my way to the peephole, and saw the electric edges of his hair framed in the dimly lighted hall. My stomach plunged into my feet, like a rock dropped into water. "Dolores, it's Julio," he said in his husky voice, which at once replaced the paranoid images and precautions I'd heaped against his name with his own, complex reality. I didn't answer, not because I hoped to convince him I wasn't there, but because I was too tired, too stunned to answer. No, that's not quite honest. I didn't answer because I was terrified—not of Julio or of what he might do to me, as I thought I'd be—but of the unexpected yearning I immediately felt for him. This yearning was not, I'm glad to say, romantic; it was not, I'm sure, a self-destructive, panting delusion posing as passion. This yearning may not even have been for Julio Bravo himself per se, his corporeal presence, but for some intense, precarious aura that surrounds him.

"Listen, Dolores. It's Julio," he said again, his staccato accent separating the syllables.

More than anything I wanted to be elsewhere, Madagascar, Bolivia, any place far from the temptation to answer, "What do you want, Julio?" and open the door. At that moment I knew that I had never stopped expecting him, never, even when I'd told myself he must be dead, back in jail, or living in Las Vegas under an assumed name. I assured myself he was never coming back, nothing to worry about, not after all this time, and I tried to forget him. Believe me, I tried, and almost succeeded. I did forget him, or if he didn't quite pass from my mind, he stopped influencing my actions. I quit scanning the papers every day, looking for the rip-off, bank robbery, murder, even the obituary I could unmistakably identify as his. I stopped dialing the Department of Corrections to find out if they had him, then hanging up after the second ring, and writing him letters I immediately destroyed. I quit jumping, with beating heart, every time I heard a knock on the door, or the phone ring, or saw a bearded Latin type who looked like him. I carried on. I met Vasco. Somehow, I miraculously picked up my career from the hole I'd dropped it in—too late for wretched Walt Whitman, for better or worse, I'll never be sure. (I still find myself reciting, "When lilacs last in the dooryard bloomed. . . .") I wrote some poetry, not about him. Yet when I heard that knock, his voice, I knew I'd always known he would come back, not because he "loved" me, not because he wanted the gun, or wanted to kill me for taking it, but because he is tied to me as I am to him—by some fatal bond of understanding. We are there to rescue one another from the inevitability of our lives.

I maintained my paralyzed silence. "Dolores . . ." he said again, anxiously. What unexplained intimacy his voice evokes in me, or the feeling that intimacy is there, between us, when all logic tells me it couldn't be possible, that what I call *intimacy* is not intimacy at all, but a distance that separates me from my usual self, the heightened life-signs of pure trepidation. He's come back to get revenge, I told myself, come back for the reason my island dream comes back, because my sick mind invokes him.

"Dolores," he said, "*nene*, let me talk to you. Open the door!" I did not open the door; powers beyond my will froze me between my irrational desire to let him in, and the opposite desire, feeble but compelling, to keep him out. My hand moved to the doorknob, lingered there, began to turn it, then did not. Something, perhaps the future I address, is saving me from myself. "Dolores," he said sadly, "are you still afraid of me? It's me, Julio."

"No," I answered, but in an inaudible whisper. Not true! I am afraid of him, or of what he inspired in me, and in spite of myself, might still inspire.

"I did not mean to scare you, *niña*, that last time," he said. So he knew he had frightened me. "I would never have hurt you, Dolores. You know that." When he said it, I felt that I had known it, that my fear had been fear for him, or fear for myself for getting mixed up with him at all, or fear for the titillating sake of fear itself. "Dolores," he said (he knew I was there, though I was perfectly still and silent). "If you cannot open the door I can dig it. It is all right. Listen, Dolores. It is cool with the parole *ahora*."

What did he mean by that? I had an intense desire to know what he meant by, "It's cool with the parole." Had he turned himself in, done a few months in jail, as I'd suggested, or managed to straighten it all out somehow? Had I really saved him by taking the gun? Or was he lying? I felt a dazed relief—if it was "cool with the parole," it would be impossible for him to be angry with me anymore. Then I realized I'd been completely pessimistic, had surrendered him, in my mind, to only disaster.

I could talk to him for a few minutes, I thought, find out what happened, wish him well, and give him back the gun, or at least tell him I still had it, without getting any more involved. I could see him, and in the process, demystify him forever, along with his role in my life. I *should* see him and resist him. I should see him in order to say a final, resolute good-bye. At last I did open the door, but the hall was empty. I hadn't dreamed it; he was actually there, but I'd hesitated too long. He had felt my fear, my uncertainty, and split—quickly, silently, like a rubber-soled phantom.

In the morning I woke up early, despite the fact I'd had almost no sleep. My head ached and the taste of hangover dried in my mouth; but I could only think about Julio. Julio came back! Immediately I began telling myself the usual conflicting stories. He was dangerous to me; no, I was only dangerous to myself, and to understand that, and why, I had to see him again. I had to see him to say good-bye, not only to him, but to what he represents in me. I had to know I could trust myself not to be tempted again, not by Julio, or another version of him. Above all, I wanted to know what he'd come to tell me. I was dying to know. To know would somehow resolve the situation; there would be no loose ends to flap forever through my brain; it would be over. In the end I was sorry I hadn't opened the door, though I knew I should be thankful.

I untaped the gun from the pipes under the sink, put it in a paper bag, and almost ran the four short blocks to the park. I didn't know why I imagined I'd find him there, but I did, perhaps because it was there we used to meet his ex-con friends when we strolled together—"Hey, man, don't I know you from . . ."—a quick glance at white me—"up *there*?" I suppose I had to do something with the ambivalent energies he'd produced, with my desire to know, to resolve it all. I fully expected to see him sitting on a bench, shoulders hunched, hands in pockets, or lying on the cold, wet ground. Irrational; no reason to think he'd be there at all. The park was nearly deserted. It was still raining lightly and a dissolving frost iced the grass and the iron bars of the jungle gym, where once, near the beginning of it all, I'd watched him pull himself up and turn somersaults, suspended by his muscular arms, and thought, No wonder my fifth floor apartment on Tenth Street was so easy to rob, and promptly felt disgusted with myself for thinking that.

Needless to say, he wasn't there. Yet I obeyed my compulsion to go out and look for him, and I am scared to realize I did that. I could have found him. I could do it again. I could spend the rest of my life looking for him, or someone like him. Now, as I sit here writing, the gun is by my left hand. It is ironic that I ran out in the rain to give it back to him, when just five months ago I risked my life to take it away. This weapon, coiled in its evil, unloaded silence, is a symbol of the desires I cannot shake from my life. I look at it, black, hard, implacable, and know there is no place secret enough to hide it, no body of water deep enough to make it no longer mine. I took it because it belongs to me, belongs to me so profoundly, I can't even throw it away. No matter what happens to me, no matter how sensible I seem, no matter how famous a poet I become, no matter what normal man I settle for, no matter how much money I make from the royalties of *High Styling Your Face* (I must finish Chapter IV by the end of the week or punish myself severely) I am stuck with this gun, and with it, the idea of Julio Bravo.